"One of the best erotic romance writers writing today!"
—*Ecataromance*

Praise for *Running Wild*

"The best anthology I have ever read! Sarah McCarty did an excellent job weaving her three passionate tales together . . . Her captivating characters, scorching love scenes and dramatic plot twists kept me on the edge . . . I could not put it down."
—*Night Owl Romance*

"Sarah McCarty delivers a well-written story with sizzling romance . . . [she] has taken paranormal romance to a whole new level."
—*Romance Junkies*

"You are going to love this trio of stories . . . Sarah McCarty definitely takes you on a wild ride . . . [with] fast-paced story lines and super-hot sex scenes."
—*Lucrezia Magazine*

"This one is a scorcher . . . If you're looking for a romance to raise the temperatures, then look no further than McCarty's *Running Wild*!"
—*Romance Reader at Heart*

"Provide[s] werewolf romance fans with a strong, heated collection. Fans will be *Running Wild*." —*Midwest Book Review*

continued . . .

More praise for the novels of Sarah McCarty

"[A] pulse-pounding paranormal."
—*The Road to Romance*

"Masterfully written."
—*The Romance Readers Connection*

"Powerfully erotic, emotional and thought provoking."
—*Ecataromance*

"Has the WOW factor . . . characters that jump off the pages!"
—*Just Erotic Romance Reviews*

"Toe curling."
—*Fallen Angel Reviews* (recommended read)

"Ms. McCarty is a genius!"
—*Romance Junkies*

Wild Instinct

Sarah McCarty

HEAT
New York

THE BERKLEY PUBLISHING GROUP
Published by the Penguin Group
Penguin Group (USA) Inc.
375 Hudson Street, New York, New York 10014, USA
Penguin Group (Canada), 90 Eglinton Avenue East, Suite 700, Toronto, Ontario M4P 2Y3, Canada
(a division of Pearson Penguin Canada Inc.)
Penguin Books Ltd., 80 Strand, London WC2R 0RL, England
Penguin Group Ireland, 25 St. Stephen's Green, Dublin 2, Ireland (a division of Penguin Books Ltd.)
Penguin Group (Australia), 250 Camberwell Road, Camberwell, Victoria 3124, Australia
(a division of Pearson Australia Group Pty. Ltd.)
Penguin Books India Pvt. Ltd., 11 Community Centre, Panchsheel Park, New Delhi—110 017, India
Penguin Group (NZ), 67 Apollo Drive, Rosedale, North Shore 0632, New Zealand
(a division of Pearson New Zealand Ltd.)
Penguin Books (South Africa) (Pty.) Ltd., 24 Sturdee Avenue, Rosebank, Johannesburg 2196,
South Africa

Penguin Books Ltd., Registered Offices: 80 Strand, London WC2R 0RL, England

This book is an original publication of The Berkley Publishing Group.

PRINTING HISTORY
Heat trade paperback edition / December 2009

Library of Congress Cataloging-in-Publication Data

McCarty, Sarah.
    Wild instinct / Sarah McCarty. — Heat trade pbk. ed.
        p. cm.
    ISBN 978-0-425-22761-9
    1. Werewolves—Fiction. I. Title.
PS3613.C3568W55 2009
813'.6—dc22   2009029051

PRINTED IN THE UNITED STATES OF AMERICA

10   9   8   7   6   5   4   3   2   1

Contents

Garrett

One

THEY were coming.

Sarah Anne stared down the hillside, her night vision casting the trees and rocks to a high contrast of black and white touched with glimmers of silver. Through the shifting mist, she watched bits of deeper darkness weave through the natural shadows. Werewolves. Biting her lip, she glanced back over her shoulder into the cave at the women and children there. She'd tried so hard to keep them safe, but there was nowhere left to run. They would have to fight.

She glanced up and then down. At least the rugged cliff surrounding their small hiding place would give them some advantage. Josiah, her five-year-old son, came up beside her, his sister inevitably trailing along. He looked down. It was too much to hope that he wouldn't see what she saw. His small canines flashed white in the night as he snarled. Though he was half human, he was wolf to the core in all aspects, his senses so acute already that she was beginning to wonder if he carried a deeper heritage—that of Protector. If he were pack, he would be assessed, protected, trained. But he wasn't, through her choice. Sarah Anne dropped her hand to his small head, desperation pulsing through her like a living nightmare. She had to keep him safe.

Her three-year-old daughter, Megan, as human as her father—tiny, delicate, ever so vulnerable—clung to her brother's hand and gave name to the emotion scenting the interior of the cave. "Mommy, I scared."

So was she. "There's no need to be afraid. We've prepared."

Three women, armed with a few guns, ammo and a mother's drive to protect, were going to hold off ten werewolf soldiers. They didn't have a prayer. Teri and Rachel left the backpacks they were organizing and came up. The soft scuff of their feet over the dirt floor scraped across her nerves in an accusation. From Rachel, a full-blooded werewolf, Sarah Anne could detect no emotion, but from Teri, there were all sorts of betraying scents. Fear, anger, determination.

"Are they the McGowans?" Teri asked from behind her.

"No." When she'd sent the letter two years ago, after her husband died, she hadn't been expecting much. Mixed bloods were never welcome. When an invitation had come from the newly formed Pack Haven three months ago, just after Teri's attack, she'd been astounded. She'd even taken it as a sign that things were changing, staying put as ordered by the Alpha, Wyatt Carmichael, until the Pack Protectors—Donovan and Kelon McGowan—arrived to escort them home. Home. She set her teeth. She should have known better than to have pinned her hopes on that word. The promise of help from the Haven pack had just been another shimmer of illusion. And while she'd sat waiting, the rogues had come calling again. She'd only had time to dash off a desperate e-mail to Haven before retreating to the caves. She'd hoped the McGowans would arrive yesterday. She'd been praying they'd come this morning. Now she was sure she was on her own, the way she'd always been since the day it became evident that her tainted genetics had left a mark. She'd come to the human world to avoid persecution. It had found her anyway. And now it endangered her children. Because she'd put her faith in pack.

Teri spun on her booted heel. "I'll get the guns."

Sarah Anne exchanged a glance with Rachel. As a human, Teri had no idea what they faced. The guns would delay, but not prevent, the inevitable.

Rachel watched Teri retreat, her near-golden eyes narrowing with worry. "We should probably tell her."

Sarah Anne shrugged and moved Meg back from the cave entrance. "She already thinks werewolves are monsters. No sense proving it and removing all doubt. Not when we have to fight."

They couldn't afford for Teri to break down now. She'd been incredibly strong for the past couple months, but it was easy to scent the tension stretching her nerves thin.

"She wouldn't be here at all except for her pregnancy."

"She wouldn't be pregnant at all except for them." With a wave of her hand, Sarah Anne encompassed the encroaching scum. She wouldn't call them soldiers. Wolf soldiers didn't rape. Wolf soldiers had honor. Integrity. They protected women. They didn't abuse them.

Behind them a shotgun cocked. Sarah Anne spun, right along with Rachel.

"I told you before, what happened isn't your fault." Teri stood, feet apart, shotgun in one hand and a rifle in the other, her tousled, short black hair and slanted green eyes giving her the look of a pixie gone bad. Dark red rows of newly healed scars peeked out from beneath her black mock turtleneck, completing the look. Shame flooded Sarah Anne anew as she stared at the furrows. Right behind that came guilt. All she'd done by running was to endanger those she loved.

"They wouldn't have found you if not for me."

Teri handed the shotgun to Sarah Anne. "That's ridiculous."

Being human, there was no way Teri could understand the

sense of unity and responsibility that was part of werewolf culture. What one member of the pack did, good or bad, reflected on them all. And the wrongs committed against Teri had been perpetrated by members of Sarah Anne's former pack.

"I still feel guilty."

"Well, don't. I wouldn't trade our friendship for the world."

The lie was in her scent. If Teri could, she'd go back in time and erase the friendship that had exposed her to the wolves who'd breathed her scent, recognized her as a potential breeder and raped her, responding to instinct rather than logic. Half-blood children had no worth. Sarah Anne couldn't blame her any more than she could bring herself to dispute Teri's claim. The woman had just regained her emotional feet. And strangely, the pregnancy had provided the vehicle.

"So what's our plan?" Rachel asked, calm as always, her demeanor as restrained as the bun that always held back her long black hair. No matter what, Rachel was always serene.

"Same as before. Shoot as many as we can."

Teri smiled a cold smile. "That works for me."

Sarah Anne cast a glance at Teri. If she was terrified, she was hiding it well. "Remember, shoot for the organs and the brain. Do as much damage as possible on each individual. Wolves don't go down easily."

Only a catastrophic series of injuries could bypass a werewolf's ability to heal.

Teri smiled again. "I'm good with that."

The scars were the tip of the iceberg when it came to the injuries Teri had sustained. Sarah Anne could easily believe she was fine with anything that had to do with taking out a male wolf. She carefully checked the trail. The shadows glided closer. Still only ten, as far as she could tell. It might as well be one hundred.

"Rachel."

"I know."

She needed to say it anyway. "Don't let them get my son."

Rachel placed her hand on Sarah Anne's arm. Her scent, her energy, all radiated comfort. Sarah Anne didn't know how Rachel held on to hope. "Things aren't going to be that bad."

They already were. "Take Josiah, shift, go out the side entrance and then run like hell."

Rachel grabbed Josiah's hand. "Maybe I can carry—"

Sarah Anne shook her head. "We already discussed it. You can't carry Meg, and she can't change." Like her mother. "She'll never be able to keep up."

Meg, hearing her name, sensing the tension, puckered up and stamped her foot. "I want 'Siah!"

Every instinct in Sarah Anne echoed Meg's cry. Sarah Anne pulled Meg against her thigh, rubbing her hands up and down her tiny ribs. How was she supposed to make this choice? She stared at the figures getting closer, the wind carrying the taint of their scent, and she knew. She just did. "Josiah's going with Aunt Rachel."

"No."

She met Josiah's stare. Someday he'd be an Alpha, maybe a Protector, but right now he was a baby, and staring down his mother was beyond his capacity. But not by much. "You go with Rachel, Josiah. You do everything she tells you and you make your father proud."

His little feet were planted shoulder-width apart. A snarl rumbled in his chest as his nostrils flared, scenting the danger riding the wind. "I'm not leaving you."

Sarah Anne blinked at the flash of the man he'd someday be. His father would have been so proud. Smoothing her hand over the rich chocolate color of his hair, she blinked again, this time in an effort to hold back the tears. "You have to go. Rachel needs protection, too, and I don't have anyone else to send with her."

His chin set. "She can stay here."

He also had her stubbornness. "No, she can't. She has to take an important message to Pack Haven."

"I do need you, Josiah," Rachel interjected.

His chin trembled, and he suddenly became a little boy again.

Her little boy, who was trying so hard not to be scared as she asked the impossible of him. Meg hugged her leg and looked up, hazel eyes big with the belief that her mother could work miracles. "Please, Mommy?"

Sarah Anne heard the faint swish of brush against clothing as the soldiers approached. They were out of time. She grabbed Josiah and drew him in, bending to hold her son and daughter close in her arms one last time—her life, her future—breathing in their familiar scents, playing over in her mind every good memory she could find, bonding them together in that moment, just in case there wasn't another. "Remember who you are, Josiah," she whispered into his hair. He nodded, the tear he wouldn't let her see seeping through the thin cotton of her shirt.

"I'm a Protector."

He was so convinced of that. "And a Stone. Don't ever forget that, or think it's not a valuable part of you."

Another nod.

"We have to leave now, Sarah Anne," Rachel interjected quietly.

With one last squeeze, Sarah Anne let Josiah go. "Be careful."

Rachel put her hands protectively on Josiah's shoulder, a small, strained smile on her face. "I'm the careful one, remember?"

Sarah Anne remembered that, along with many other things.

Teri looked out the entrance. "It's now or never, guys."

A bolt of pure fear stabbed through Sarah Anne. Josiah's escape out the side entrance had to be perfectly timed so he wouldn't be seen or scented, and even with perfect timing the plan had only a scant chance of success. The weight of impossibility strained Sarah Anne's voice as she lifted her daughter up. "Run very fast, Josiah."

He nodded, looking like a little boy again as he asked, "And you'll meet us at the south ridge, come morning?"

Nothing short of death would keep her away. "That's the plan."

It was enough for him. She caught Rachel's hand as she turned away, tugging her around. She had to say it. "Thank you."

The words were so paltry compared to the emotion backing them. If they got out of this alive, Rachel could ask anything of Sarah Anne, anything at all, and Sarah Anne would grant it.

Rachel inclined her head. "Anything for the Alpha female."

"I'm not pack." Even after eight years, it still hurt to say that. "Let alone Alpha."

Rachel sighed as if the truth were a deception. Teri looked at them both and shook her head. "If pack means family, then I think we're it." She hefted the rifle. "Now, if nobody objects, I've got some damage to do."

GUNFIRE echoed through the canyon.

"You can't fault them for courage," Garrett murmured as a woman and a boy slipped out the side entrance of the cave, shifted and then started to run perpendicular to the hillside, blending into the night, the female shielding the cub. The gunfire from the interior picked up in a rapid spate, no doubt in hope of keeping the main group distracted.

Beside him, Cur snarled as two bigger shadows slid into the night behind the woman and child. "Can't fault the woman and kid for a damn thing, but I've got a hell of a bone to pick with those SOBs hunting them." He touched his hand to the transceiver attached to his ear.

"Daire, you've got two friendlies in fur heading your way."

Daire's distinctive, gravelly voice rumbled over the connection that linked all five Protectors on this mission. "I've got them."

"They've got company following."

Daire's satisfied growl preceded his, "Good."

"Nice to know his reputation isn't inflated," Cur grunted over his and Garrett's private frequency as he angled wide to cut off two soldiers heading up toward the side entrance.

Garrett supposed it was. He moved to the left, flanking the two soldiers who comprised his targets. The scum didn't know it yet, but they were surrounded. Whoever had sent the note had been a bit vague on her directions, causing a critical delay. But they were here now and the matter would be settled.

"I'm just glad he's on our side." Daire was a big son of a bitch, even for a were, and he wore the violence of his history in the scars on his body. It took a hell of a lot to scar a were.

"Thought when he went freelance, he went rogue?"

"I'm not sure he hasn't."

Garrett wasn't sure of anything when it came to this new pack, least of all Daire's reasons for joining this mission. His and Cur's motivations were easy to see. Neither had chosen to become part of the packless lost, and when the McGowans had approached them in the bar and offered them pack status, they hadn't hesitated; they had run to accept. The McGowans were legend. Fierce fighters. Old-school Protectors, who put pack and honor first. It would be a privilege for any Protector to be asked to join forces with the McGowans. For outlawed rogues like him and Cur, it was a prize without equal.

Below, there was movement. Garrett sighted his rifle on one of the soldiers closing in on Kelon McGowan, just in case. He switched his transceiver back to all frequencies. "You've got trouble on your tail, Kelon."

Through the sight, he could clearly see the smile of anticipation flash across Kelon's face. "Thanks."

The enemy leapt straight for Kelon's seemingly unprotected back. The rogue might be a soldier, but Kelon was a Protector, and that much faster, that much stronger, that much more pissed. He spun and caught the wolf midleap, evaded the swipe of the soldier's claws through the simple expedience of breaking his arm, and then, in the split second while the man hung helpless, delivered justice with a graceful, lethal simplicity that Garrett admired. When the signal came, he'd do the same to the two men marked as his. These men hunted women and children of his new pack. They would not survive the night.

The sense of rightness strengthened as Garrett slid the rifle into the scabbard on his back and moved forward, ears tuned for the call to battle, adrenaline pumping through his body in a familiar rush, enhancing the drive of muscle, the acuteness of his senses. For the first time, he entered battle not to defend himself, or an ideal, but in defense of his pack. Satisfaction and pride blended with cold calculation as he crouched and waited, his marks in sight, one moving up the slide of rock to the cave entrance, the other tucked behind a tree ten feet away, gun aimed at the cave mouth. Garrett smiled, claws extending. The bastard would never get that shot off.

"Everyone in position?"

Donovan McGowan's question whispered through his earpiece.

Four echoes of "Go" whispered back.

Garrett looked up toward the entrance. His second target had reached it, fanatically dedicated to his mission, clearly confident he could overpower the women inside. Garrett couldn't wait much longer.

Gunfire flashed from the mouth of the cave.

A second later the McGowan war cry split the night, reverberating across the valley. Garrett leapt for the sniper, the element of surprise making the kill simple. Too simple for the rage pumping through him. Without hesitation, he picked up the battle cry echoing around him and raced up the hill. A hint of a woman's fear blew down on the wind, catching on some instinctive recognition inside, pulling it forward, centering his rage, his focus. A baby screamed. A woman cried out.

He sent his promise ahead on another howl.

Touch them and die.

Two

THE enemy was on them.

Sarah Anne shoved more cartridges into the shotgun as a shadow became the broad-shouldered silhouette of a man. Beside her, Teri fired the rifle. Meg screamed, the terror in the sound an echo of the emotion churning inside Sarah Anne. Damn the bastards. Just one more thing to lay at their feet. Until that moment, Meg hadn't known real fear.

The silhouette stuttered, but didn't stop. Teri fired again. This time the shadow didn't hesitate. As it came closer, Sarah Anne could make out the face of a wolf in battle heat, face slightly morphed, claws extended, death in his dark eyes. Teri's next shot produced only a metallic click.

Shit.

"Drop back to Meg and reload," Sarah Anne ordered, yanking up the shotgun.

"You can't fight them off alone."

No, she couldn't, but she couldn't stand Meg's screams. "The shotgun does more damage."

Another scream from Meg. The note in this one different, whipping her around. "Mommy!"

A quick glance over her shoulder showed another man in the cave reaching for her baby, claws extended. "Meg!"

She swung around, aimed the shotgun, knowing even as she did she couldn't risk the shot. From behind her, down the hill, came a wild cry. Feral, primitive, deadly. A Protector's challenge. Help was coming. Too late. Teri was already in motion, running for the man, gun held up like a club.

"Teri, no!"

The soldier turned, and waited, meeting Sarah Anne's gaze over Teri's shoulder. A sense of horror washed over Sarah Anne. She knew him. Colin. The werewolf from an affiliated pack whose suit she'd rejected. Teri didn't stop, just issued a challenge as feral as any Protector's.

"Get away from her!"

From outside the cave, more battle cries rose, so close, yet too far away to do any good. Stone scraped over dirt behind her. Her breath locked in her throat, she braced for the tear of the other soldier's claws, diving desperately for her daughter and Teri. She heard the impact of two heavy bodies colliding, followed by snarls. She didn't care. Nothing going on behind her mattered. All that mattered was her daughter and the woman so fiercely determined to pit her fragile, human body against a full-blooded were-soldier.

From behind, a man's voice barked, "Get back."

Her soul picked up the silent litany. *Get back! Get Back! Get back!*

It was as futile as her last burst of speed. Colin caught the rifle stock and with a cold smile ripped it out of Teri's hands. Sarah Anne froze, knowing what he was going to do, begging with everything in her for mercy, a fruitless "please" shaping her lips. *Please don't kill my daughter. Please don't hurt Teri. Please, please, please.*

She watched helplessly as Colin's claws swept downward toward her daughter.

"Mommy!" Megan's shriek etched its horror into her soul.

Oh God! She wasn't going to make it in time. "No!"

"Fuck." A hand hit her shoulder, tossing her to the side as a man surged past her. "Get back!"

Time slowed to a crawl as she seemed to float, her gaze locked on the vicious curve of claw as it swiped down toward her screaming daughter. Too late. They were too late. Yet still, she prayed.

Please, save her!

She heard a scream, disembodied, that floated with her and then the impossible. Teri, dear God, Teri somehow managed to inject herself into that small space in time, between prayer and contact, covering Meg's body with her own, taking the devastating impact instead of Meg. Teri's cry cut off in a strangled gurgle as the deadly claws bit deep into her side. Blood sprayed. Sarah Anne hit the ground, the impact whipping her head back against the stone wall, and for a few precious seconds she saw nothing but stars.

When her vision cleared, she could see Teri lying in a motionless heap, blood pooling around her still body. She couldn't see Meg. With another battle cry that reverberated painfully around the cave, the stranger slammed Colin into the wall. Colin retaliated with blows that, had they landed, would have killed the stranger, but the stranger was a Protector. Faster, meaner, deadlier than a soldier could ever dream of being. One of the few genetically superior werewolves born to every generation.

Legend was that nothing could come between a Protector and his goal. Watching the stranger pulverize Colin as she struggled to her feet, Sarah Anne believed it.

The room spun as she crawled toward Meg and Teri. Grief dragged behind every flex of muscle. She'd already lost her pack, her husband. She couldn't lose her friend and her daughter. She couldn't. There was another disturbance behind her. She didn't look, didn't care. She reached Teri's side. For all the blood beneath her torso, Teri's shoulder was clean. It gave her a place to put her hand.

"Teri, get up."

The other woman didn't move, didn't moan—just lay there. And under Teri's deadweight lay her daughter. Little Meg who was too fragile to take that much weight without suffocating. Sobbing, praying, cursing in one big jangle of panic, Sarah Anne pulled Teri off, hoping the act wasn't the fatal last straw. Her stomach heaved at sight of the blood. As soon as Teri rolled to the side, Meg started screaming. Nothing had ever sounded so good. Sarah Anne snatched her up, holding her blood-soaked body to her chest, feeling her tiny arms hug her neck, her screams dying to sobs before she reached back for the woman lying on the ground. "Auntie Teri. Auntie Teri."

Sarah Anne tucked Meg's face against her shoulder, away from the grisly sight, as she moved to the pile of rocks in the corner. At the front of the cave, the fighting continued. She set Meg down in the dirt behind the biggest rocks.

Holding her gaze, she ordered, "Stay here. Don't move. No matter what."

Meg nodded. Sarah Anne figured she had about five minutes tops, and only that, because her intrepid daughter was terrified. She turned back. Nothing had changed. Teri was still lying there, still bleeding, and she still had to think of something to do. Except she couldn't. She wasn't a surgeon and humans didn't mend from the inside out.

The three steps back to Teri's side seemed to take a lifetime. Teri stared up at her with pain-filled eyes, blood trickling out of her mouth. Her best friend in the world and all Sarah Anne could do was kneel bedside her, take her hand and give her a pale shadow of a smile. "Thank you."

Teri shook her head. Her hand lifted toward Meg, and then dropped to her stomach.

"Okay?"

She meant Megan. "Thanks to you."

A flick of her fingers dismissed the gratitude. That was so much like Teri. She always put others first, which was probably what had led her to become a doctor. This time, she'd put Meg first. Because she saw her as family. For all that she was human, Sarah Anne always thought Teri would make good pack.

Teri's hand dropped to her stomach, and she asked again. "Okay?"

She wanted to know if her own baby was okay. Growing up with no one, Teri had come to see her baby as a start of a long-held dream of family. From the moment she'd realized that she was pregnant, despite how the pregnancy had come about, she'd loved her baby. Focusing on that love had given her a road out of hell. And now she was in danger of losing it.

"She's fine." At least Sarah Anne hoped so. She checked on Meg. She was still out of sight behind the rocks.

Teri looked over Sarah Anne's shoulder. Her eyes flew wide. Her lips worked. Her hand pressed weekly against Sarah Anne's arm in a parody of a shove. In the next split second, Sarah Anne felt what Teri saw. A male presence. Snarling, she spun, swinging for the point she thought his groin would be. She was wrong. He was taller than she'd thought, and, looking up from this angle, extremely intimidating.

Catching her hand, and using her momentum to move her a step aside, the werewolf knelt beside Teri, giving Sarah Anne a gentle smile as he informed her, "Your aim is off."

Sarah Anne bared her canines—the only wolflike conversion she could manage—as he released her hand. "I'll do better next time."

"Good." He turned that smile on Teri as he lifted the bottom edge of her shirt. "Your baby is fine and will be fine as long as you are."

When Teri attempted to view the wound, the man blocked her effort with a finger under her chin.

"Rather than looking, I need you to close your eyes and focus on slowing your heartbeat."

Teri shook her head, coughed and squeezed Sarah Anne's hand, pleading with her eyes.

"She's not wolf. She's human. She can't—"

The stranger cut her off with a shake of his head that sent his black hair sliding over his shoulder. "She can do it."

It wasn't so much what he said, but the way he said it. As if there was no doubt that the impossible could be achieved simply because he commanded it. And because she desperately needed to believe in something, Sarah Anne whispered to Teri, "Try. Please."

Teri nodded.

The man reached for the buttons on the bloody shirt. "That's my girl."

The growl surprised Sarah Anne, coming out of instinct rather than plan, hovering in her throat, too soft for human ears to hear, but the man heard the betraying sound.

"I'm not here to hurt."

She snarled again. Teri couldn't bear to be naked. Not after what had happened to her.

"Get yourself under control."

No one had ever told her that before. It had never been necessary.

After one more assessing, sidelong glance, he turned back to Teri. "Close your eyes now and do as I say. You're safe now." Touching his finger to the device in his ear he murmured, "Daire, did you find the other two?"

He had someone hunting Rachel and Josiah? No matter how Sarah Anne strained, she couldn't hear the answer to the vital question.

The man looked at her, the near black of his eyes more pronounced as his rage faded. "The boy and the woman—do you have a plan to meet up with them later?"

She met him glare for glare, fighting the instinct to drop her eyes before him, so clearly an Alpha. "Who wants to know?"

"Kelon McGowan."

Her gaze dropped. Immediately. One did not challenge a Protector. Especially one of the legendary McGowans. "We've arranged to meet tomorrow."

He spoke into the transceiver again. "We'll pick them up tomorrow. They should be safe until then, since the threat has been eliminated. I need you back here."

She looked at the bodies around the cave. *The threat has been eliminated.* That was one way to put it.

There was a pause in which Kelon was clearly listening to something else, and then Kelon smiled again at Teri before saying, "Daire?"

"What?"

"Make it fast."

"What can he do?" she asked, getting to her feet, realizing she didn't know where the first man had gone. When she saw him, a snarl rumbled up from her toes. Kelon's hand on her arm prevented her from lunging at the stranger who had picked up her daughter.

"I don't know, but I'm banking he'll come up with something. He's an inventive son of a—" He glanced at Meg, who stared at the man holding her, caught between terror and fascination. "He's inventive."

Sarah Anne knew just how her daughter felt as the stranger approached. She couldn't take her eyes off the man who walked toward her with the lethal grace of a predator. She couldn't look away from the strength in his broad shoulders, move away from the haunting lure of his scent, step back when he reached out and caught her hand, his eyes glittering with a combination of silver and black.

Electricity flared from her hand up her arm, flashing down to her center in a wave of heat. As he met her gaze, his smile sent another jolt through her. She had the strangest sense that she knew him, but they'd never met. She would have remembered meeting someone like him. Meg issued a startled little noise as Sarah Anne's shoulder bumped her side as he drew her in.

Meg quieted as the man whispered, "Shh . . ." never taking his eyes from Sarah Anne's as he wrapped his arm around her back, enveloping her body in his strength and her senses in a rich, luscious scent. Masculine. Pleasing. Addictive. She inhaled. He smiled.

His face was equally as luscious, with chiseled features harboring an impressive strength. His eyes were neither round nor oval, but somewhere in between. They were incredibly compelling beneath the aggressive slash of his eyebrows, which clearly reflected the force of his personality. This was not a man people trifled with.

"Let's get the little one away from here, okay?" He pulled her toward the back, and for all that he was fascinating, or maybe because of it, she still felt that start of fear as he tried to take her and Meg away from Kelon and Teri. It was not unheard of for male weres to kill the offspring of women they were interested in, and the scent of this man's interest surrounded her as strongly as his arm supported her. The snarl ripped from her toes. "Let me go!"

"Way to go, Garrett," another male scoffed as he came up and knelt beside Kelon.

Garrett. The overwhelming man was named Garrett. In her night vision, the newcomer's hair was a charcoal color streaked with silver, which meant that in the sunlight it would be brown mixed with blond. Only mixed-bloods had blond in their hair. Pure weres always had dark hair.

"Shut up, Cur."

She gasped at the insult. Garrett's thumb stroked over the back of her hand. "Relax. That's his name."

That didn't make it any less a horrible thing to call someone. She barely kept from blurting that out.

"What's Garrett done now?" A man who looked remarkably like Kelon asked as he ducked into the cave.

Cur applied more pressure to Teri's wounds. Her groan was so weak. "Ticked off our newest pack member, Sarah Anne."

Her, he was talking about her. Sarah Anne had forgotten she was no longer packless.

The man walked over, a smile on his handsome lips. "Want me to teach him a lesson?"

"You're welcome to try," Garrett countered, handing Meg to her while moving her back another step—away from the other men, she noticed.

This had to be Donovan McGowan. She just stared, hugged Megan, and shook her head, swallowing hard. Wyatt Carmichael hadn't lied. He had sent them for her. "You really came."

"Of course. We at Haven take our promises seriously." He glanced at Kelon, who was working on Teri, before asking, "Your friend?"

"A very good friend," Garrett rumbled from behind her, his drawl slipping along her nerves like honey, soothing the ache of watching Teri die, tucking the stress behind an invisible cover of calm. "She jumped between the rogue and the baby, taking the blow."

Sarah Anne found her voice. "You can't let her die. The pack is in her debt."

Donovan cocked a brow at her. "Humans aren't subject to pack law."

Yet another man entered the cave, ducking under the low ceiling of the side entrance. Sarah Anne could only stare in shock as he straightened and crossed the dirt floor in a soundless stalk, his long black hair blowing back from his heavily scarred face. Werewolves didn't scar, but as he pushed past her, there was no mistaking his scent. Wolf. Maybe even an ancient. Whatever had happened to scar this male must have been horrendous. She stepped back and ran up against Garrett's chest. His arms instantly came around her. This time, rather than resenting it, she was grateful for the protection. This newcomer was terrifying in the raw power he exuded.

"Her baby is wolf," she whispered.

Silence dropped like a lead weight into the already heavy tension.

"Where's her mate?"

The question, asked in a deep, gravelly voice, came from the newcomer as he reached for Teri's cheek, not quite touching her skin. His hands were as big as the rest of him, but there was tenderness in the near touch that made her blink.

Teri was unconscious, dying. It didn't matter what Sarah Anne revealed now. "It wasn't a voluntary pregnancy."

She expected curses, anger, questions at the heinous revelation, anything except the continued silence. Then it started, almost too low to be heard, a low rumble that grew, taking on intent as it emanated from the big were kneeling at Teri's side. The vicious snarl didn't stop, even as he slid his hand under Teri's head. It just continued to rumble ominously, stopping only when the man snapped at Kelon and Cur as he turned to Teri, "Keep the pressure steady!"

"In case you haven't noticed, there isn't much left to hold on to," Cur grumbled.

"Shut the hell up."

Donovan took something from his belt and set it on the floor. With a snap, the room flooded with light. "Can you save her, Daire?"

Daire looked directly at Sarah Anne. "Not without sacrifice. How badly do you want this?"

She wanted Teri to live more than she wanted her next breath. "Do whatever you have to."

This time, his hand touched Teri's cheek, conforming to the soft curve, cradling it. On a murmur she couldn't understand, he leaned in.

Teri moaned. Sarah Anne echoed the sound. There was so much blood.

Garrett turned, taking Sarah Anne with him. When she tried to look around him, he blocked her with a hitch of his shoulder. "You don't need to see that."

"She's my friend."

"And she's in good hands."

She elbowed him in the side. He didn't even grunt. "And I'm supposed to take your word for that?"

His eyes were a fascinating mix of browns, golds and greens. A slow curl of heat, totally inappropriate, totally uncontrollable, stretched lazily out from her core.

"Yes."

Meg reached up, as fascinated as her mother. Sarah Anne caught her hand and pulled it back down, needing to put distance between them and the werewolf. He didn't let her, and when Teri moaned again, Sarah Anne lost the impetus. She needed someone to lean on right now. "Why?"

"Because you'd know if I lied."

There was only one circumstance in which that could be true. "You're not my mate!"

His gaze never left her mouth, watching her shape the words, making her so nervous that she licked her lips. That inner heat intensified as his eyes followed every flick. His mouth crooked up, along with his left brow, as he asked, "Want me to prove it?"

Three

*W*ANT *me to prove it?*

Sarah Anne shook her head as the brief moment of weakness that had her leaning on Garrett's strength passed. No woman in her right mind would. There was nothing safe in the energy coming off the man who held her. He was everything she'd run away from her former pack to avoid. Wild. Dominant. Aggressive. "No."

"Maybe later."

That didn't imply acceptance of her rejection. The pounding in her head increased. She didn't need this complication. All she needed to know was what was happening to Teri, but she couldn't see anything but the ancient's broad shoulders. She didn't trust the big wolf any more than she trusted Garrett. Leaning back, she could just make out Kelon and Donovan. They were her new pack Alphas. She didn't trust them, either. She took a breath and squared her shoulders. That being the case, she needed to gather some semblance of control.

"Let go of me."

To her surprise, he did.

He countered her look with a smile. "I'm not a monster. I can give you time."

There was no point arguing with a male werewolf intent on mating, so she didn't waste her time. Stepping around Garrett, she tried to get a better view of Teri. All she could see was a spreading dark stain and the ancient's back as he shifted position right along with her. Was he deliberately blocking her view?

A touch came on her shoulder, almost too much for her heightened senses to bear. So much blood.

"Sarah Anne . . ."

She shrugged off Garrett's hand. "What I need is for you to leave me alone."

For a moment she didn't think he would, but then he gave a short nod. "I can do that, too." There was another short pause, before he added, "For the moment."

He made her feel so threatened. Physically, emotionally, mentally. She balled her hands into fists, still staring at that pool of blood. Was it getting larger? "Thank you."

The sarcasm bounced off Garrett's confidence like a ping-pong ball off a hard surface. "You're welcome."

Donovan looked up and motioned to Garrett. Garrett glanced at her, then Meg, and hesitated a split second before crossing the small distance with an easy grace. Despite her tension and her fear, Sarah felt a tiny trickle of desire.

Dear God, was he really her mate? If he was, it would be ironic. She had left the pack eight years ago to avoid a werewolf mating, and the second she found a new pack, what happened? She took a deep breath and let it out. Meg leaned her head on her shoulder and wrapped her arms around her neck.

"Josiah?"

Sarah Anne kissed the top of her little head. Meg smelled of dirt, sweat and fear. She needed a bath. She needed safety. Sarah Anne glanced at the men surrounding them. Big men all, radiating the power that was unique to Protectors. Her eyes moved to the two dead men lying in the cave. These men were now her pack. They'd come for her and her children. They'd fought to protect them. She remembered the awful moment when Colin had prepared to bury his claws in Meg's fragile body. Glancing over at Garrett, she remembered the snarl when he'd lunged, the brutality with which he'd fought, for her. And as the sounds of the battle refreshed in her mind, along with that moment of utmost horror, she realized something else. Apparently the word was out that she was a female who was capable of producing offspring with more than one male. A rarity in the werewolf world. Colin would not be the last werewolf who would try to mate with her by force. Or the last to try to murder her children. As long as she remained packless and unmated, her children were in danger.

Along with the bath, she admitted to herself with a sense of inevitability, her daughter needed protection. She rested her cheek on Megan's head and studied the men in the cave, starting with the McGowans. The dark hair and dark eyes common to werewolves were a striking asset to the sharp-edged profiles of the twins, giving weight to their reputation. The McGowans were the most feared and respected Protectors in centuries. They were legendary for their ruthless defense of those under their protection. Tension gathered in her gut, spreading outward. Her daughter would need the protection of such strong men. Her mind reluctantly went to the next logical conclusion as her gaze moved to Garrett. Any wolf running with such men would share the same code of honor. And even if he didn't, as much as they wouldn't interfere between mates, pack hierarchy would ensure that they would for her offspring.

Want me to prove it?

She studied Garrett's hard face. Dear God, she didn't want him to prove it, but it looked as though she couldn't afford for him not to.

MEGAN'S sense of empathy chose that moment to kick in. Her little hand touched Sarah's cheek. "Mommy sad?"

Megan's voice carried in the cave. All the men except Daire looked at her. She wasn't sure how to answer. No doubt, any response would be interpreted according to the needs of the man hearing it.

"No, baby. I'm just tired."

Tired of the prison of her heritage. Tired of being damned if she did, damned if she didn't. She sighed. Garrett frowned, and ran his eyes over her from head to toe. Looking, she knew, with a potential mate's obsessive need to regulate and control everything surrounding his woman. She gave him what she hoped was a reassuring smile.

Her acting skills must not be up to par because Garrett walked away from Donovan, something one never did to his Alpha. Donovan frowned. Part of her had the panicked thought that maybe the Alpha didn't think she was worth one of his Protectors' trouble. That would be very bad. An Alpha could prevent a mating. Garrett stopped in front of her. His fingertip came to rest against her jugular. A threat?

"There's no need for you to worry. We will take care of everything."

"My son is out there. My friend is out there. My other friend is dying, so you tell me—how do you expect me not to worry?"

Garrett grimaced. "I guess, when you put it like that, I can't."

Beneath Garrett's finger, Sarah Anne's pulse raced like a freight train. Her anxiety rose around them in an acrid addition to the coppery scent of blood. Inside Garrett, the need to fix things for her increased in a silent howl. He wanted to pick her up, carry her to his home, settle into the big recliner in his living room, wrap a blanket around her and, well, coddle her. Which was a hell of a note for a man who'd never coddled anything.

The little girl stuck her grubby thumb out, looked at it and then popped it into her mouth. In all his speculations about his future, his mate coming to him with children by another man had not been a scenario he'd envisioned. As confident as he was about his ability to make Sarah Anne happy, he had no confidence in his ability to shine as an instant father. The little girl smiled at him. A strange emotion churned in his gut. He frowned. Her smile faded and she turned her face into her mother's neck. He felt like a heel. More so when Sarah cupped her daughter's head in her hand and held her close. Her lips lifted, showing her small canines in warning. What in hell did she think he intended to do?

He didn't get a chance to find out as Donovan called, "If you can drag yourself away from your flirting, Garrett, I'd like to finish our conversation."

Megan turned her head when Garrett grunted. After what had happened last time, he would have expected a frown. Her smile was a total surprise. Incredibly sweet, it touched, again, something inside him. He reached out. Sarah Anne growled, and hunched her shoulders protectively around her daughter. He dropped his hand to his side and stepped back. Donovan called him again. Garrett turned on his heel and headed toward Donovan.

"You'll have to make your peace with that," Donovan said as soon as he got alongside.

There was no question what "that" was. "I like children."

"Just not the child of your mate, fathered by another man?"

Garrett didn't appreciate the implication. "What makes you say that?"

From the floor where he cradled Teri, Daire offered, "Any werewolf would have that moment of jealousy."

"The question is," Kelon interjected, "what are you going to do about it?"

The scent around him changed. Despite their outward appearances, the men were on guard. Prepared to attack should he threaten the child. He should be used to this by now. No one ever gave a mixed-breed the benefit of the doubt. He lifted his lip in a sneer.

"Don't worry. Your newest pack member is safe tonight. I only eat little girls for breakfast."

Too late, he caught Sarah Anne's scent. It came riding the accusation in her snarled, "Bastard." He closed his eyes for a second, fighting down the violent flare of anger. The others had to have known she was there. He tracked her progress across the room, frowning as she tucked herself behind the small outcrop of rock, as if it offered some sort of protection.

He turned to the nearest Protector, who just happened to be Kelon. "You set me up."

Kelon snarled right back at him. "Only because we thought you'd have enough sense to say you wouldn't have a problem with the child."

"I don't have a problem with the child."

"You're going to have a hell of a time convincing that woman of that," Daire offered without looking up.

"Shut up, Daire."

Donovan cocked an eyebrow at him. "You know who you're talking to?"

"At this point, I don't care." All he cared about was Sarah Anne. It was going to take him years to remove the suspicion that he wanted to kill her daughter. He wanted to hit something, someone. Preferably Daire. The ancient's superior manner of speaking irritated the shit out of him. Unfortunately, Daire didn't rise to the challenge, so it was either provoke a fight or find something else to do. He settled for the latter.

"I'm going to go scout and make sure there're no more rogues around."

No one pointed out the obvious—that they knew there weren't. For that, he was grateful. Killing a member of his new pack was bound to put a dent in his acceptance.

Four

GARRETT didn't need to look to know who followed him out of the cave. He and Cur had been together so long that Cur's scent was barely distinguishable from his own. Metal grated against stone as Cur leaned against the cave wall.

"I guess you can take the wolf out of the pack, but you can't take the pack out of the wolf."

Garrett shrugged. "We knew the acceptance would be limited."

He scanned the valley below looking for any sign of life. He didn't find any. More was the pity. He was in the mood for a fight. He picked up a rock.

Cur pushed his hair off his face. "What are you going to do?"

Garrett tossed the rock up once, twice, before catching it in his fist and squeezing—remembering the expression on Sarah Anne's face. She really thought he'd hurt her child. "About Haven or my mate?"

"You choose."

He couldn't. That was the problem. "We could leave."

"Away from your mate? I don't think so."

Garrett dropped the rock and pressed it into the ground with the sole of his boot. "A mate I'd have to force. You saw her face."

"I also saw the way she leaned into you during the rogues' attack."

"That was fear."

He shrugged. "It doesn't matter. We've created success out of less."

Yeah, they had. They were a good team. Cur, given an edge, could manipulate any situation. And Garrett could always find an edge. He leaned back against the opposite wall. "Anyone ever tell you you're a goddamn optimist?"

Cur smiled, revealing his canines. "No matter what happened in there, whether you decide to stay with Haven or not, there's no denying that you're better off tonight than you were when we rolled out of bed this morning."

"How do you figure that?"

He hooked his thumbs into the pockets of his jeans and leaned his head back against the stone wall. "Tonight we have choices."

"All of them bad."

With a jerk of his thumb, he indicated the interior of the cave. "Only a pessimist could call that pretty little thing in there bad."

That pretty little thing was the scariest thing he'd ever seen. She made him hope. "That pretty little thing cherishes the same prejudices as the McGowans."

"That pretty little thing belongs to you, body and soul, by pack law. It doesn't matter what she thinks. All that matters is what you want to do about it."

Yeah. As if it would be that easy. He'd snap his fingers and everything would fall into place. "You think the McGowans are just going to let me walk out of there with her?"

Cur smiled, baring his canines. "I don't imagine we're going to give them much of a choice."

It was tempting. And it wasn't as if taking what they wanted wasn't the norm for them. Packless wolves had to scavenge the best they could, for what they could. Some thrived. Some died. Some went mad from the loneliness. He and Cur had found a way to thrive. Sarah Anne was a fighter. From every indication, she'd learn to thrive, too. "Tempting."

Cur pushed off the wall. "So, why are we still standing here?"

Garrett remembered Sarah Anne's courage as she'd fought to the bitter end, the disbelief when she'd thought she'd run out of options, the rebirth of hope as she realized her pack had come for her. The wonder when the McGowans introduced themselves. He'd been a lot of things in his life, some of them less than flattering, but he did not want to be the man who took away Sarah Anne's dream. As much as he longed for pack, a woman with children would long harder. "Because I like to think we're not total bastards."

"Fuck."

"Yeah, fuck."

"Couldn't you wait to try out decent until after we get what we want?"

The "we" made Garrett pause. "Apparently not." The coldness built in his gut. "However, there's nothing holding you here if you want to pick up that job we turned down for this one. It's pretty doubtful anyone else has jumped on it."

It was pretty much a suicide mission for a human.

"Nothing except my pack."

"I'm not sure Haven is going to accept us."

"Who the hell was talking about Haven? We've been pack our whole lives." Cur dismissed the distance between them with a wave of his hand. "It's enough for me."

No, it wasn't. Though they'd been telling themselves that for years, werewolves were made to belong to a bigger whole. He and Cur might have human blood, but they were wolf to the core, Protectors, and despite the life they'd made for themselves, they were only half alive. Garrett felt the pain of it every day. He knew damn well that Cur did, too. If Garrett walked away from this opportunity to belong, he'd have his mate, but Cur would have nothing but knowledge of what could be but might never happen. And yet, he'd make the sacrifice for Garrett. Because they were friends.

Garrett glanced back inside the dark interior and saw Donovan arguing with Sarah. Whatever they were discussing, neither was pleased. He hoped to hell the McGowans knew what they had in Cur. He was a fierce soldier, a loyal friend, and he deserved a heck of a lot better than to be cast out because his father had mated a human. If the McGowans could deliver belonging, Garrett was willing to make a few sacrifices of his own. Cur was right. They were all the pack each of them had. And pack put pack first.

Garret straightened. Sometimes a man had to fight for what should be his. "Well, I'm thinking we're going to take more."

"Your mate?"

Garrett nodded. "And our place is in this pack."

It felt good to say it.

"I'm glad to hear it."

The statement came from the interior of the cave. Garrett turned and Kelon was there. That fast, that startling. Not a sound had betrayed his approach. Yet another difference between the Protectors and themselves. He and Cur were self-taught. Their skills were limited to what they could improvise and piece together, the taint of their human blood prohibiting the assignment of a mentor to teach them the skills of their birthright. Not that it had stopped them from stealing a few, but there was so much more they could learn.

"Don't worry," Garrett sneered, driven to lash out by the resentment he couldn't shake. "It's our policy not to leave a job until it's done."

Kelon's right brow lifted in clear mockery and the corner of his mouth twitched. Anger twisted in Garrett's gut. If Kelon kept pushing him, he'd find out just how many of the Protectors' secrets he and Cur had managed to uncover for themselves.

"We appreciate that." He jerked his head toward the interior. "Donovan wants you back inside."

"Why?"

This time there was no mistaking the other Protector's amusement. "Sarah Anne is freaking out."

He hadn't claimed the woman, and Kelon knew it. "So why is that my problem?"

Another cock of the brow accompanied by a flash of canine. "Because Donovan wants it to be."

What the hell did that mean? Was Donovan sanctioning the mating? He glanced at Cur. After a hesitation that indicated his own doubts, Cur shrugged.

Garrett was finished being a pawn in the McGowans' games. "Tough."

Kelon straightened, aggression whipping out in an acrid scent. "Are you challenging me, pup?"

The one thing Garrett knew how to deal with was aggression. All it took was a lift of the mental barriers he normally kept battened down. "Call me 'pup' again and there won't be any question mark at the end of that sentence."

Cur took a step forward, ready as always to cover his back. Garrett shook his head. This was his battle.

Kelon glanced at Garrett. Then at Cur. Then back at Garrett. His expression was impossible to read. "Fair enough." He motioned to the interior. "But Donovan is still your superior, and he's still waiting."

"Let me guess—he doesn't like to be kept waiting?" Cur asked, shouldering past.

"Nearly as much as he likes dealing with hysterical women."

Despite himself, Garrett felt the leap of concern, the need to protect. "Sarah's hysterical?"

"From her scent, she's about to go over the edge."

It shouldn't have bothered Garrett. It did. "Shit."

He followed Cur.

Behind them, Kelon chuckled. "I thought that would get you moving."

"Shut up."

All the order inspired was an outright laugh.

Five

SARAH Anne was facing Donovan, chin up, shoulders squared, her daughter tucked behind her. From the impatient slash of Donovan's hand, it didn't look as if he liked what he was hearing.

"He'll go after them now!" Sarah Anne's order carried clearly.

If she was intimidated by facing down her Alpha, she was hiding it well. In another second, Garrett expected her to release her wolf and, at the very least, lash out with her claws. That wouldn't do. Attacking the Alpha incurred severe consequences.

"You forget yourself." And from the snarl that punctuated that statement, Donovan had reached the end of his patience.

Sarah Anne was anything but cowed. "I haven't forgotten a thing. Not about how my son is out there at the mercy of any rogue who finds him. Or how my friend, who's with him, is just as defenseless, and most especially as to how you took your own sweet time showing up with our protection."

"You were told to continue to lie low until we could get here and provide escort "

"We couldn't."

"You disobeyed a direct order."

Sarah's hands fisted at her sides. "The rogues came for Teri."

"That wasn't your problem."

"Like hell. She's my friend. She was in trouble."

Donovan raked his fingers through his hair. "She's in even more trouble now."

"And whose fault is that?"

"Whose do you think?"

She came up on her toes in a direct challenge "Yours!"

Behind Sarah Anne, Meg whimpered and hunched back against the rock. Garrett told himself this wasn't any of his business. Sarah had, for all intents and purposes, rejected him. Her fear and her daughter's fear were not his to soothe, but he might as well have been talking to the wind when Meg's lip quivered and she looked at him.

Help me.

She might as well have screamed the words, they bored into his brain so hard. He blinked. She was telepathic?

He held out his arms. *Come.*

She didn't just come; she ran across the dirt floor, long hair flying, tears streaming.

Sarah's "Meg, get back here!" was pointless, as the little girl was clinging to his neck before the last syllable got out.

Instinct had his arms wrapping around her tiny torso as her legs wrapped around his waist. He braced himself to be repelled by her scent, but all he felt was a cataclysmic urge to protect.

"Don't let him hurt my mommy."

He knew, from Donovan's start, that he heard. And Sarah, too, from her gasp of "Meg!"

He ignored them both. "Donovan is your mommy's Protector. He would never hurt her."

"What's a Protector?"

What was the human equivalent? "You know the police in your town?" She nodded. He moved to put her down, but she clung tightly. Not sure what to do with his free hand, he cupped her head as Sarah Anne had. Megan sniffed. Was she getting snot all over his neck?

"They're good guys," she said.

"Well, Donovan is like a super good guy."

"He yelled."

He shot Donavon a glare. "A super good guy with a big voice."

Apparently that didn't soothe her because when Garrett started to put her down again, she clung tighter. And from the way her nose slid against his skin, she *was* getting snot all over his neck.

Donovan touched his finger to her arm. Meg whimpered. Garrett's lip curled in warning.

"I would never hurt your mother, little one."

Meg froze. Garrett snarled.

"Or you," Donovan added calmly.

Meg rubbed her nose on the back of her hand. Her lashes ticked Garrett's collarbone. Just a foot away, Sarah Anne fussed, her arms crossed over her chest, her fingers biting into the puff of her jacket sleeves, betraying the tenuous hold she had on her control. In another minute, she'd rip her daughter out of his arms.

"You're one of them," Meg accused the big Protector, in a tiny voice.

Donovan's tone gentled to an impossible level. "One of who?"

"The bad ones who hurt Auntie T."

Donovan ignored Garrett's warning and placed his hand on Meg's back. "No, little one. I'm the good one who's going to kill the ones who hurt your auntie T."

That got her nose out of Garrett's neck. Cold air rushed over the spot. "Really?"

No one that sweetly innocent should sound so bloodthirsty.

Sarah Anne reached for her daughter. "No, he's not."

Garrett didn't hand Meg over, but he did give Sarah a piece of advice. "You don't tell your Alpha what to do."

It was too dangerous. Donovan would be totally within his rights to cut her down.

"The hell I don't."

Meg perked up. At the tone, or the opportunity to learn a new word?

"Watch your language."

Sarah Anne's mouth opened and then snapped closed as she looked at her daughter. He turned to the right. Sarah Anne went with him, following her daughter. With every inch between her and the other man, he breathed easier. Cur moved in on Donovan's other side. Garrett caught Donovan's eye. However he felt about the situation, protocol had to be observed. "I apologize for my mate."

Donovan's eyes narrowed. His nostrils flared. Something like satisfaction lit his expression. "You claim her, then?"

Garrett looked over, taking in Sarah Anne's pale face, even features and that determination that belied the fragility of her gender.

"You take her as your mate, her children as yours?"

The ancient sanction settled like a balm over his soul.

"No," Sarah Anne gasped.

"Yes," he said, the inevitability of it flowing through him, even as Donovan smiled.

"Then your apology is accepted." Donovan ruffled Meg's hair. "Enjoy your new family."

"You can't do this," Sarah Anne protested, her head whipping back and forth, looking for help. She wouldn't find it in this all-male crowd. No male werewolf would mess with the advantages bestowed upon them when it came to claiming their mates.

"It's already done," Daire rumbled from where he sat on the floor.

"It can't be." Sarah Anne grabbed for Meg. This time Garrett let the child go. She clutched Meg to her as though the child was her one last link to sanity. "I left to escape this."

The words had a hollow, disbelieving quality.

Donovan's didn't. "You can't escape destiny." He bowed slightly. "Welcome to my pack and my protection."

Sarah Anne's lip curled. "It didn't last long."

"Long enough."

"What about my son?"

This time it was Cur who answered. "I'll bring him home to you."

"Rachel—"

Cur nodded, his too-long hair rasped across the leather of his coat. "Your friend, too. Consider it a wedding present for my newest pack member."

Sarah Anne's fear cut into Garrett like the edge of a blade. He wanted to give her something to hold on to. "The one thing Cur can do is keep a promise."

"That's an awful name," she whispered in that shell-shocked way people had when they just couldn't take any more. She looked at Garrett, her big brown eyes full of pain. "I want my son."

"I know."

She looked at Teri, her gaze bouncing off Daire's imposing presence, skimming over Kelon and Donovan, before returning to Cur. "You two are friends."

It wasn't a question. "Yes."

"And you're insisting on your claim?"

He didn't hesitate. "Yes."

"And you'll protect me?"

"Yes."

"No matter what?"

What was she up to? "Yes."

She ducked under his arm. "Then keep them off me while I find my son."

Six

How the hell had she ended up back where she'd started, mated to a wolf she didn't know, with everyone expecting her to smile and be happy? Sarah hugged Meg to her as she stepped out into the night. She took a deep breath, inhaling the cool air, blinking back tears when she couldn't find a trace of her son's scent. For five years, it had never been absent, but now it was nowhere to be found. The night sky, normally a thing of beauty, stretched over the landscape in an endless mocking expanse of empty black. Josiah was out there somewhere, along with Lord only knew how many rogues chasing him. She closed her eyes.

Keep him safe, Rachel.

Oh, God. What was she saying? Rachel was just one woman, not even trained in battle skills. Sarah Anne closed her eyes and tried again. Reaching out into the vastness of the night, searching for a connection with something bigger than herself. *Please, keep them both safe.*

A feeling of peace settled over her. She blinked. Meg cupped her cheeks in her tiny palms.

"We find 'Siah now, Mommy?"

Sarah hitched her up. The feeling of peace disappeared as if it had never been. "He'll be waiting for us at our special spot."

With everything inside her, she hoped he would be.

"What if he's losted?"

He couldn't be lost. "Auntie R is with him."

"What if they got hurted?"

Dear God, Megan had to stop bringing up all her fears. She didn't have the strength to fight them when so starkly presented. "Then we'll make them better."

"What if—?"

"Megan Lea, be quiet!"

Meg gave that little huff that preceded a full-out squall.

Oh, God, now she was snapping at the child she did have. Sarah Anne pulled her close, kissing the top of her head. "I'm sorry, baby. Mommy's just tired."

Meg's lip quivered. "I don't like yelling."

She'd been impervious to it until the rogues had broken into Teri's apartment, beating and raping the other woman while Meg lay in her crib listening. As much as she wanted those wolves dead for what they had done to Teri, she wanted them dead for the fear of men they'd put into her child. Except for Garrett. She bit her lip. Meg had no fear of Garrett.

"Then I won't yell anymore."

Meg's lower lip stuck out. "I don't like it when you yell inside, either."

Oh, dear heaven, she couldn't say things like that where anyone could hear. Among pack, differences like Megan's were not tolerated. "Sometimes people just get angry."

"But your mother doesn't have to be angry anymore," Garrett said as he came up to them.

Sarah Anne should have known he would follow.

"Why?" Megan asked.

"Because it's my job to make sure she's not upset."

"And if she is?" Sarah Anne asked.

Garrett's gaze met hers. The green in his eyes seemed so much more pronounced. "Then I take care of it."

It was a predictable male response. "I can take care of it myself."

Megan frowned at her. "But he's bigger."

Yes, he was. Much bigger. With broad shoulders, lean hips and enough muscle layered over both to make any woman's mouth water. "Might doesn't make right."

Megan clearly didn't get the reference. "But he's bigger."

Garrett's smile took on the depth of full amusement. "At least your daughter understands the natural order of things."

Natural order her aunt Fanny. That totally chauvinistic attitude was the main reason she'd left the pack. "She's not full wolf."

Garrett's feet settled shoulder-width apart. "Which is more than enough reason that she should stay pack. A wolf mate could protect her."

"And who will protect her from the wolves?"

His head tipped back. Arrogant man. "The same ones who will protect you. Cur and myself."

"You'd have no right if her mate claimed mate privilege."

Tilting his head to the side, Garrett hooked his thumbs in the pockets of his jeans. "Damn, I must have gotten all respectable-looking since joining Haven if you think I care about pack law when it comes to what's mine."

"You're a Protector." And Protector loyalties are always pack.

"I'm your mate first." Though his position didn't shift, she felt his attention home in. "And I protect what's mine."

And he considered her his. He wasn't going to be easy to shake, down the road, but for now, maybe she could use it. "Then you have to protect my son."

"That's already been taken care of."

Why couldn't he understand? She put her hand over Meg's ears. "Nothing is 'taken care of' until I have him back."

"You'll have him back tomorrow."

"And until then?"

"You'll have to have faith in your friend's training."

"What makes you think she has training?"

"What makes you think she doesn't?"

Her arms ached from holding Meg. Her heart ached with worry for Teri, Josiah and Rachel. And now he added the niggle of concern that maybe she didn't know Rachel as well as she should?

"I don't."

His hands came out of his pockets. "How well do you know her?"

Truth was, she didn't know anything about Rachel's past. They'd been outcasts together, clinging to each other through the common bond of their heritage, but she did know that Rachel was one of the most trustworthy people she'd ever met. "Well enough."

He clearly didn't believe her. "Why did she leave her pack?"

It didn't matter. One of the things she'd learned after leaving the pack was how to think for herself without the prejudice that saw outsiders as people not to be trusted.

"I don't know, but what I do know is that my son is safer with her than he is with you."

His chin came up and his eyes narrowed. "You have trouble with the fact that I'm mixed blood?"

It would be easier if she did. She dismissed his statement with a wave of her hand. "I have trouble with your arrogance."

"I'm not arrogant."

"Arrogant enough that you blithely dismiss my instincts."

He didn't exhibit any of the anger she expected, just asked in an almost conversational tone, "Do you trust your instincts?"

There was a time when she'd never questioned them.

"Sometimes."

But the times they'd failed her had left scars too big to ignore.

He tipped her face up. "That's a shame."

Yes, it was. Especially now when she needed them to tell her that her son was fine, and they weren't telling her anything at all.

"You need to find my son."

Cur's broad-shouldered frame filled the mouth of the cave, looking bigger silhouetted by the light behind him. "I was planning on doing that very thing."

Garrett nodded to Cur. "Sarah Anne will tell you where they're meeting."

"I will?"

Garrett reached for Meg. "Yes, you will."

She took a step back, feeling an unreasonable bite of hurt when Meg reached for him. "You have a habit of thinking you know a lot more than you actually do."

"I know you're going to tell me."

"The same way you think I'm mated to you?"

"Yes."

"Then you're wrong." She shifted Meg's position to ease the ache in her back. "I'm not joining Haven. It was a mistake to think I could."

"Haven won't have a problem with your children's bloodlines," Cur said, setting his pack down before squatting beside it.

"That's what everyone says . . . now."

Garrett smiled at Meg. It was a little stiff and a touch awkward, but from the way Meg beamed back, it didn't matter.

"Do you know something I don't?"

"I know it's never a good idea to take anything at face value."

"So you've decided you're going to go it alone."

"I've decided you don't own me." When he didn't contest her claim or look concerned, her stomach knotted.

"I guess there's plenty of time for you to learn that I don't often say what I don't mean."

She turned to Cur. "What do you do?"

He smiled and leaned against a boulder. With a flick of his fingers he motioned to Garrett. "Pretty much whatever he tells me to."

The brief moment of freedom she'd felt when she'd stepped out of the cave disappeared. "I hate you."

"I get that a lot."

An emotion as powerful as hate should have an impact. She turned and started walking down the hill, Meg nearly deadweight in her arms.

Garrett fell into step beside her. "You're a stubborn woman."

"You're an irritating man."

He was everything she'd run away from. An arrogant wolf who was convinced that he knew best, expecting her submission and obedience simply because he was male. He reached for Megan again. Sarah Anne gave him her shoulder.

"You're just tiring yourself out."

She planted her feet. "Go away."

He stopped and arched a brow inquiringly. Behind him, she could see Cur getting something out of his backpack.

"You should know I fully intend to contest your claim," she challenged.

"Uh-huh."

"There are probably a hundred women at Haven who want your attention."

"Probably."

She snorted. "You could've at least pretended modesty."

The corner of his mouth tipped up. "Probably. Where are you supposed to meet Rachel?"

Her mouth worked. Her distrust burned deep.

"Where?"

He repeated the question with such calmness. In the end, she didn't really have any other option but to tell him. "The south ridge. Are you happy now?"

"Not by a long shot. I shouldn't have had to ask twice."

Her head came up. Megan grunted, disturbed from her dozing by the sudden move.

"You might want to save your claiming until later, hot stuff. When you have all the facts."

The "hot stuff" scraped across Garrett's nerves. What the hell was the point in waiting? Did she have someone else in mind? "I never have been a man for taking chances, and waiting won't get me anywhere but dead. Just like that useless human husband you mated up with. You're a breeder, dammit."

She had to know what that meant. A woman who could produce children without a mating bond. Every werewolf alive would want to claim her.

She glared at him. "Don't you ever say that about him again. John was a good man who loved his children, and he was strong in ways you can never be."

"But you weren't mated to him." It was a shot in the dark.

She blinked. Her face paled to a ghostly white. "How did you know?"

Shit, that put a whole new spin on the situation. "I didn't."

"Oh, God."

Oh, God, was right. "We wondered why the rogues came after you so aggressively."

Her chin came up. "Well, now you know."

Now he knew. "You should have told Wyatt." The alpha wouldn't have waited until a home was ready for the family before sending for them. But he had waited, knowing that transporting them would expose them to suspicion. Since they'd been hiding successfully for eight years, he hadn't thought another couple months would matter. Of course, Sarah Anne hadn't told him about the attack on Teri. And she hadn't told him she was a breeder—a woman who could bear a wolf child outside a mating bond. A woman every werewolf would want because only the drive to mate was stronger in a wolf than the need to reproduce. Shit.

"You kept a hell of a lot secret."

"With good reason."

Maybe. "Did your husband know you were a breeder?"

"He didn't even know I had wolf blood."

"He wasn't worth much, was he?"

She jerked back as if he'd struck her, and a terrible shadow of pain whipped around her. "I loved him."

But she hadn't trusted him to handle the truth about her heritage. "Tell me, what were you going to do if your children showed signs of their mixed blood?"

She took a step back. "Tell him the truth."

"And you think he would have accepted that?"

She took another step back. Did she think it was that easy to run away from the truth?

She glared at him, her brown eyes dark with the pain of what she didn't want to admit. She might have loved her husband, but she hadn't believed in his love for her.

"He was five times the man you are."

He wasn't going to argue that. A lot of men were better than him. Men who'd had the luxury of developing a love of rules while growing up, whereas he'd survived outside them. "Be that as it may, currently you and your children are at the mercy of whomever is strong enough to keep you. Right now I'm the one with the claim, so until you find someone stronger, running away ends now."

"No."

Another step and she'd be out of his reach. He grabbed her arm. An immediate awareness of her mixed heritage slammed into him. There wasn't a hard muscle within the spread of his fingers. Shit, he was probably hurting her.

He let her go. She hunched her shoulder and rubbed her arm, glaring at him accusingly.

"That's right." She sneered. "I'm not pure wolf. I won't bring you prestige. I'll always be a liability and my children, too. So are you very sure you want to go forward with this claim?"

He let her go, reeling from the revelation and the waves of pain that flooded from her to him. She marched back to the cave. He followed more slowly, anger burning as hot as anything else. Over Sarah Anne's shoulder, Megan watched him with sleepy eyes and a whole lot of expectation.

He ran his hand through his hair. Shit. He'd spent his whole life thinking that, when he found his mate, he'd finally find acceptance.

Cherished images, framed in his youth of his life "someday," shattered. Sarah disappeared into the mouth of the cave.

Cur stood, his gaze following Garrett's. "You can see she's teetering on the edge."

"Yeah." Well, so was he. "She's not pure."

Cur would know more than anyone else what that meant to them. "Could see that." He continued to repack his pack. "She's got two kids."

"She's not pure wolf."

"Could see that, too."

Garrett spun around. "How do you know?"

"A pure wolf or a mix with wolf talent would have used a wolf's speed to save her daughter."

He was right. "Why the hell didn't I see that?"

"I'd say you were a bit distracted."

He had been. The woman had knocked him off his feet from the moment he saw her. And it got worse the more he saw her. He ran his hand through his hair again. "Hell."

"So tell me, are you pissed because she's not pure, or because you don't know what to do with her?"

Garrett dropped his hand to his side. Cur always had a way of paring things to the bare essentials. "The latter."

"That's what I thought." Cur stood and shouldered his pack. "Just remember, when that rage gets eating at you, she's yours, and the only way you lose her is if you hand her over to whatever yahoo thinks he's got the balls to take you down." Cur smiled at him. "And I'm still waiting to meet the wolf who can match you in a fight."

More of the wildness settled as that fact filtered through emotion. Though he had yet to mark her, Sarah Anne was his. And it would be a cold day in hell before he lay down in a fight.

"She is, isn't she?"

"Yup. So where am I meeting up with this woman and kid?"

"Rachel and the boy will be waiting on the south ridge tomorrow morning."

Cur grunted and hefted his gun. Before he could walk away, Garrett added, "I get the feeling Rachel isn't going to be that happy to see you."

Cur smiled over his shoulder. "Well, we wouldn't want it to be easy, would we?"

"Nope. Have a care, Cur."

"Going soft now that you have a little woman?"

"Got a bad feeling." A very bad feeling.

"How much trouble could a woman and a cub be?"

Garrett scented the wind. Trouble was definitely coming. "A bit more than you're expecting."

Cur's grin flashed white in the night. "Well, good, then. I hate to be bored."

"MEGAN!"

The cry was Sarah Anne's. In a heartbeat Garrett was in the cave, Cur hot on his heels.

Inside the cave, Sarah stood ten feet away from Teri. Meg was taking the final steps to Teri's side. Between her and her destination was Daire. The big man looked up, his dark face starkly impassive as she offered him a tentative smile. He didn't smile back.

Sarah tried again. "Get back here."

Meg took another step forward, her head cocked to the side, studying Daire's battle-ravaged face until she got close enough to touch.

"Oh, my God."

Garrett caught Sarah with an arm around her waist.

"Daire won't hurt her."

Sarah shook her head and dug her nails into his arm.

"Let me go."

It was too late. Though werewolves had hurt her aunt and killed her dad, and Daire must look, to the little girl, like the worst of them all, Meg reached out and placed her tiny hand against his cheek. The ancient didn't move as her fingers explored every inch of scar tissue. Neither did the child. For a heartbeat they stood face-to-face. Then Meg gave his cheek a pat.

"I'm sorry."

Daire didn't say a word, just watched her as she went back to her mother. And sticking her thumb in her mouth, she leaned against her mother's chest when Sarah Anne pulled her close.

"Damn," Cur murmured. "Things are getting interesting."

Seven

SARAH Anne took a breath and held it. She didn't like the way Daire was still watching Meg, as if he could see beneath her skin. "I'm sorry; she's always doing things like that."

His lips didn't move but there was the slightest crinkle around his eyes. Daire just shook his head and held up his hand. It annoyed her that he didn't even deign to speak until she realized he was still concentrating on Teri, doing something—she didn't know what, but something—to her. A smooth stroke of his thumb across her lips and Teri's frown melted away.

"What are you doing to her?"

He didn't look up, just said in that gravelly voice of his, "She's dreaming."

Could he read minds?

He looked at her. "Would it bother you if I did?"

"Of course."

"Your daughter is talented."

It sounded like a reprimand, but she couldn't be sure, since he didn't take his eyes off Teri's face. Garrett's arm tightened around her waist. "She's not wolf."

"Didn't say she was. Doesn't change the fact that she is talented."

She did not want any of the Protectors' attention on her daughter's odd ways. "Is Teri going to live?"

"I don't know yet."

God, she needed good news. The brush of Garrett's lips over her head should have been an irritation, but instead, it was a comfort. "When will you know?"

Daire looked up. It was funny—when she could really see his face, she didn't see the scars. Instead she saw those black-as-night eyes and the endless depth of energy behind them. She grabbed Garrett's arm against the black-magic lure. It wasn't a sexual pull, though there was a sexual component to it. The sensation was more like the type of vertigo she got when looking over the edge of a high cliff. She had the unsafe urge to lean farther, get closer.

"Your daughter doesn't fear me."

"No." And that was a mystery unto itself.

"How long have you been living with humans?"

"Eight years."

"You didn't teach her wolf protocol."

"There wasn't a need." She'd never intended her daughter to grow up among wolves.

"She shows no respect."

"If you touch her—"

This time his lip did twitch. "I know. You'll kill me."

Garrett pulled her back against the hardness of his thighs and chest. "Stop threatening the pack members, Sarah Anne. They'll get to thinking you don't like them."

"Maybe I don't." The retort was weak because she couldn't get past the fact that Daire was right. Meg didn't show the proper respect and as such could find herself quickly ostracized. Her bright, shining little girl snubbed. It broke her heart.

"She'll be fine, Sarah."

What did Garrett know about little girls and how they needed to fit in? In her peripheral vision, she could see a pair of scuffed black leather boots. She couldn't remember which Protector wore those. Kelon or Donovan. She didn't care. She wanted her son. She wanted her daughter. She wanted her life back. She wanted this all to end.

"Actually," Kelon said, "Daire hasn't declared allegiance to anyone yet. We're trying to win him away."

"From whom?" She wished the question back the second she said it.

Donovan walked up. "If you believe the rumors . . . from the devil?"

She could believe that.

Donovan's gaze raked her from head to toe. "Garrett."

"What?"

"Your mate is tired."

"I'm fine."

Garrett's hands on her shoulders moved subtly. The tight muscles relaxed and a comforting haze settled over the worry in her mind.

"I can't leave Teri." She looked so still, so lifeless, so close to death.

"You can't do her any good in here."

She swatted at his hands. "Stop telling me what I can and what I can't do."

His response was to lift her and her daughter into his arms and carry them over to a boulder. Easing her forward, he slid his big body behind hers. She had to admit that it was much more comfortable resting against him than the rock. And it felt so good to have his strength to lean on.

The last brought her up short. She couldn't let herself rely on Garrett's strength. She didn't even know if she was going to stay with Haven.

Meg struggled in her arms.

"Megan, stay still."

Daire held out his hand and beckoned with a twitch of his fingers. "Let the child go."

"She'll just be in the way." It was too dangerous. Meg would reveal too much. She felt a pull on her consciousness. Daire looked up and, once again, she was staring into those bottomless eyes.

"You know that's not true."

"She's just a baby. What can she do?"

He didn't blink. "More than you understand."

That was probably true. Megan's gift had been growing along with the rest of her. She looked at Teri, remembered that moment when Teri had thrown herself between Megan and certain death. Whatever Teri needed, she would get. Sarah Anne would just deal with the consequences when they came calling. She let Meg slide down her body.

Garrett's fingers slid down her forearm. Shivers chased up her arm. She whipped her head around. Garrett's eyes had that same bottomless feel as Daire's.

"If I thought there was danger, I wouldn't let her go," he whispered in that calm manner.

She believed him. Kissing the top of Meg's head, she whispered, "You do as Mr. . . ." She didn't know his last name. "You do as Mr. Daire says."

"Yes, Mommy."

Sarah Anne let her daughter go. Meg rushed to Teri's side, sinking with a peculiar grace to the floor beside her.

"Oh, God . . ." *Please protect her.*

Garrett's hands slid up her arm and around her shoulders, giving her something to brace against as Meg revealed all.

"What do I do?" she heard Megan ask.

"Pick up her hand."

Megan did, stroked her little fingers over it with an eerie competence and then brought it to her cheek while Daire watched.

"What is he doing?"

Garrett looked at her. "I don't think he's doing anything."

Which meant Meg was doing everything. Whatever that was. "What are you doing, baby?"

Meg glanced in her direction as if it should be obvious. "I'm giving Teri happy dreams."

There was no way anyone could misinterpret the child's meaning. No way anyone could mistake the otherworldly concentration in her expression.

Daire looked up at Kelon and Donovan. "She has a lot of talent."

The look Kelon and Donovan exchanged did not give Sarah Anne a warm fuzzy. Neither did Garrett's curse.

Megan was different, and now they all knew it.

Eight

IT was her worst nightmare come true. It would be hard enough for the child to live among werewolves as a human, but anything more different from the species would just be too much. Weres were not tolerant of "different."

Garrett's hand tightened on her shoulder for an instant as his thumb rubbed at the top of her spine, seemingly finding the tension within her and dispelling it in outward shivers of relief.

"Easy."

There was an odd depth to the order. If Sarah Anne hadn't been focusing so hard on Megan, it would have stolen her attention away. She shook her head. She couldn't afford that. Megan and Josiah were the only things she had in the world. It was up to her to keep them both safe. Even if she had no idea how she was going to do that.

Easy.

The command came again, more forceful, so imperative that she couldn't find the strength with which to fight it. She leaned back against Garrett, just wanting to close her eyes as the rightness of his scent enfolded her. With a wave of her hand she motioned Megan over. "Come here, baby."

Megan was so slow to respond that Sarah Anne wasn't even sure she'd heard her, but then she turned. Her eyes were very large and they looked like . . . Dear God, they looked like Daire's, compelling and haunting, with endless depths. "I stay here with Auntie T, Mommy. Daire needs me."

Sarah Anne had the eerie impression that Megan was slipping away from her. Everything was slipping away. "You don't need to, Meg. Mr. Daire is taking care of her."

Megan shook her head. "He needs me to help Auntie T."

No!

"Sarah Anne," Garrett soothed, "it's under control."

Nothing is under control.

The wild denial whipped through Garrett's head. Cur was right. Sarah Anne was at the edge of her control. He turned her in his arms. Catching her chin between his fingers, he turned her face to his. Her thoughts were no wilder than her eyes. "Yes. It is. Haven is not a normal Pack."

She strained against his hand, trying to keep Megan in her sight. He could feel her desperate belief that, if she just didn't look away, nothing would change.

In reality, everything had changed, but that was a big truth to swallow all at once.

"Megan will be accepted as she is."

"What makes you so sure?"

"Because they accepted Daire."

And him. Gentling his touch on Sarah Anne's shoulders, Garrett soothed her with a physical connection while he stretched the mental connection carefully. It was a touchy business trying to surround most of her anxiety without revealing his ability to do so to anyone else in the room. Among werewolves, some things were best kept private. Like his ability to manipulate minds.

Garrett continued to massage Sarah Anne's shoulders, probing backward along the torrent of emotion for the source. Garrett was a strong telepath. He didn't know if his talent came from his father or his mother, but psychic skills were not valued by most packs because a psychic with the skills of a fighter could win most battles. There weren't many pack leaders comfortable with a pack member who could wrest leadership from them at any time by right of challenge. Especially a half blood. He had no reason to believe Haven was any different. "You need to calm down."

She twisted in his grip, her gaze searching his. "Where will we go if they don't accept her?"

"With me."

Garrett turned her around and held her still. Though her muscles were as rigid as steel, it took minimal effort on his part to keep her there.

"Haven will accept your daughter," Donovan interjected. His gaze lingered for a fraction on Garrett. "Haven will accept all of you."

Shit. Did the Protector suspect?

Sarah Anne sighed, drawing his attention away from the Protector. Her hand turned into Garrett's, the act of trust striking deep. "I hope so."

No more than he did.

"Give us a chance," Donovan said. "You'll see."

Garrett answered for them both. Haven was a last chance for them both. "Don't see where we have any choice."

Donovan's response was a grunt that could have meant anything. Sarah Anne didn't say anything at all. Her glance slid to Teri and Megan, to where Kelon was attempting to clean up the blood. She took a shuddering breath. "God, I hope so."

Garrett took advantage of the relaxation to pull her against him. He needed to hold her to soothe the rage that surged at her distress.

"Why don't you relax and try to rest? You're going to need your strength later."

"I couldn't."

He tipped her face up. The underside of her chin was very soft against the calluses on his fingers. "Humor me."

"Why should I?"

"Because I don't want to force you." But he did want to persuade her.

A brush of his thumb across her temple released the scent of wildflowers into the air. It was a manufactured scent, but pleasing nonetheless. The floral tones complemented her natural allure. He wasn't surprised. Sarah Anne's heightened sense of smell would ensure such compatibility. The ridge of her collarbone pressed against his fingers. Fine bones, under fine muscles, under finer skin. He liked the way she felt in his arms and in his mind. Soft, yet possessing an impressive inner strength. The only thing he didn't like was her hair. It was too short. "Did your human husband allow you to cut your hair?"

Leaning back, she met his gaze. "Why? Are you planning on yelling at me for it?"

He smiled at the weak attempt to provoke him. "Nah. Just curious."

Little Megan turned and looked at him from under her brows in a fair imitation of her mother's autocratic way. "No yelling."

She was a pretty child with rounded cheeks and a sturdy little body, but she was so very tiny. Too tiny to be holding the hand of a dying woman, a look of such purpose on her face.

Garrett nodded. "No yelling."

Sarah Anne snorted. "Maybe I should get her to tell you to let me go."

He stroked his fingers up over her neck, smiling at her involuntary shiver. She could deny him all she wanted, but she was aware of him.

Teri moaned. Sarah Anne straightened. Garrett took the opportunity to hook his arm across her chest and his hand over her stomach and pull her back. He'd never tried to influence someone as he was trying to influence Sarah Anne, but the more contact there was, the clearer the path felt. He probed the unstructured energy surrounding her, finding a glimmer in the back. An opening?

Sleep. He sent the command into her mind, accompanying it with a subtle press of his hands. Her body settled slightly against his. Had he gotten through? He tried again. Daire glanced over. As usual, his expression gave away nothing of his thoughts. Garrett hoped to hell the ancient didn't have psychic abilities and didn't feel the ripple of his energy in the field around them. There was no way to tell. Daire could very well be a master psychic and was just better at masking them than Garrett was at detecting them. That was the trouble with ancients. They accumulated so much in their lifetimes they became almost unknowns.

"What's the plan?" Donovan asked with complete calm, coming to their side, bringing in the scent of the forest but nothing else. The McGowans could hide all emotion and scent in a way Garrett and Cur had yet to master. One of the benefits of being raised to their birthright. Garrett set his teeth as the old resentment welled. Both Donovan and Kelon looked over. He cursed under his breath. He would learn that trick.

"Tomorrow, before first light, when Teri gets a little stronger, even if we have to carry her, we'll head back to Haven."

Sarah Anne jerked upright. "Josiah."

Garrett pressed her back against his body, murmuring in her ear, "Cur knows the way to Haven."

The mental soothe bounced back on a wave of anxiety. "It's not safe for them to be out there alone. They—"

Daire cut her off. "Teri needs more help than I can give her here. If we leave at first light, we'll get back to Haven before the rogues realize these"—he waved toward the entrance, where Donovan had dragged the bodies—"aren't coming back. We'll need that head start to get Teri to safety."

It all made sense, but Garrett knew Sarah Anne was weighing the pluses and minuses with a mother's heart and wasn't surprised when she reiterated, "I'll wait here for Josiah."

It about killed him when she gave him that look that was half defiance and half plea. His instinct was to give her anything. Logic said he couldn't. Kelon and Donovan remained silent, letting him be the bearer of the bad news. He sighed. There were downsides to this mate business. "The place where you're planning on meeting Rachel and Josiah is in the opposite direction from where we're heading. Cur is laying a false trail and will be doubling back, but once we leave here with Teri, we'll be fair game."

Sarah Anne chewed her lip, her eyes on Megan, who sat holding her friend's hand. "Because the scent of blood carries almost as well as the scent of fear."

"Yes. We may need to split up if we're discovered. We can't afford to leave anyone here with you."

"You could stay."

"As much as I would like to make you happy . . ." Her brown eyes widened as if that fact surprised her. He shrugged. "Your way would put four lives in danger, including yours and Megan's. I can't support it."

Sarah Anne blinked rapidly. Oh, hell, she was going to cry. Nothing had ever prepared him for the effect of a mate's tearful gaze. The way her panic and fear would hit him in the gut like a Protector's fist. How inadequate he'd feel in the wake of the first tear's slide down her cheek. He cupped her face in his palm. "I promised you that your son would be safe. Wyatt promised you a home within his pack. Donovan and Kelon have promised to get you there safely. All you have to do is remember your place and follow orders and believe."

"Oh, God . . ." He felt her control break like a rubber band stretched too far. He turned her face into his chest. She didn't fight, just went with his direction. He could smell the salt of her tears as they gathered, and what it did to his insides wasn't comfortable. He braced himself for the onslaught of sadness that had to come.

It wasn't the gentle build he expected. Instead, she just ruptured into huge, rib-wrenching sobs. Her right hand doubled up into a small fist and she struck him, once, twice, a sob punctuating each blow to his shoulder. "I want my son. Go get him."

He'd never held a crying woman. He didn't know what to do with the emotion battering him any more than he knew what to do with the way her crying made him feel. All he knew was that he had to make it stop. Putting his hand over Sarah's head, covering her ears to block outside stimuli, he shot an order deep into the morass of emotion. *Sleep!*

She fought for three gut-wrenching sobs and then she went limp, her hands sliding off his shoulder, down to his wrists. Her pretty pink nails were a delicate contrast to the hard muscle and sprinkling of dark hair covering his forearms. Standing, he held on to the fragile link he'd forged, blocking out the distraction of her beauty, her scent, for the simple reason that losing it meant she'd wake, and if she woke, she'd cry again. He couldn't stand that.

Donovan didn't say anything as he passed. Neither did Kelon.

"Mommy?"

The one person Garrett couldn't ignore. Finding his voice was harder than it should have been. Megan watched him with too-old eyes that made him feel irrationally guilty. "She's tired."

"She's going to take a nap?"

He took the excuse offered. "Yes."

Megan kept stroking Teri's hand with that faraway look in her eyes. Teri moaned. Megan smiled. "I like you."

He didn't know what to do with that any more than he knew what to do with Sarah Anne's tears. He settled for a "Thank you."

As soon as Megan turned back to Teri, Teri visibly relaxed. There was no mistake—the child was connecting to the woman. While he struggled to connect to his mate, which theoretically should be easier than connecting with anyone else, this toddler was connected telepathically with a critically injured woman. The implications of that blew his mind.

Sarah Anne had to know her daughter had powers. That being

the case, she had to be as worried as he was about the implications of her new pack finding out. No matter how progressive, every pack had limits to their tolerance. Nothing was more important to pack than balance, and a child who could mess with their minds while in a tantrum would definitely be seen as a threat.

"Megan . . ." Sarah Anne protested as he walked away. Shit. He was so deep in Sarah's mind, his thoughts were bleeding over. He quickly masked any thoughts of Megan and replaced them with the sensations of how good she felt in his arms, how satisfied he was to have found her, how sexy she looked with the buttons of her shirt straining open across her breasts. Desire whispered from him to her as he settled down behind the rocks in the corner. Partially shielded, he whispered his magic word once again. She fought, rising above the seduction he offered, pushing back, adding her energy to his. He put more force behind the suggestion. As his back hit the stone, he felt the give in her brain, and then there was nothing impeding the flow of energy.

Sleep. The need washed over him as strongly as it washed over her, followed quickly by a sense of warmth, and unexpectedly . . . belonging. He couldn't help smiling as his eyes closed. Belonging felt as good as he'd always imagined.

Nine

HE was on fire, burning from the inside out. Every nerve ending straining toward the source of the scent filling his nostrils. Warm, willing woman. Garrett inhaled again as the woman shifted on his lap. And not just any woman. There was something special about her scent. Something intoxicating, the way whiskey only dreamed of being—spicy, earthy, right. He growled in his throat, turning her more fully into his embrace, not opening his eyes, just enjoying the flood of lush feminine delight into his senses as her ass slid over his groin.

Come here, darling.

She did, with a little sigh that went straight to his cock. Her arms wove around his neck. Had she heard his thought or was she just responding to the pressure of his hands? Was she real or was he dreaming? He wasn't sure, but either way, he didn't want to wake up. There was a depth to the connection he'd never experienced before. A seamless transition from his consciousness to hers. As he recognized that, he recognized something else. He could not only scent her desire; he could also hear it. The soft little sighs as her breasts melted into his chest, the need for his touch, the mental wish.

Touch my breast. Please.

The request whispered into his mind. She didn't have to beg. There was nothing he wanted more than to take those soft mounds into his hands, his mouth. He cupped her gently, not wanting to startle her and break the magic. She fit his palm perfectly. The resilient flesh conformed to the hard surface.

"Perfect."

The hard nub of her nipple slipped into the crease between his fingers in an erotic invitation. He squeezed, catching her gasp in his mouth, her surprise in his mind.

"So good. It's going to be so good between us."

"Yes."

It was a breathless sigh of surrender. Everything that was wolf in him snapped to attention. Everything that was male in him surged to the fore. His cock ached and his mind screamed. *Mine.*

She stirred. In protest? It was too late for protest. She'd already given herself to him in the most elemental way that went far beyond the physical. She'd given him access to her thoughts. Physically joining their bodies would complete the tradition, but the victory was already his.

A growl rumbled in his throat as he lowered his head, catching her lips with his, tasting her for . . . the first time? As sweet as honey, with a hint of pepper, her flavor spread though his mouth, enhancing the song of his senses. His. Only his. Her arm came around his neck, her breast pushed farther into his hand and her tight little rear slid across his cock in a sensual prelude. He had a vague sense of others around. A growl rumbled in his chest. The need to claim rose right along with his desire. He broke the kiss, trailing his lips along her cheek, nipping the line of her jaw.

Her pleasure poured over him in a liquid rain. He didn't close his lips as he found the cord on her neck. Her scent was stronger here, more addictive. He breathed deeply. Her little mewl of protest stroked across his desire, shredding his complacency. She was his. His teeth scraped down her neck, a tiny promise of the claiming that would soon take place. She shivered and turned her face, arching her neck.

Yes. Make it easy for me. Invite me.

He lowered her to the floor, easing her gently against the packed earth before following her down. Her body was so much smaller than his, yet somehow fit him perfectly. Her head twisted to the side. It was natural that his mouth found the hollow between her shoulder and neck, natural that his canines lengthened as primitive emotion overrode caution. He didn't care that they weren't alone, didn't care about anything except this moment in which she would become irrevocably his. He fitted his teeth to her shoulder, getting drunk on her scent, her taste. Now. She had to be his. Now. It had to be now.

Ten

"GARRETT!"

A hand touched his shoulder. The scent of another male stole past the pleasure in which he was drowning. He snarled, jumped up and lashed out. Kelon swore and leapt back.

Donovan grabbed Garrett from the other side. "Stand down."

Garrett shook his head. Too close. They were too close to Sarah Anne.

With a snarl Garrett broke Donovan's grip. The energy in him gathered. Head lowered, he took a deep breath. Aggression laced the air, layering over Sarah Anne's sweet scent. Burying it.

"Get back."

Kelon closed in on one side, Donovan on the other. "Not until you have yourself under control."

Only one word ground past the primitive rage. "Mine."

"Not yet," Donovan countered. "And you're not claiming her against her will."

"She's not complaining."

In reality, Sarah wasn't doing anything but lying on the floor where he'd placed her, her soft little body twisting with the yearning for his mark. The knowledge flowed through him. He shook his head, the flood of emotions not abating—his, hers . . .

Kelon knelt. Garrett lunged, only partially in control. Donovan knocked him aside. Sarah Anne gasped and moaned. Linked. They were still linked. He felt her scream build. A woman's reaction to rage pouring from him to her. He tried to sever the connection. *Easy. Easy.*

He sent the command to her, unable to break their link. She held him too tightly, wanting the security. How long had she felt this scared?

I've got you, darling.

It was himself he had to get under control. Kelon reached for Sarah Anne.

"Don't touch her."

Kelon's glance darted between Sarah Anne and Garrett, narrowed. "Shit."

"What the hell?" Donovan asked.

Kelon looked over at his brother, and Garrett knew his secret was out. "Looks like Megan isn't our only talent."

"Let her go, rogue."

Rogue. The hated name. "It's not me."

Donovan snarled. "Like hell."

"Maybe to start, but now it's her. She won't let go."

"Why the hell not?" Kelon snapped. "You're not that good-looking."

Because she was scared, and had been for a long time. But Garrett wouldn't tell them that. One thing Sarah Anne had in spades was pride.

Kelon leaned in. Garrett snarled, the urge to kill drowning all but a remnant of sense. "Stand back now!"

"Don't get fussy with me, rogue."

He ground out the truth. "I can't control my instinct with her in my head."

It galled his pride to give that explanation, but without space, he wasn't going to be able to last much longer.

From the back came Daire's deep rumble. "He's not lying. If she's linked with him, he's dangerous."

"Back off, Kelon," Donovan ordered.

Kelon stayed put, canines showing. "He's not in control."

"Neither is she. They are together, though."

Kelon paused and then cut Garrett a glare. "Don't mate her."

He wouldn't. Not yet; not here. "Just stand back."

Sarah's whisper twined through his mind, a siren's call for contact. A hunger. Need.

Casting Kelon a snarl, every sense on alert, Garrett crouched over her. "Sarah Anne."

She fought awareness, preferring to stay linked inside him. Hell, he didn't want the link severed, either. She was so right inside him. So safe.

"Mommy?"

But her daughter needed her. "Sarah Anne, Megan needs you."

Agony seared along his consciousness as Sarah wrenched free.

She cried out. He held her closer, absorbing her pain along with his.

"Careful."

He let her go when she struggled. Her big brown eyes were wide and her scent a wild mix of fear and confusion.

Donovan offered her his hand. Garrett's teeth snapped together when she took it. She did that too easily. She'd spent too much time among humans to touch another male so readily. They were going to have to talk about that.

Eleven

SARAH Anne rushed to Megan. The child was pale and wan. Sarah Anne snatched her close. "What did you do to her?"

Her small canines flashed in the dark. Too small to inflict real damage. Garrett wondered if she could actually manage to change. Was that why she hadn't run with her son?

"Nothing was done to her," Daire said wearily, from where he sat beside Teri. "She's just tired. What she did took a lot of strength."

"What exactly has she done?" Sarah asked.

The answer came short and sweet. "Kept Teri alive."

Garrett knew the strength of his own power, but he hadn't felt its existence until he'd reached puberty. How strong must the little girl be, that she could do so much, so young? And what would that mean to her future in the pack? She lay against her mother's side, her thumb stuck in her tiny mouth, eyes drifting shut. The flickering resentment at what she represented drowned in a flood of protectiveness. She would need someone strong to stand between her and prejudice. He brushed his mind over hers, experimentally. Without hesitation, it opened for him. With no shields, anyone could rip her apart. He hadn't ever been around children. Were they all this trusting?

"She will be very valuable." Daire looked pointedly at Garrett before returning his attention to Donovan. "Too valuable to chance."

To a packless rogue, he meant. Garrett shifted his position and bared his teeth in a silent challenge. "Fuck you."

Sarah Anne gasped.

"Watch your language," Donovan snapped, glancing pointedly at the baby.

It took Garrett a moment to recognize the surge of emotion that flooded him. Shame. Son of a bitch. He'd vowed never to feel that again.

"Sorry."

The guilt only increased when he saw the disappointment in Sarah Anne's expression. Hell, she already didn't trust him. She probably thought he'd never make it as a father for her kid. He would, though. Including watching his language.

"It won't happen again," he told her gruffly.

"Good."

There was a distinct lack of subservience in the retort. The defiance skittered along his raw nerves, bringing forth more aggression. He didn't need that right now. The rumble in his throat was soft, a warning she recognized, if the dropping of her lashes was an indication. He had all he could handle right now, with the other werewolves.

"Megan is not Haven's concern. She's mine, by right of mating."

"No one argues that."

"He's not marked her yet," Daire pointed out.

Donovan dismissed that with a quick wave of his hand. "Semantics."

Daire's response came too casually. "It is only custom, not law, that says a child goes with the mother."

Donovan spun as fast as Garrett did. "Take a child away from its mother?"

Hell, no. Garrett dropped into a fighting crouch. "Sarah Anne, get behind me."

Kelon caught her arm. "Stay."

"Now, Sarah."

The snarl that rumbled from Sarah Anne's throat was no less feral than the one building inside of him. "Let me go, Protector."

"No."

"You have no rights over me."

"Wyatt, Pack Haven's alpha, does, and until I get you back to Haven, I speak for him."

"Not in my opinion."

Kelon cocked an eyebrow at her. "Fortunately, your cooperation is not required."

Garrett smiled. "But you do need mine."

With a burst of mental energy, he broke Kelon's grip.

Move. He shot the command into Sarah Anne's mind.

Sarah Anne did, leaping behind him with gratifying speed.

Donovan slid in beside Kelon. Daire stood. Damn, he wished Cur was here. The odds weren't good.

Take Megan and run. Now.

He could feel the energy pouring off Sarah Anne in a wave of anxiety. Stress, fear, indecision.

His claws extended, the bones in his face ached and stretched and his canines cut into his lower cheek. The cold, hard clarity that always preceded battle settled into his stomach as he met the other Protectors' gazes. "My mate. My law."

"Haven doesn't work that way."

"Mommy?" Megan was waking.

"Then f— Screw Haven."

"You defy us, rogue, and we'll kill you."

He smiled at Kelon. "You can try."

Go, Sarah Anne.

Her boots scraped across the floor, but instead of going backward, she was in front of him, her slender shoulders squared. "No one is killing anyone. And no one is taking my baby from me."

Damn, he was going to have to take her in hand. From the shocked disbelief on the other men's faces, they likely wouldn't interfere.

"You don't have a say in this," Donovan said, almost gently.

"I have all the say. I've run before."

Shit. "A good time to run would have been thirty seconds ago," Garrett pointed out. When he'd told her to.

A flick of her fingers dismissed his reprimand. "I'm sick of chauvinistic men telling me what to do."

"Then you'll just have to readapt." He did not like the way Daire was shifting position.

Sarah's eyes flashed red as she snapped back at him, "Don't you tell me what to do. I don't wear your mark."

"Is that all that's holding you back from obedience?"

She bared those little canines at him. "Not at all."

"The child should be secured," Daire interrupted. "She's too important to risk."

"Garrett says he has her," Donovan countered.

Nice to know someone was willing to give him the benefit of the doubt.

"Garrett wasn't raised pack."

"Meaning?" Garrett wanted the prejudice out in the open.

Daire met his gaze squarely. "Your instincts aren't to be trusted."

And nice to know who wasn't.

"Like the one that says to take you down now?" he asked, taking Sarah's arm and moving her behind him. A downward cut of his hand told her to stay.

Daire nodded, as calm as ever. "Yes."

Power eased over the barrier of Garrett's thoughts, cutting

through his shields like a hot knife through butter. Shit. Daire. The merc *was* a telepath. And an incredibly strong one.

"Shit." With a hard mental shove, Garrett expelled Daire from his mind.

Daire's eyes narrowed. "You need more training."

"I had all that was available." To a half werewolf with no future.

"You trained yourself?"

Daire sounded surprised. Who the hell else did he think there was? "Yes."

Daire's eyes narrowed a fraction more before he nodded at Kelon and Donovan. "Don't kill him."

Donovan sighed. "He's not going to let us take the child if we don't."

Daire nodded. "Understood." He held out his hand to Garrett. "Give me your hand."

Give a physical conduit to a telepath who could rip his mind apart? The hell he would. "I'm not feeling sociable right now."

Not a muscle shifted in the other's expression. "If you want the woman and your child, you'll warm up."

Shit again. The ancient was powerful enough to make him do anything he wanted.

"Don't."

Sarah's whisper poked at his hesitation. She stood there, clutching her baby, agony in her eyes. She knew as well as he what would happen. Wolves were not tolerant of telepaths. Sooner or later they'd kill him. Especially if Daire was able to discern the full extent of his "talents." However, his safety was secondary to her safety and he couldn't stay with her if he didn't do this. He held out his hand. Daire took it. There was that slightest whisper of power and then . . . nothing, except the collective tension of everyone in the room.

Daire released his hand and grunted.

"What the hell does that mean?" Kelon snapped, his long black hair sliding over his shoulder.

"It means the McGowan instincts are sound."

Without another word, he turned and headed back to Teri.

Kelon frowned after him. "The man delights in talking in riddles."

"I get the impression that he feels he said all he needed to say," Donovan countered.

Garrett wiggled his fingers. Not the slightest remnant of power lingered. Had his shields held or had Daire read his mind? The wolf knelt beside Teri, touching her cheek with the same tenderness as before.

"Well, I need more." Kelon lifted his lip in a snarl. "Can we trust him or not, Daire?"

"For now."

Kelon rolled his eyes. "What the hell does that mean?"

Garrett didn't care. He grabbed Sarah and pulled her into his side. He felt better immediately. When Megan fussed, he took her into his arms. Her weight was as nothing against the unfamiliar weight of responsibility. For a moment, he wondered what the hell he was doing; then her little arms came around his neck and her breath blew across his skin. When Sarah Anne's hand slipped into his, he knew. He was accepting his destiny. His family. His place.

"It doesn't matter what he meant."

Both Donovan and Kelon stared at him with that impassive way they had. And then they nodded. The way they would when any pack member gave his word.

It was all shit, but somehow good.

Twelve

"I'M not leaving without my son."

Sarah planted her feet at the cave mouth and tugged on her arm. Garrett paid her no mind, merely switched his grip to her waist and hefted her up. "Cur's bringing him."

He said that as if it settled everything. "I don't know Cur."

"You will."

"What does that mean?"

"We pretty much share everything."

She'd lived among humans, seen rogues at their worst. "Like hell." They weren't sharing her.

His green eyes cut to hers and that strange tingle went down her spine, as if he'd touched her deep inside. "You'll do as you're told."

"Not hardly."

"You lived too long among the humans."

And that was supposed to cow her? She'd left behind the pack behavior that said she had to submit to a male's will when she'd married John. "Well, maybe I'll go back."

He didn't even look at her as he stepped over the large rock at the edge of the cave. "No, you won't."

The morning air was damp with dew, redolent with scent. No matter how deeply she breathed, there was no scent of Josiah or Rachel. Her stomach clenched on an agony of anxiety. Was he all right?

"Rachel might not go with your friend Cur."

All that got her, as he set her down, was a cock of an eyebrow and a curt, "One way or another, she'll go."

She dug in her heels. "He'll force her?"

A small smile flirted with his lips. "Never yet known Cur to have to resort to force."

She assumed he referred to how handsome Cur was. "There's a first time for everything."

With a tug of his hand he pulled her along. From her perch against his other shoulder, Megan giggled. "True enough," Garrett responded.

"But you're not concerned?"

"No."

"I'm not leaving Josiah."

At that he turned. With her hands still captured in his, he brought both to her cheek. "I'm bringing him to you, baby."

"I'm not a baby."

His eyes did a rapid but thorough perusal of her figure, starting at her head, lingering on her breasts, before traveling to her feet and then back up. She braced herself for the obvious retort. Instead he asked, "You walking, or am I carrying you?"

"I'm not leaving my son." She couldn't.

With a move so rapid her mind only cataloged it afterward, she was facedown over his broad shoulder. And with the same graceful strength he again picked up Megan, effectively mitigating her struggles with the fear of hurting her daughter.

"I figured you for a stubborn one."

He didn't sound at all put off by the idea.

Thirteen

HAVEN wasn't what Sarah Anne had expected. She was used to the rigid community structure of werewolves, with the houses set out by hierarchy, but Haven was actually charming. There were capes mixed in with Victorians and bungalows. Some of the houses were in a state of disrepair, but the majority of them were in the process of being rebuilt.

"How big does Wyatt expect his pack to be?" she asked as the SUV they'd picked up three hours ago left the town behind.

Garrett cut her a glance. "I didn't get the impression that he thought in terms of limits."

She thought of all the weres who had been displaced for a variety of reasons. "He can't expect to take them all in."

"Where would you suggest he draw the line?"

Donovan's low drawl from the front seat made her blush. The most likely place would be with half bloods. Like her and her children, who were not even that.

"I don't know."

"Yeah, neither does Wyatt."

"So he's just taking in whomever?"

The seat creaked as Donovan turned. His hard gaze raked her face, leaving her feeling like less than nothing for asking a perfectly valid question. Garrett's arm came around her shoulder. He was always doing that. Touching her when she needed it most. Whether she wanted it or not.

"The pack is always protected."

"Meaning?"

"Meaning we investigate anyone who applies."

"You investigated me?"

There were a whole lot of things she didn't want them to know about her.

The half smile on Donovan's mouth raised the hairs on the back of her neck. "We left that to Garrett."

The sick feeling in her stomach grew. The hairs at her temple stirred. There was the softness of a "Relax" couched inside an exhale. "There was nothing unexpected in your background."

Then he hadn't discovered everything. She let out her breath. His lips brushed her temple again in what almost seemed like . . . approval?

"Of course," Donovan continued. "In light of what we now know, those findings could be suspect."

Garrett cursed.

Donovan laughed. "Relax, cub."

"Fu—" He glanced at Megan, who was leaning against his other side. "Screw—"

Sarah gasped. Donovan laughed as the car pulled into a driveway that wound through the trees, and said, "You might just want to let that trail off."

He did, thank the Lord. The wolf in Sarah went on alert as the SUV wound down the driveway. Her nostrils flared, seeking the scent of danger. All she could smell was a hint of leather, the underlying scent of Donovan—wolf, but wrong. The fragrance of her daughter and the overwhelming perfection of Garrett's scent. Which was slightly stronger in response to the tension.

She bit her lip. If she was worried, how much more so must he be? Not only was his own talent putting him in jeopardy, but as he truly believed she was his mate, he had to worry for Megan. Even if he wanted to escape, she and Megan tied his hands. And who knew what Kelon and Daire were saying to Wyatt? They had a twenty-minute jump on her arrival, as Donovan had stopped for supplies. She glanced up at the flat set of Garrett's mouth.

He definitely knew they were in trouble. But he wasn't running. She shouldn't be surprised. He was a Protector and had claimed her as mate. The one thing a wolf woman never was was alone or vulnerable. Living among the humans, she'd forgotten how good that could make a woman feel. When Garrett looked down, she offered him a smile. The one he offered in return didn't shake. It was full of the confidence with which a Protector was born, and it settled over her uncertainty with that uncanny yet so welcome calm.

She lay her head against his shoulder. Whatever was going to happen, he was the one who could best handle it. Beneath her ear, she heard his rumble of satisfaction. Her conscience pinged her sense of guilt, but she was tired, worried and, as they pulled in front of the house, more terrified than she'd ever been. The car stopped. The front door of the big Victorian cracked open. Fear chased hope. Suddenly, coming here didn't seem like such a good idea. A big man stepped through the door. Right behind him came a medium-height woman with brown hair.

Garrett opened the door and stepped out before reaching back to give Sarah Anne a hand. "Too late to change your mind."

"You're supposed to support me in whatever I do. Even if I choose not to swear fealty."

His hand on hers sent that scintillating rush of pleasure down her spine. When he brought the back of her hand to the heat of his lips, the sensation doubled. "So I did."

She pulled her hand from Garrett's. A big werewolf who had an expectation of obedience that exuded from his very being caught her eye. That had to be Wyatt. Only the true Alpha had that. He was watching them—no, Garrett—very closely.

Her lip curled up. A snarl rumbled in her throat. Garrett's hand on her arm held her back when she would have stepped in front of him. Wyatt's left eyebrow went up.

"So it's true. You're mated?"

She tossed her head, not wanting her options closed off so early. "I don't wear his mark."

Wyatt's lips twitched as he glanced over her shoulder. "I see."

A glance showed why. Garrett stood, head up, shoulders back, glaring at his Alpha. Sarah Anne elbowed him in the gut. He didn't even grunt.

Wyatt's lips twitched again. "But I'm thinking that's just a matter of time."

The woman behind Wyatt cuffed his shoulder. "Wyatt, remember when we had the discussion about rude assumptions?"

"Not at the moment." He reached back and drew a woman with long brown hair pulled back in a ponytail forward. "This is my mate, Heather."

Heather was of medium height with a svelte build, gray blue eyes and a restless energy. Sarah Anne took a breath, confirming what she already knew. "You're human."

Heather smiled brightly at her. "To the core."

"And you're Alpha." Wyatt's warning skittered down her spine. She immediately remembered protocol and lowered her eyes. "Nice to meet you."

Garrett's fingers brushed her back. Heather frowned at Wyatt and then at Sarah Anne. "What?"

Wyatt folded his arms across his chest.

"This is one of those wolf things, isn't it?" Heather asked.

"Yes," Wyatt replied.

A blush burned Sarah Anne's cheeks. So much rode on this introduction going well and she'd already insulted the Alpha's wife. "I'm sorry," Sarah Anne said.

Heather threw up her hands. "For what?"

Sarah opened her mouth. Heather cut her off with a slash of her hand. "Whatever it was, forget about it."

"It was disrespect," Wyatt drawled, displeasure still in his tone.

Heather snorted. "More like shock, I expect."

That jerked Sarah's eyes up.

Heather's smile made her look so much more approachable. "Wyatt's not nearly as uptight as he appears."

"I'm not?"

Heather patted Wyatt's hand. "Nope, and as I told you before, if we're going to have a community—"

"Pack," Wyatt corrected.

"Community," Heather reemphasized. "Of humans and were-wolves, then you're going to have to allow for cultural differences."

"Sarah Anne is a werewolf—"

"Who has been living among humans for eight years." Heather walked down the four steps, her smile never faltering. "And I, being human, prefer to be treated as one." She held out her hand. "Welcome."

Sarah Anne took her hand, slowly letting out her breath as the relief flowed through her. She hadn't offended her Alpha female.

Heather included Garrett and Megan in the welcome before coming back to Sarah Anne. "I thought you had a son?"

"Cur's bringing him," Garrett cut in.

He didn't know that. Cur hadn't had time to call in. The familiar despair clawed at Sarah's stomach. Heather squeezed her hand.

"There's no one better than Cur."

Words were beyond her, so she just nodded and stepped back.

Wyatt stepped down beside her and put his arm around Heather's shoulder. The other woman looked totally content as she leaned into his side. "Welcome to Haven."

It had to be a good sign that Heather was so at ease with her mate. "Thank you," Sarah said.

"Did Teri arrive?" Donovan asked.

"About half an hour ago." Heather looked toward the tall upstairs corner windows. "Daire has her upstairs. He says she'll be fine."

Sarah Anne followed her gaze, dread and hope vying for dominance. "Do you believe him?"

Heather didn't pull her punches. "As a human or a woman mated to a werewolf?"

"Both."

Heather sighed. "As a human nurse looking at a human patient, I don't see how she could be. As a werewolf's mate, I have hope. Daire is an impressive man."

Garrett's fingers pressed the center of her spine and said, "Yes, he is."

"Thank you."

Wyatt cocked his eyebrow at Donovan. "I still think that's one dangerous wolf."

"Not to us, I don't think."

"Don't think?"

"Hard to tell," Kelon said, walking up.

"But you brought him here?"

Kelon hauled gear out of the back of the SUV. "You find a way to tell him no and make it stick."

Wyatt glanced at the second story of the house. "That powerful?"

Kelon put the packs on the suitcase. "That mean."

Teri must be in that room. Sarah debated handing Megan to Garrett, but with whom would she be safer? The man had muscle on top of muscle and the wherewithal to use it. And he saw the little girl as his to protect.

She shoved Megan into Garrett's arms before he could figure

out what she was doing. She kissed Meg's cheek. "I'll be right back, baby."

Megan plucked her thumb out of her mouth long enough to ask, "Stay, Garrett?"

Sarah Anne looked up into Garrett's hazel eyes. She hoped trusting her daughter to him wasn't a mistake. "Yes."

Fourteen

SARAH Anne made it to just inside the door, but no farther. Daire stood at the foot of the stairs, arms folded across his chest, looking broader and somehow a lot bigger than she remembered. The scars on his face lent a feral cast to his features.

"I want to see Teri."

"No."

Just that. A "no" with no explanation. She wanted to gnash her teeth. "Why not?"

He motioned toward the doorway to the right. From the dark wood paneling and the big desk, she figured it must be Wyatt's office. "We need to talk."

"After I see Teri."

The hair on the back of her neck lifted as the floorboards creaked behind her. Wyatt stepped past. Where had he been hiding?

"We have some things to sort out first," Wyatt said.

"Whatever it is, it can wait."

The soft smile he gave her did nothing to cover the order. He motioned to the room. "I'm afraid it can't."

A touch on her thigh had her looking down. Megan clutched

her leg, blue eyes wide as she stared at Wyatt. She made a soft sound of distress.

Sarah Anne glanced over her shoulder for Garrett. He strode up the porch steps, wearing that slightly baffled look everyone had the first time Megan slipped their grip.

Wyatt's gaze dropped to Megan. And that fast, his expression softened.

"Hello, Megan. Welcome to your new home."

Sarah Anne blinked again. Was he being . . . charming?

"My name is Wyatt."

"Mr. Carmichael," Sarah Anne corrected.

Wyatt cocked an eyebrow at her. "That's a mouthful for a bit of a thing like her."

Sarah Anne licked her lips. "Manners are important."

Daire nodded. "So are traditions."

She licked her lips again. That didn't bode well. Tradition would have her packless. Tradition would have her daughter killed. "I'm not that fond of tradition."

Wyatt's golden brown eyes met hers. The corner of his mouth twitched. In annoyance or a smile? "I've never been overly impressed with pack tradition, either. That's why we're starting new traditions here."

She decided to take the bull by the horns. "If they involve you kidnapping my child, they're not going to fly."

His mouth twitched again. And it was definitely a smile. He motioned her into the room. She didn't have any choice but to go. Thank God Garrett was right behind her.

"Is that a threat?" Wyatt asked.

She squared her shoulders as she passed. "Yes."

Two things happened simultaneously. There was the sound of a scuffle and the door closed, trapping her in the room with Daire, Wyatt and Donovan.

"Not much of you backing that threat," Wyatt commented as she spun around.

"Wyatt," Heather gasped from the other side of the closed door.

Garrett's energy pulsed against the edges of Sarah Anne's mind in a relentless wave. He was telling her to stay calm. That he was there. She took another gamble, holding hard to that energy. "I'm not alone."

"You've accepted Garrett as your mate, then?"

She looked at Daire's stony expression. She didn't doubt for a minute that he'd take her daughter if he saw a need. She looked at Wyatt. He still had that half smile on his face, but she didn't have any illusions there, either. He'd take Megan, too, if it meant pack safety. Donovan was the wild card.

"Yes."

The walls closed in around her. Energy whirled. She could feel Garrett's intent. He was coming in. She held tighter to his energy, needing him.

Stop it.

The order came out of nowhere, echoing in her mind. Startled, she gasped and spun around. Daire?

There was a series of hard thuds against the wall. Daire warned, "He's not going to wait much longer."

Wyatt shrugged. "He doesn't have much choice. If I say he waits, he waits."

"He has mating lust. She's telegraphing like crazy. I give him about two minutes before he stops giving two hoots who you are."

Wyatt smiled. "Then I guess we'll have to make it fast." He turned back to her. "You sure about accepting Garrett as your mate?"

She nodded again. "Yes."

Garrett cursed. *Not like this.*

What does it matter? she shot back.

She couldn't believe that she was the only one who heard Garrett's thoughts.

With a pointed glance toward Donovan, Wyatt said, "Then it's settled."

Settled? What was settled? She wasn't even aware there had ever been an option. "What does that mean?"

The sense that events were spiraling out of her control increased.

"It means just that. Your relationship is settled."

"And Megan?"

"She's your mate's responsibility."

"And Josiah?"

"He's pack, and will be brought home."

She couldn't ask for a more solid promise than that of her Alpha. A bit of her anxiety faded.

"And Garrett? You'll leave him alone?"

Wyatt shook his head. "Him I haven't decided about yet."

For a moment Sarah Anne was torn, but she owed the debt of her daughter's life to Garrett. The least she could do was to insure he had pack. "If I decline the mating, would that help you to accept him?"

A snarl erupted behind the door. She felt the surge of Garrett's energy.

Wyatt's expression was sympathetic. "No, it won't."

"So I chose him with no certainty?"

"Only the certainty any wolf is born with when meeting their mate," Donovan answered.

How could she trust that?

Another surge of energy and a mental warning. *Stand back!*

Sarah Anne jumped back. Megan spun around as the door hit the wall. Her face lit up with joy as soon as she saw Garrett.

"Gar!"

All the males watched as the little girl ran, with total trust, toward Garrett. He scooped her up in one arm and then put the other around Sarah Anne's shoulders. The gesture of possession summed up the one word that slipped past his lips. "Mine."

Instead of reacting with a snarl and a challenge, Wyatt just laughed and leaned back in his chair. "Apparently no one, least of all her, is contesting that."

Garrett whipped around to look at Sarah. She forced herself to meet his eyes.

"Sarah Anne was in the process of accepting your mating claim when you . . . interrupted," Donovan said.

Garrett studied her for a heartbeat. The probe in her mind was as gentle as his thumb's touch to the corner of her mouth. There was hesitation but also . . . joy? His "Finish it" was beyond arrogant.

He was so irritating. She folded her arms across her chest. "I'm not sure I want to now."

Another bark of laughter from Wyatt and a chuckle from Donovan.

Garrett's thumb slipped between her lips, teasing the inner lining. "Do it anyway."

She wanted to melt into a puddle at his feet. She wanted to kick him in the shins. Neither was the option a mature woman would pick. More was the pity. Which left her only one. With as much dignity as she could muster she said, "I accept his claim."

Garrett leaned in until his breath caressed her lips, mingled with hers, inviting her to taste what he had to offer.

"Good girl."

She stood on tiptoe, closing the distance between them. As his lips parted against hers, she kicked his shin. There were some things that needed to be understood from the get-go. "I'm not a girl."

His chuckle puffed into her mouth in an erotic invitation. "Good."

Good. She shivered from head to toe as his kiss flowed through her. Yes, it was very good.

Megan giggled. Wyatt tossed an envelope on the desk.

"What's that?" Garrett asked, watching Sarah Anne's mouth

so intently as she ran her tongue over her lips that it felt as if he had kissed her again.

"Keys. We have three houses currently available. The addresses are in the envelope. Pick one and return the others."

A house? They were going to have a house? It was more than Sarah Anne had dared to hope. A house spoke of permanence, acceptance. Garrett slipped his hand from around her back and reached for the envelope. She held her breath. Would he accept? "Just like that?" Garrett asked.

"Yup." Wyatt folded his arms across his chest. "Just like that."

Fifteen

SARAH Anne liked the cape the best. Garrett could tell from the way she lingered and trailed her fingers across the few pieces of furniture in the living room. He hitched a dozing Megan up higher onto his shoulder. Her mouth pressed against his neck. There was a suspicious dampness.

"Is she getting drool on me?"

"Yes, she is."

He grimaced.

Sarah Anne laughed. "Suck it up."

"Easy for you to say. You're not wearing kid drool."

She paused and turned, facing him. "Do you really mind?"

She meant more than just the drool. She was worried that he resented her children.

"Can't say that I didn't expect to."

"But?"

There was a world of hope in that "but."

"Apparently, it's not in me. Maybe I'm more human than wolf in some ways."

Her head cocked to the side. Her hair swung around her face. She looked very pretty standing there, studying him.

"Do you think saying that will make me more comfortable with you?"

"I hope something will."

Her gaze dropped to Megan. "You're growing on me just the way you are."

"You sure?"

"Don't make me think on it too much, okay?"

"Why?"

"Because if I don't think about it, I'm more comfortable."

"Deal." He rubbed Megan's back. "How about we lay this one down for a bit?"

"You don't think anyone will mind?"

"Why would they?" he asked, carrying Megan to one of the two downstairs bedrooms. "This is going to be our home."

Sarah Anne trailed behind him. "You liked that Victorian."

"It was nice, but this feels like home." Mainly because Sarah was comfortable here, and he liked to see her comfortable.

"Thank you."

"For what?"

He laid Megan on the pastel yellow comforter that brightened the sunny room. She immediately turned on her side. Her thumb popped into her mouth. She looked like a tiny angel. Too tiny to have so much trauma in her life.

Sarah Anne took the pink-flowered throw off the bottom of the bed and drew it over her daughter's shoulders. "For claiming an association with humans to make me feel better."

He chuckled. "It was that obvious?"

"You're all wolf, Garrett."

He pushed her hair out of her face. "And you don't like it."

"Sometimes it scares me."

"Only sometimes?"

"Just sometimes."

That was an improvement. She hovered by the bed. He took her hand and tugged. "Might as well let her get some rest."

Sarah Anne nodded, but her lower lip slipped between her teeth. No doubt, she was rethinking the wisdom of telling him so much. No doubt, she worried he was getting ideas. And she'd be right.

He caught her hand. "Let's check out the backyard."

They passed through the neat kitchen on the way to the back door. Garrett could easily imagine sitting at the glass-top table sipping coffee with Sarah in the morning while the kids ate breakfast. It was a very settled image of a future he'd never thought would be his. The feeling of being on the outside looking in slipped some more. He squeezed Sarah Anne's hand. To his surprise, she squeezed back. And smiled. He opened the back door and looked out, kissing her hand as she stepped through onto the small deck. Her smile faltered, but didn't slip. Maybe she was warming up to him.

The backyard was fenced in. The grass was freshly mowed. Situated in the deep rectangular yard was a small jungle gym and a barbecue, along with a brightly colored play house. Something for a girl and a boy.

"Looks like Wyatt thought you'd like this one, too."

Sarah Anne's hand lay unresponsive in his. "Maybe."

She was staring at the jungle gym. He knew what she was thinking. It was all too easy to imagine a little boy playing there. "Cur will be calling anytime now with news of Rachel and Josiah."

"Thank you."

He stepped in front of her, blocking her view. "You don't have anything to be nervous about, Sarah. I'll take care of you."

She glanced up, startled. "I know you will."

Yeah, he guessed that was a given seeing as he was wolf, but she could sound more enthusiastic. That lack gnawed at him. What had her human husband been able to give her that was so wonderful? Had the mating heat been stronger with her husband? Did he kiss better? Hell, what did that matter when the man hadn't even been able to protect her? Garrett tugged Sarah out onto the deck, closing the door. When he turned back, he was struck by how small she looked standing there. She lacked the sturdy structure of a female wolf, the sleek muscle, heavier bone. He remembered the flash of her small canines.

"Can you change at all?"

Her eyes flew wide. She shook her head as her gaze ducked his. It wasn't hard to figure out why. A werewolf who couldn't change was like a human without limbs. Trapped. Often ostracized. He remembered the small wolf fleeing with the male child. "Josiah can?"

She nodded.

"He's only a quarter wolf."

She shrugged. "He can change."

"Megan?"

She took a step back. "So far, no."

He followed. "There's still time." Sometimes it took years for werewolves to come into their full powers. "Besides, she has other strengths."

She frowned. "That Daire wants to use."

"Daire can want forever. It's not happening if you don't want it." In case she didn't understand he had value that was directly applicable to her needs at the moment, he added, "One of the benefits of having a werewolf for a mate."

"I think it was a mistake to come here."

"I think that has yet to be determined."

"You've sworn loyalty to Haven. My loyalty is to my children."

"In about five minutes we're about to be mated and my loyalty to you will take precedence."

Another step back for her. "Pack law says 'pack above all.' "

Another step forward for him. "Does it?"

"You know it does."

One more step and she'd be back against the side wall, with nowhere to go but into his arms. "I haven't read the law."

She swallowed hard but didn't take that step. "It still applies."

He tipped her chin up. "Not to me. I never thought I'd have a pack or a mate and I've thought about it enough to know what matters to me more."

"Which?" She needed to hear the words.

"Nothing will ever matter more to me than you."

"Promise?"

He stroked his mind over hers, letting her feel the depth of the truth. "Promise."

Her hands slid up over his shoulders and her frown softened. "You're a good man."

"Not that good."

"Meaning?"

"There's no sense putting the marking off, Sarah. The longer you do, the more danger the children will be in. Wyatt will be checking for the change in your scent, looking for my mark."

And not just Wyatt. Other males would, too. Sarah was a good-looking woman, obviously capable of producing children. Any un-mated male who could would want a chance with her. She took a breath and blew it out. "Can't we even wait a day?"

He remembered Daire's enigmatic stare, Wyatt and Kelon's silent communications. "No."

She closed her eyes. "I was hoping we could get to know each other."

"I'm sorry."

She didn't say anything.

The brick was warm against his palms as he flattened them against the wall on either side of her head. "How do you know mating with me is going to be so bad?"

"I'm beginning to think mating with you might be very good."

"Then why the hesitation?"

She opened her eyes. The brown of her irises seemed deeper, warmer. Cupping his cheeks in her palms, she sighed. "There won't be any going back."

"There's no going back now." He would never let her go.

She dropped her hands to his upper arms, grazed the muscle there, returning them to his face for a second before dropping away again. "No. There isn't."

He wanted those soft hands back on his cheeks. Tucking his finger under her chin, lifting her face to his, he studied her expression. Her worry was clearly etched in the fine lines at the corners of her eyes, the tightness of her lips. He slid his fingertips up her jaw, feeling the delicacy of the bone. He could probably snap it with just a squeeze of his fingers. No wonder she'd gone to a human. Were matings were often violent. She had to be terrified that she wouldn't survive it. He touched his thumb to her lower lip, feeling her start ripple across her skin in a subtle protest. There was nothing he could say that would convince her. "You're worried I'm going to hurt you."

She shrugged, as if it didn't matter, but she also didn't deny it.

He didn't like her fatalistic acceptance. Didn't like the way a lot of things stood between them. She wanted him, but she didn't like it. She needed him, yet she resented it. Maybe there had been werewolves who had started out with worse marriages, but he wasn't sure he'd ever met one.

"I won't hurt you, Sarah Anne."

Her eyes flashed at him. "If you do, I'll make you pay."

He should have been offended. Forced her to retract the threat. Instead, he found himself smiling. He took that last step in. She took the inevitable step back, right to where he wanted her. "Good."

He knew the exact minute she became aware of his intent. Her scent spiked with a teasing musk and her eyes flew wide. He watched her throat work as she swallowed. And smiled. Shifting his hands to either side of her shoulders, he pressed his mouth to the smooth muscle, his smile broadening at her soft gasp. Sarah Anne might distrust him intellectually, but instinctively she knew who he was. The other half to her whole. The one to whom her value was immeasurable. The one who would always keep her safe, always put her above all else.

Her throat muscles worked against his lip. Catching the soft skin between his teeth, he nipped softly. He caught her as her knees gave out, pressing her against the wall. The violent need to possess welled. She moaned. The taint of fear spread through her scent. He didn't want her afraid.

"I'll take care of you." If it killed him, he'd take care of her. He had pack, a mate, a family. Three things he'd always thought would be denied him. He wouldn't insult the gifts by abusing them. He brought her hand to his mouth, inhaling her scent, feeling the softness of her skin. "And I'll pleasure you."

Sixteen

SARAH Anne shivered from head to toe as his lips brushed the back of her hand. Yes, he would. She could feel it in her mind, in her bones, in her womb. Electric shocks of pleasure traveled from her neck to her clit, coming faster and harder as the nip turned to an erotic bite. Pain mixed with pleasure. His thigh shoved between hers. Her knees gave out. His thigh was there to offer support. And pleasure.

"Rock on me."

His hand on her hip guided her in the motion he wanted. She followed his lead only to discover she wanted it, too. His hand left her hip, moving onto her breast, enveloping the full curve with strength, heat. Promise. He squeezed, his thumb flicking across her nipple. She ground her pussy down on his thigh.

"Damn, that's good," he growled as her nipple swelled to his command. With another growl, he yanked the scoop neck of her T-shirt down until it cupped her breasts, holding them up for his pleasure. Her bra dissolved beneath the slice of his claw. Her will dissolved beneath the heat of his mouth. With a moan she pulled his mouth to her. He was being so gentle when she needed more.

"Harder. Oh, please, harder."

His eyes glowed red. "Do you know what you're asking?"

Yes, she did. She wanted to be taken by her mate. She wanted his passion, his wildness. His possession.

"Yes, I do."

"Damn." His fingers tightened to near pain around her breast. His hand tangled in her hair pulling her closer. She opened her mouth for the thrust of his tongue, the power of his kiss. His mind brushed over hers, leaving the image of how he saw her. Lush, beautiful, a siren in a T-shirt and jeans. She'd always dreamed of being seen like that, wanted like that.

"Oh, God."

His teeth closed around her nipple, pressing into the sensitive flesh slowly, carefully, until the pleasure speared so deep, she gasped and dropped her head back in an agony of pleasure. Her womb clenched in need. Her pussy ached. Her legs spread. He growled.

There was the sound of tearing material and then the tip of his claw grazed the well of her vagina.

Pleasure ground up through her pussy.

"Open, seelie."

Seelie, the ancient endearment that a werewolf reserved for his mate. She spread her legs wider. Material ripped further and cool air whispered over her heated flesh. Garrett growled his pleasure as his finger slid along the soaked slit. She shuddered from head to toe as the calluses of his finger rubbed across her pussy. Another shiver preceded the beginning of an orgasm.

"You're ready for me." There was wonder and satisfaction in the statement.

She nodded, digging her nails into the back of his neck. "Touch me again."

She needed him to touch her again so she could come. She so needed to come.

"Don't come," he grunted, fumbling between them. "Not yet."

She didn't know if she could help it as his finger teased her clit, probed her pussy, tantalizing with the promise of possession but not delivering. Spreading her legs wider, she tried to force the union. "Why?"

"Because this first time, you come on my cock."

Oh, shoot. The trembling started deep within. "Garrett!"

"Shit!" His mouth bit at hers as he lifted her. Her legs wrapped around his waist. His cock settled into the well of her vagina. For a moment, she hesitated—he was so big—but then his fingers dug into her buttocks, spreading them as he squeezed, pulling her down as he thrust. She screamed as the pleasure rode the slight pain while he stretched her, filled her. He held himself high within her as he pumped almost helplessly, forcing more and more of his cock into her tight sheath, not giving an inch, not letting her resist, grunting as she moaned and tightened her legs, pulling him deeper, not caring about the pain, caring only that she have him all. She had to have him all. It was wild. It was crazy. It was perfect.

His teeth snapped by her ear. "Present."

The order whipped along her desire, sending it higher. She hesitated. Keeping her back pressed against the wall, he tucked his shoulder under her right leg and then he did the same to the left, leaving her suspended between the wall and his passion. His cock ground deeper; the pleasure spiked higher. One more thrust and she was impaled fully on his pleasure. He ground against her as her orgasm gathered.

"Present!"

She did, arching her head to the side, giving him access to her neck. Within her, his cocked flexed. His mind sought hers. She could feel his passion, his pleasure, his climax building right alongside hers.

His canines grazed down her throat. He pulled out just enough to leave her gasping as the canines reached the hollow joining her shoulder and neck, and then he thrust, bit, and her world exploded in an agony of pleasure.

GARRETT carried Sarah Anne inside and sat on the couch, settling her across his lap. She lay her head against his chest, listening to his heartbeat, absorbing the reality of what had just happened. The spot on her neck pulsed and burned. They were mated. He brushed her hair.

"Tell me, do you resent being forced to mate or the mate you were forced to accept?"

"I'm not into the whole traditional werewolf thing."

His beautiful mouth flattened to a straight line. She had the insane urge to kiss it softer.

"Well, you're mated." His fingers curved around her neck and settled over the mark. The humming warmth she'd noticed increased to a burn that spread outward to her breast. "Not only to a very traditional male, but to a mixed-breed at that."

"With something to prove?"

All breed males had something to prove. The few she'd seen exhibited it in a very tight hold on their mates.

His head cocked to the side and that smile she didn't trust chased the tension from his mouth. "A thing or two." His pinky stroked over the mark. "One of which being I'd like to prove to you I can be tender."

"You had needs." Which she'd thoroughly enjoyed.

Pressure at the back of her neck pulled her in and up. The hazel of his eyes deepened to dark green. Tiny fires lit behind them. Flames that matched the growing heat within her as his mouth lowered to hers.

"Nothing comes before you, Sarah Anne. Nothing."

Not even her son? The thought popped into speech.

He paused his mouth a scant breath from hers. "Not even him."

For some strange reason the honesty soothed her. There was a lot to be said for knowing where one stood with a man. Her arms slipped up around his neck. "Thank you."

His eyes narrowed. "You're a strange woman."

"And you're an honest man."

"Who is going to kiss you."

"So I gathered."

"Any objections?"

About a thousand from her sensible side. Not a one from the primitive one calling the shots. But she didn't want him to know that, so she said nothing, and then it was too late. His lips met hers softly yet firmly, giving her time to pull away, daring her to pull away. She'd always been a sucker for a dare. Rising up, she let the explosive passion of before roll over her. Parting her lips, she offered a challenge of her own. He accepted with a low growl. Beneath her hands, she felt the rumble of his response. His tongue thrust past the barrier of her lips, claiming her mouth with a totality to which everything feminine in her rejoiced. Her breath caught; her nails dug in. His fingers wrapped in her hair. To pull her closer? Oh, yes, she needed to be closer.

From the hall came a cough.

Or to pull her away? Garrett lifted his head.

Donovan stood in the door. "Sorry to interrupt."

"Ever heard of knocking?" Garrett growled.

"Door was open."

Garrett's hand pressed Sarah Anne's burning cheek against his chest, covering her face protectively. For that she was extremely grateful. She was vividly aware of the slice in the crotch of her jeans.

"What do you want?"

"Daire wants Sarah Anne."

Garrett's muscles went rigid. "Why?"

"Teri's awake and calling for her."

Seventeen

TERI wasn't just calling for her; she was screaming her name in harsh, horrible blasts of distress that grated down her nerve endings. Thank goodness Meg was with Donovan's mate and not witness to this. As soon as she opened the door to the main house, Sarah Anne lunged in. Wyatt caught her arm.

"Hold on."

Behind her Garrett snarled. Donovan stepped forward. In the corner, Heather wiped at her cheeks.

Sarah Anne flipped her hair back over her shoulder and met Wyatt's gaze. "What is it?"

The concern in his eyes stilled her anger. Whatever he needed to tell her was important. Another scream ripped through the interior and she felt Wyatt flinch through his touch. There was a pause, as if he didn't know how to say what he had to. Heather came up beside him, tear tracks shining on her blotchy face, and caught his free hand in hers.

"I'm sorry."

Sarah Anne reached back. Garrett's hand swallowed hers and squeezed.

"She's dying?"

Wyatt took a breath. But it was Heather who answered. "No. Absolutely not." Donovan opened his mouth and with a wave of her hand, Heather shut him up. That amazed Sarah Anne. That a small, helpless human woman could control so many Protectors with nothing more than her will.

"She's not dying. But she did lose her baby."

"Oh, my God." That baby had meant the world to Teri. She'd clung to that coming life as if it were the only link to her sanity. And now it was gone. "This is bad."

"We gather that," Wyatt said.

"What would you think Sarah Anne can do about it?" Garrett asked.

"Daire thinks a lot."

"Who is this Daire?" Sarah Anne wanted to know that more than anything. The man scared her, intrigued her and worried her. In a very short amount of time he'd made himself very important to her friend, yet he was the deadliest thing she'd ever seen. And, if anyone asked her, incapable of giving the love that Teri needed to heal.

"Right now, he's the one thing standing between Teri and death," Wyatt said.

Sarah Anne was getting very sick of the Alphas using that to hush her up. "Well, he doesn't seem to be doing a very good job."

Donovan looked over his head to Garrett. "Don't let her talk to Daire like that."

She took advantage of a distraction to yank her arm free of Wyatt's grip. "He doesn't have any say in how I talk to anybody."

Her freedom was only momentary. Garrett caught her hand again. As if she hadn't made her point clear, he spoke over her head. "She's still got some adjusting to do."

The next scream stole the urge to argue right out from under her. She headed for the stairs, expecting Garrett to hold her back, but he didn't. The heavy weight of his footsteps on the stairs behind her was comforting rather than threatening. At the top of those stairs was Teri in terrible emotional distress and Daire with his cold gaze and scarred face and very deadly manner. She could be walking into a nightmare and it was good to know that if she was, Garrett was there to back her.

As if he heard the thought, his hand caught hers. With a tug, he spun her around. His free hand anchored in her hair at the base of her neck, tilting her head back. The flare of excitement that she always experienced whenever he touched her went through her, opening her senses and her nerve endings. He held her as if he expected her to fight, but the reality was that in a world that was full of danger and totally topsy-turvy, he was the one thing she could count on. He pulled her body into his. The tip of his head blocked out the light but it couldn't block out her awareness. She breathed deep, taking his scent into her lungs, holding it there as his teeth nipped at her bottom lip. She had no intention of fighting. She might be half human. She might've turned her back on her heritage, but right now, at this time, in this moment, not knowing what was beyond that door, just knowing whatever was happening was bad, it was very good to have this man at her side. She relaxed into his grip, feeling his start of surprise as her hands slid up his chest and wrapped in the material of his shirt, holding them to her. She did not want to be alone, always fighting battles alone. She wanted someone by her side. Someone up to the fight ahead, not someone she felt she had to protect.

His hesitation lasted only a moment, but in what she was coming to accept was his normal behavior of taking what he could when he could, he plundered her mouth. And for once in her life, she surrendered with no reservations. This was her mate. Her choice.

The kiss was over in a matter of seconds. Garrett held her at arm's length. She couldn't recover as easily as he. She stared at him while he studied her, eyes narrowed, assessing. Behind her, beyond the door, Teri screamed again. It was followed just as quickly by a man's harsh curse.

"If you don't do what I tell you right now, I'll tie your ass down."

Sarah Anne lunged for the door. Garrett caught her around the waist and set her back. He opened the door, quietly slipping through. She ignored his motion to stay back. That was her friend screaming in there. She came to a halt just inside the door. The room reeked of blood and fear and desperation. There was no sorting from scent who was afraid and who was desperate, but it was easy to see who was bleeding. Teri might be wounded but the white bandages covering her abdomen were pristine. The same couldn't be said for Daire's face. Deep gouges raked across his cheeks and his neck. Another furrow went across his chest and down the arms with which he was pinning Teri to the bed.

"What are you doing?" Sarah Anne gasped.

"Keeping her from killing herself," Daire snapped.

Garrett rolled up his sleeves and stepped into the room. "What do you need?"

"I need you to hold her feet." With ruthless efficiency Garrett grabbed Teri's feet and pinned them to the bed. Daire's hair slid over his shoulder as he snapped his head around to look at Sarah Anne. The impact of his gaze was like a blow. Sarah took a step back, the power overwhelming her.

"You, I need you to come here and tell her I didn't kill her baby."

"Oh, my God." Sarah Anne ducked under Daire's arm when he lifted it. This close, it was impossible to miss who was afraid and who was desperate. She glanced at Daire, surprised. She never would have thought the so-controlled ancient capable of desperation.

"Hold her."

From the way Teri was thrashing about, Sarah Anne had real questions as to whether she could. "Maybe you'd better continue."

"I can't."

The bald truth sat between them.

"Now, put your hands over mine."

She did, feeling the violence of Teri's fear. "Teri, calm down."

Teri's eyes flew open. Focused. "Sarah!" she gasped.

"Yes, Sarah Anne."

"He killed my baby."

Beside her Daire flinched. He pulled his hands carefully from under hers and took a step back.

"No, he didn't."

Teri glared at Daire over Sarah Anne's shoulder, her fingers clenching into tight fists, anger vibrating through her body. "Yes, he did. Ask him."

Sarah turned her head and added her glare to Teri's. "Tell me you didn't say that."

His chin came up as his eyes narrowed. "I do not lie."

Oh, for heaven's sake. "You saved her life!"

He straightened and backed away from the bed. Teri continued to glare at him. Energy crackled between them.

"I made a choice."

Beneath her hands, Teri's fingers curled to claws that would have gone for Daire's face if he were close enough.

"You had no right. It was my decision."

She and Garrett might as well not be there. This war was between Teri and Daire. It was personal, and it was hurting both of them.

Daire squared his shoulders. He looked every bit the powerful ancient as he countered, "My mate comes first."

Teri arched and twisted. "I hate you."

Daire nodded and accepted the verbal blow with a passivity Sarah never would have expected in an ancient. "I know."

He took another step back. He was only a few feet from the door.

"Where do you think you're going?" Garrett growled.

"She needs to heal. It can't be done with me here."

"You can't leave." The only life in Teri was her anger. Beneath the flush she was ghastly pale and so weak. The one thing standing between Teri and death was Daire and the anger she felt toward him.

"You can't leave your mate when she's sick," Garrett said.

Daire's gaze clung to Teri. For all he was hiding his feelings, Sarah Anne had an impression he was suffering. "Don't tell me what to do, pup."

"She won't survive without you."

"She'll do better without me."

"You didn't kill her baby," Sarah Anne added.

"It doesn't matter what I believe. All that matters is what she thinks she knows."

And what Teri knew was that Daire had taken away her hope of family.

Sarah shared a glance with Garrett. Dear God, this was such a mess.

Eighteen

SARAH Anne was going to think he lied. Garrett stood in Wyatt's office two hours later and stared at Wyatt uncomprehendingly. "What do you mean you couldn't find them?"

He'd promised Sarah Anne that Cur would bring her son to Haven, and Wyatt was telling him Cur had lost him?

"Cur went to the meeting place. There was no sign of Rachel or Josiah."

"Sarah Anne has complete faith in Rachel."

Kelon snorted. "Well, maybe she shouldn't."

"Rachel would know how worried Sarah Anne would be about Josiah. She would have left a sign."

"They were never there."

Garrett raked his fingers through his hair. Goddammit, he would not start his life with Sarah Anne with failure. "There has to be an explanation."

"Not a good one," Donovan said almost gently.

Kelon pushed his chair away from the wall. "How good a tracker do you think Cur is?"

Garrett didn't like the sick feeling in his gut. It blended too well with the bite of suspicion in the other men's scents. "There's none better. Why?"

"According to Cur, he's found Rachel and lost her . . . twice."

"Not possible." No one ever ducked Cur.

"Cur is not happy."

Garrett just bet. He headed toward the door, determination settling in his gut. "I'm going after them."

"Not yet, you're not," Wyatt ordered.

Garrett turned, his hand on the knob. "What's to stop me?"

"Well, for one, I forbid it."

Wyatt was going to have to do better than that. "And two?"

Kelon tossed a folded piece of paper on the table.

"What's that?" Paper rustled as Garrett opened it.

"To me it reads like an eviction notice from Pack Carmichael. They say we're on their turf."

Garrett scanned the note. "Cheeky bunch, aren't they?"

"The Carmichael pack has always had an inflated sense of their own importance."

Wyatt should know. His father had been the head of the pack for as long as anyone could remember. Wyatt had been in line to assume leadership before he'd broken away.

Garrett handed the note back. "This is a sanctioned pack. They have no standing."

Wyatt shrugged. "I have some enemies in the Carmichael pack that would like to see my pack fail. Since my father died, they've made it their mission to discredit the sanction."

"They've taken it to the level of obsession, if you ask me," Donovan cut in.

Wyatt shrugged again. "They believe they have the might to make right."

"What did you answer?" Garrett asked.

"I told them to fuck off." Wyatt smiled. "In the most diplomatic of terms, of course."

"And their response?"

Wyatt gazed out the window. Garrett didn't need to smell his anger to know what it was. War.

"They've called a blood feud."

"Shit." Worse than war.

"We knew it was coming," Donovan cut in again.

"War, yes," Wyatt snapped, "but not a blood feud."

A blood feud with the Carmichaels. One of the strongest packs around. Garrett looked to Donovan. "How tough are they?"

"I trained them to be the toughest."

Kelon and Donovan had been Carmichael's Protectors before Wyatt had formed Haven.

"How tough is Haven?"

Kelon folded his arms across his chest. "We're outnumbered, unproven and only roughly trained."

"Shit." Garrett couldn't leave Sarah Anne, Megan and all the other wolves who'd come to Haven unprotected in the face of a pending attack.

"How close is Cur to Rachel?"

"Close enough he claims to be able to offer her protection if the rogues slow her down long enough for him to catch up."

Garrett shook his head. He couldn't imagine a woman evading Cur.

"Has Sarah Anne mentioned Rachel having any training?" Donovan asked.

"No." Actually, she didn't know herself.

"There had to be a reason she trusted her with Josiah."

"I got the impression it was because there wasn't another option."

Wyatt put his hand on Garrett's shoulder. "I'm sorry, Garrett. I know you promised Sarah Anne to bring Josiah home."

"It can't be helped."

"Cur will be calling in again in a couple days."

"Good." And he'd better have good news. Garrett looked out the window to the woods beyond, fanning his senses outward, feeling the odd vibrations at the edges. "The Carmichaels have been watching?"

Kelon nodded. "And waiting."

"For what?"

Donovan's mouth set into a straight line. "We don't know."

Shit.

Nineteen

GARRETT didn't have to say a word. Sarah Anne knew from his expression that the news wasn't good.

She didn't move, just stood in the doorway, her knuckles showing white against the dark wood of the jamb.

"Just tell me."

He pulled her to him, ignoring her struggles, buffering the turbulence in her mind as best he could.

"How well do you know your friend Rachel?"

"What does that have to do with anything?"

"Just answer the question."

"I know her well enough to trust her with my son."

"Because you had no other option or because . . . ?"

Sarah Anne didn't hesitate. "Because she's that trustworthy. What happened?"

"We weren't sure before, but now we are. She's on the run."

"Oh, God." She cuffed his shoulder. "Is that all? I told you she wouldn't trust your friend Cur."

"It might be more than that."

"No." She shook her head, her denial as strong in her mind as it was in her voice. She had complete faith in Rachel.

Garrett didn't have the heart to argue with her. "Does Josiah have any special powers?"

"Like Megan's?"

"Yes."

"No."

"What do you know about his father? Did he have any strange abilities for a human?"

"No, he was perfectly normal."

"What about the extended family?"

"They used to tease about his grandfather. They called him Mr. Know-It-All because he always seemed to know what was happening. Or so the stories go."

"He had precognition?"

"I don't know."

"Did your husband ever talk to Josiah about his grandfather?"

"Why would he? I mean, it was a joke. A story they told at Christmas and Thanksgiving."

"Those might have been based on fact." And that fact might be why the rogues were so relentlessly pursuing Rachel and Josiah. "Maybe his grandfather had some power."

A werewolf father would have prepared his son with the knowledge to survive, whether that knowledge meant emphasizing a trait or hiding it. Maybe even from his own mother. He found it hard to believe a human father wouldn't do the same.

"I don't know. You need to go get him. You promised me you would go get him."

"And I will, but I promised to keep you all safe."

Her lip curled. "But not now. Because Wyatt forbid it. Because the pack needs me more than Josiah does."

She spun away. "I knew it. I knew it was pack first."

Garrett caught her arm and pulled her back to him. Her hands slammed up against his chest. "There will never be a time when my Alpha can command me to put my family at risk."

Sarah Anne pushed against his chest. "It seems to me he just did."

Garrett didn't flinch away from her glare. "No, he didn't. But the threat to Josiah is not as great as the threat to you and Megan."

"But Josiah—"

"Will be safe."

"How do you know that?"

"Cur is watching over him."

Her hands clenched into fists against his chest. Her pain rose in a mental haze around them. "You just said he couldn't find them."

He brushed his mind over hers, muting her distress as best he could. "A better phrase would be to catch up to them."

She tossed her hair out of her eyes. "So how can you tell me not to worry?"

"Because as good as your friend Rachel is, Cur is better."

"You sound so confident."

"I am."

Her eyes searched his. "What are you going to do?"

He wrapped his hands around her fists and brought them up to his lips, first the right and then the left. "I'm going to take care of the threat here, and then I'm going to get our son."

"And what am I supposed to do?"

"Take care of Teri."

"I don't know how to help her."

"Just talk to her."

And pray.

Twenty

THERE was no talking to Teri. She grieved for her child to the point of obsession. Over the next few days, she fought Daire. She fought Sarah Anne. She fought life, but there was nothing that could stop her body from healing. As soon as Sarah Anne saw the mark on her neck, she understood that. Daire had bonded his life to Teri's. As long as he lived, so would she. Sarah Anne balanced the breakfast tray and kicked the bedroom door closed. Teri lay on the bed in the dark room, the covers pulled up to cover half her face. She didn't even turn her head when the door clicked shut. Sarah Anne sighed. Daire had left two days ago, and Sarah Anne was no closer to breaking through the wall of Teri's anger than she had been the day she stepped into that room, but something had to give. And soon.

How far are you willing to go? Daire had asked Sarah Anne that the awful night Teri had been injured and she'd given him permission to do what he had to to keep Teri alive. As a result he was bonded to Teri. And Teri, who hated werewolves, was now bound to another for life. No matter how much space Daire gave her, there would never be another man for Teri. No other option for a future. No other path to take but that of mate.

Sarah Anne had never seen Teri like this, even after the rape. Teri was a born fighter, always coming up swinging no matter what life threw at her, but it seemed there was no fight left in her anymore, just the defeated acceptance that she had nothing left to live for. Sarah Anne set the tray of food on the table beside the bed.

Teri turned her face away. "I'm not hungry."

Sarah Anne drew open the curtains on the window beside the bed. "You have to eat."

Teri glared out the window to the sunshine beyond. "I don't have to do anything."

Not even take the next breath. The thought was whispered into Sarah's mind. She blinked. Had that thought been real or imagined? She shook her head and sighed.

"Death is not an option for you."

That snapped Teri's head around. Her hand clenched in the blanket. "Don't tell me what to do."

"I'm sorry. I'm not; it's just that . . ." How did one go about telling someone they had a werewolf husband? Sarah Anne sat on the side of the bed. "This may be hard for you to understand, but to save your life, Daire took you as mate."

"How did that save my life?"

"Bonded mates share a life force. Daire is a very strong were. As long as he lives, you will, too." Sarah took the napkin off the tray and settled it across Teri's legs. "So you're starving yourself for nothing."

Teri met her gaze. The dark circles under her eyes made the green of her hazel eyes even brighter in her pale face. "John died."

Yes, he had, because Sarah Anne had never given him her mark. Because she hadn't told him who she was. Because she'd been pretending her wolf side didn't exist. The guilt of that would haunt her the rest of her life. "I didn't bond with John."

"He loved you."

And she had loved him. Not to her full capacity, but she had loved him enough. She blinked and the guilt surged in. She'd cheated him on so much and he hadn't cared. He'd just been happy to be with her, and she couldn't help but wonder if it was because he didn't know what he was missing or if he'd loved her so much he'd taken what he could get. "I cheated John."

"You cheated on him?"

She shook her head. "I cheated him of the love he should've had. He was a very good man. He gave me two wonderful children, and I cared very much about him, but I didn't love him enough to mate with him the way Daire mated with you."

"You're saying Daire loves me?"

"Love is a human concept."

"One I'm fond of."

"I know. But a werewolf is born knowing there's one person out there for him or her. One perfect match. A werewolf lives with that sense of perpetual loneliness every day of their life. It grows year after year as they wait for their mates." She took Teri's hand and squeezed it. "Daire is an ancient. His life has been very long. So has his wait."

Teri's expression became guarded. "So what's that mean to me?"

"It means the instant he saw you, he knew what you meant to him. He knew he'd found the other half of his soul. It means he wasn't going to let you die."

"I didn't ask him to save me."

"I know, but your life is now bound to his. You won't die until he dies, barring a catastrophe."

The horror that filled Teri's eyes marked her as very human. "That's crazy."

Sarah decided it was time to speak plainly.

"No, that's what it means to be loved by a werewolf. You will never be alone. You will never be undefended. You'll be always be guarded, pampered and protected. Your children will be loved, guarded, protected. So I guess it's safe to say, no one will ever love you more."

Teri's hand went to her stomach. "That has to come at a price."

"Yes." There was a price for everything. "Your mate will expect obedience, and he will expect the same devotion back."

Teri shook her head and pulled her hand free. "I can't love anybody like that."

Sarah Anne disagreed. "I don't think you know how to love any other way."

"I hate him."

Sarah nodded. "I know that, too. But you have to find a way to get around that, because from here on he's going to be the biggest part of your life."

Just as she had to accept that Garrett was the biggest part of hers.

———

FOUR hours later, Sarah Anne descended the stairs, a sense of anticipation humming in her blood. As he had for the last two days, Garrett was waiting for her, standing in front of the big windows. He looked so handsome with the setting sun reflecting off the hazel of his eyes, making them more green, amplifying the emotion inside.

No one will ever love you more.

The words she'd spoken to Teri came back to her as she crossed to him. No one would ever love her more than this man. He would take everything she had, demand everything she could give, but in return . . .

Garrett reached out, and in that gesture she was beginning to recognize implied comfort. He ran his fingers down her cheek.

"But in return," he finished the thought for her, "I'll give you everything I am."

"You read my mind."

"You make it easy."

Maybe she did. And maybe she did it on purpose. Garrett was

nothing like she'd thought a wolf husband would be. He was so much more. Legend was that each mate was created for the needs of the other. She thought of Teri up in the room battling depression and loss, refusing everything Daire offered, including comfort. She thought of how hard she'd tried to make John happy while holding herself back. She thought of how Garrett never held back, just making the most of what he had, as if it was about to be taken away.

She caught his hand in hers. "I'll try to give you what you want."

She needed him to understand she'd accepted this mating.

There was a flicker of something in his eyes. Disappointment? Hurt? It was impossible to tell from his tone.

Squeezing her hand, he tugged her toward the door. "This is enough."

He could tell himself that, but there was no way that it could be. A male wolf needed his woman's complete devotion. Garrett might be a mixed-breed, but everything in him, every instinct from the one that had him defending her to the one that dictated their marking was pure, unadulterated wolf. She reached up and covered her mark. Their lives were bound. There was no going back. Not for him. Not for her. Was that why he said it was enough? Because neither one of them had any choice? How could that be enough for either of them?

"Where is Megan?"

He steered her down the stairs, stopping her at the last step before stepping down himself, leaving them at eye level. "I want my kiss first."

There was no smile on his face as he made that statement. From anyone else, she would have considered it a tease. From Garrett? Darn! She wished he was easier to read. Taking a chance, she looped her arms around his neck and smiled at him. "Okay."

His start was almost a reprimand. Had she really been that cold to him? She threaded her fingers through his hair. She liked the way it felt running through her fingers, cool and silky.

"A kiss, huh?"

His palm opened over her spine. She pushed away her worry for her son, pushed away everything except this man and this moment. Feeling as though she were stepping off a cliff and tumbling into the rest of her life, she said, "I can probably arrange that."

Again that start, on his part, that whipped through her like guilt. He was guarding her child, searching for her son, putting his life on the line for her, and she had done so little in return.

"I'm sorry."

"You have nothing to be sorry for."

Yes, she did. "You deserve better."

His hand in the small of her back pulled her up. "I have what's mine."

Mine. She'd always hated that word before with all the loss of self she'd assumed it implied. Now it settled with disturbing comfort over her raw nerves, more wolf in her than she'd ever expected rising to accept the claim.

No, she realized, he didn't. And he'd go to his grave fighting her for the bit he had, but there was no going back from this. If that held true for Teri, then it held true for her.

"Yes, you do."

With her fingers at the back of his neck, she drew his mouth to hers.

His fist knotting in her hair froze her a mere breath from her goal. "What are you saying?"

"I'm saying you're my mate."

"You finally letting go of the idea of an 'out' clause?"

"Yes."

"Good." He let go of her hair. "Then prove it."

Here in the middle of the street? No sooner did the thought enter her mind than she knew the answer was yes. Here where all could see. His pride would need that, this man who'd always grown up an outcast, who'd been born a Protector and always been denied his status. This man who'd just realized his dream and had sworn to give it up for her if necessary.

When Garrett's hands cupped her buttocks, she didn't say a word, just pulled him closer, kissed him deeper. His growl reverberated down her spine before spreading outward in a heated vibration that swelled her breasts and sensitized her clit. Her mark burned. Wrapping her legs around his waist, she held on, letting the passion flow through her, letting acceptance flow through her. This man was her future.

"Nice to see I'm not the only one that puts on the spectacle."

Shock should have had her feet hitting the floor, but even knowing someone watched was not sufficient to gather her wits. Fortunately, Garrett had more fortitude. His fingers clutched in her hair. Every cell in her body moaned a protest as he put her away from him. Two layers of clothing, his and hers, were not enough to prevent sensation shooting through her as her nipples dragged down his chest. When her feet hit the floor, her knees didn't get the message to support. If it hadn't been for his hand on the small of her back, she would have collapsed. Heat flared in her cheeks. Above her, she heard Garrett chuckle. Behind her, she heard a feminine counterpoint.

"I'm sorry to interrupt, but Lisa sent me over to let you know Megan's taking a nap and she'll bring her by in a couple hours when she wakes up."

There was no hope for it. Sarah Anne was going to have to turn around. She took a step back. Garrett allowed it, but he didn't let her go far. His hand on her stomach kept them connected, kept the fire burning. Before her stood a pretty woman with long brown hair. She looked a lot like Heather but there was an innate softness about her. And her smile guaranteed the recipient wanted to smile back. As if she wasn't blushing hot enough to start a bonfire, Sarah held out her hand. "I'm Sarah Anne."

Amusement danced in the woman's eyes as she took her hand. "I'm Kelon's wife, Robin."

Automatically Sarah breathed her scent. Robin wrinkled her nose. "I'll save you the effort. I'm human. Heather is my sister."

She knew that. Somewhere in the depths of her beleaguered brain she knew that Wyatt, Donovan and Kelon had married human sisters.

Robin tilted her head to the side and put her hands on her hips. "If you have a problem with that, we can have a chat."

Garrett's hand pressed warningly. "She has no problem with that."

Robin cut Garrett a glance. "It's nice to know you don't think so, but your opinion is not the one I'm looking for."

"My opinion is hers."

Robin rolled her eyes and shook her head. "I do not understand how werewolf women put up with this."

"Kelon doesn't tell you what to do?" Sarah Anne asked.

Robin waved her hand. "Oh, he tries, but I just listen to what pleases me and negotiate the rest."

Sarah Anne could just imagine the negotiations that serious, dark Kelon got into with this cheerful sprite of a woman. It was the first time she was happy her face was already red.

"You'll like this about this pack. Women have a lot of say in a lot of things. Heather insists on it."

"She does?"

"Yep. And I've got to tell you, the woman is in her glory. She's finally got enough to manage."

Robin put her hand on her full hip and pushed her hair back. "For ten years, you see, she only had Lisa and I to rule."

"From what I hear, she could've been stricter."

With a wave of her hand, Robin dismissed Garrett's reprimand. "You heard about the waterfall incident."

"No Protector hasn't."

Robin sighed. "One skinny-dipping session and a woman's branded a troublemaker for life."

"It wasn't the skinny dipping that got you in trouble."

"There was no way to know Donovan would be training the new soldiers over there that night."

"Had you told your mate, you would have been informed."

Robin rolled her eyes again. "And guarded. Which would have totally defeated the point of a girls' night out."

"You endangered yourself."

Robin sighed and glanced at Sarah Anne, clearly looking for support. "That single-minded devotion to protection gets old fast."

"I used to think so."

She felt a surge of Garrett's energy that indicated surprise. Stepping out of his arms, she held her hand out to Robin. She had a feeling they were going to be good friends.

Robin shook it. "But you came back?"

Sarah nodded, and stepped back. "I had this crazy idea it could be managed."

Across the compound, she could see Kelon approaching. Robin's gaze followed hers. A lovely soft smile touched her lips. "It can, but it's a delicate balance."

"Woman, you were told to wait for me," Kelon growled as soon as he got close.

"I knew you'd be along shortly and Heather asked me to deliver a message."

"It's not safe for you to be out alone."

Robin rolled her eyes. "Could you excuse us?"

Kelon reached for her arm. Before he could grab her, Robin slipped her arms around his waist, kissed his chest through his open shirt. "Not here."

His big hand anchored in her hair. Sarah Anne would have feared for her except for the fact that no scent of tension flowed off Robin. And when she thought about it, Kelon wasn't throwing stress, either. "I think here would be very appropriate. You have been very defiant of late."

Robin whispered against his chest, "I totally lack discipline."

Behind her Sarah Anne felt Garrett's start. Wolf hearing was extraordinary, something Robin had forgotten.

Robin pressed her body closer to Kelon. Her smile as she looked up was total seductive amusement. "You might even need to take me in hand."

Kelon's face didn't change, but his scent grew muskier with desire. "I was thinking the same thing."

Robin's sigh was exaggerated. "Of course, you know how I get when you discipline me, but if you don't mind others seeing . . ."

Kelon swore and swung her up in his arms. She looked very small there, but very at home. "You have no shame."

She linked her arms around his neck. "I'll work on it."

As he turned, he smiled. "Don't bother on my account."

Robin's laugh trailed behind them as Kelon carried them toward the big blue house next door.

Sarah Anne watched, a smile tugging her own lips. Human or not, there was an aura of invincibility about Robin. She looked at Garrett. "Maybe I wasn't so crazy after all. Maybe you can be managed."

***

SARAH Anne thought she could manage him. Garrett watched the swish of Sarah Anne's hips as she preceded him down the sidewalk. She was in a strange mood. He didn't trust it. Something had happened in that room with Teri. Had Daire said something to the other woman over the course of her care? Something that scared Sarah when Teri repeated it? A frightened woman would have reason to cozy up to her Protector. The idea didn't sit well.

With a slight lengthening of stride, he reached the door to their house before Sarah Anne did. A hand on her arm stayed her.

"I'll check it out first."

She smiled calmly as if every other time he'd insisted on checking the house she hadn't rolled her eyes. A quick mental and physical scan of the interior revealed no one waiting.

"Okay."

That "okay" was entirely too easy, increasing his suspicions that something must have gone on in that room with Teri today. He couldn't imagine what it was. But whatever it was needed to be dealt with. Sarah Anne had enough stress waiting on word about her son.

"Did you have a good visit with Teri?"

Her immediate frown confirmed his suspicions.

"It was enlightening."

Enlightening. There was a broad term. He'd begun to understand how she protected herself. While she thought in terms of absolutes, she shielded herself with vagaries. He could probe her mind for the information he wanted, but he rejected the idea as soon as he had it. He wanted her to give to him on her own.

With a motion of his hand, he waved her into the house. She stepped past without her usual care. Her shoulder grazed his chest. The door closed behind them with a soft click. His eyes dropped naturally to the gentle swish of her rear. Inside, the heat rose. Despite his suspicions there was nothing tense in her posture. Sarah Anne picked up the day's mail, sorted through the letters. He already knew there was nothing of import there, but a couple pieces of junk mail had been forwarded. She tapped the envelopes against her arm.

"Looks like my mail is beginning to be forwarded."

"That's good." Though in reality he'd prefer that all contact with her past was severed.

"It still makes me nervous."

"Why?"

She waved the envelopes. "They know where we are."

"They've always known where you were."

He'd made sure of it, announcing far and wide his claim on Sarah Anne. If any more wolves wanted a chance at the widow, they needed to know they were going to have to go through him and Pack Haven first.

"It just seems . . ."

"Obvious?"

"Yes."

She'd been living among the humans too long. Werewolves always dealt in the obvious, always dealt in absolutes. He studied her, feeling the flux of her energy. Scenting her nervousness. Again it struck him she was different from other females. But for once the sense of dissatisfaction didn't follow, because he was coming to realize her differences gave his differences a certain acceptance that he might not have found with a traditional werewolf woman who dealt in absolutes.

"Sometimes obvious is good."

She glanced past him out the window bordering the door, her hair falling over her shoulder in a rich swath of brown, and frowned. "Maybe."

They were back to whatever happened in that room to alarm her.

"Did Teri say something to upset you?"

"As I said, it was enlightening."

He took one step forward and then another. Expecting her to retreat. She didn't. "So you said before. I'm just not sure what that means."

Her head cocked to the side and her face took on that expression he was used to seeing on others' faces. A mix of fear and uncertainty that said they were searching for the words to break bad news.

"Whatever it is, just spit it out."

"What?"

Garett sighed. "Whatever it is you think I'm going to take wrong."

Her sigh echoed his. "You're always expecting the worst."

"Habit."

Sarah Anne cocked her head to the side. "For a pessimist you have some amazingly optimistic tendencies."

"Like what?"

"Like thinking this between us is going to work out."

"It will."

"Because you won't accept any less?"

Garrett shook his head. "No. I'm not fool enough to think I can force feeling where there is none."

Her mouth opened, then snapped closed. She tossed the mail on the table. "What *are* you fool enough to think?"

It was just like Sarah Anne to challenge when she should back down.

"I think I have a mate."

"Even if I was forced on you?"

That stopped him in his tracks. "You were the one that was forced."

"I'm not blind, Garrett. I've seen how much you value pack. A full-blood mate would suit your ambitions more."

"The thought had crossed my mind, but . . ."

"Then why did you mate with me?"

He took the two strides that closed the distance between them. Reaching out, he cupped her cheek in his hand and stroked his thumb across her lips, catching her gasp against the pad of his thumb.

"But that was before I met you," he finished.

"You wouldn't have looked at me twice if the circumstances were different."

Was she trying to convince him or herself?

The image of her in that cave, so determined to protect her children, so ready to throw her fragile body into a battle she couldn't win, stuck in his head. She was brave, resourceful and loyal. Any man would be proud to have her. "What makes you say that?"

"Your distinct lack of enthusiasm for my company outside the bedroom."

He blinked again, absorbing that. "I didn't think you wanted my attention."

She shrugged. Her gaze skirted his.

He rubbed his thumb across her lips. "Seelie, rest assured, had I met you anywhere, I would have set to courting you immediately."

"Courting?"

She didn't have to say it as if it were the most unlikely event on the planet. "Yes, I would have courted you." He bent, moved his thumb to the sensitive corner of her mouth and pressed until her lips parted before teasing the seam with the tip of his tongue. Another gasp kissed his lips. "What's more, I would have enjoyed it."

Her tongue came out and touched his. "Prove it."

"What?"

"Court me."

"We're already mated."

She took a step back, her gaze locked on his, a very feminine smile on her lips. "Then you've got some catching up to do."

With a toss of her head she turned and headed for the kitchen. As he watched the sassy twitch of her hips, he smiled. "I guess I do."

———————

His smile lasted all of about two seconds. Right up until he remembered the look of surprise on her face when he'd said he'd court her. She didn't look up when he entered the kitchen. He leaned against the doorjamb, watching her make a pot of coffee.

"I may be only half werewolf but that doesn't mean I lack any finer feelings."

She shrugged. "I guess I never . . ."

"Never what? Thought I had any softness in me?"

She shrugged, filling the pot with water. "It's not immediately visible."

"I thought it was very visible in bed."

That drew her up short and put a blush in her cheeks, but it didn't remove the speculation from her gaze. "No, I think you're right. That's one of the things that occurred to me while I was talking to Teri today."

"What? That there's no going back for us?"

"No, that I've never given *you* a chance." She measured in the grounds. "I just had it in my head how it was going to be and I couldn't seem to see anything else."

"That must have been some conversation."

Her smile was sad. "In some ways, it was. And in others." She shook her head. "I'm afraid it wasn't enough."

"I don't understand."

"I don't know if Teri can take this."

"Take what?"

"So much change on top of so much loss. Being mated to Daire won't be easy and Teri hasn't had an easy life."

"Neither have you."

"But when I was young, I grew up protected. I know what it's like to have someone care about you."

"You also know what it means to lose."

"But the loss was my choice."

"You were disowned."

"It was still my choice. I'm not saying it wasn't a bitter blow when my parents disowned me when I wouldn't accept Colin as my mate, but it stemmed from my choice. None of this is Teri's choice."

"You couldn't have expected them to go against pack law?"

"No."

But she had. He could tell from the way she rubbed her arms, as if still needing to shield herself from the blow. "You had siblings."

She nodded. "I know."

"Your parents had to protect the family for them."

"I know."

"It would have been easier for you to adjust than for them to throw away everything."

"Garrett, I understand the logic behind their decision." She closed the coffeemaker and jabbed the on button. "It just doesn't help me to accept the decision."

Garrett couldn't hold out anymore. He pulled her into his arms. "I'm sorry."

He liked the way she leaned against him. The softness in her eyes when she met his gaze. "For what? It was my decision to leave the pack."

"Why did you leave?"

"I didn't want to mate with the one chosen for me."

"You had a chosen mate?"

"I seem to be one of those rare women who has many options."

Not anymore. "None of which you seem to like."

He felt the press of her lips against his chest. Pressure built in the spot, bleeding outward in a lush spread of desire.

"Well, don't be too hasty. I might have it right this time."

The pressure exploded into flames of desire. It was the first time she'd made a move toward him. "You do. What happened with the proposed mating?"

"I refused the mating. My parents threatened to disown me."

She was lucky that was all they had done. In the most traditional families, a woman would be beaten for such defiance and carried unconscious through the ceremony. And Sarah Anne came from a very traditional pack.

"And they carried through with their threat?"

"Yes."

"So you went to the human world."

"It's where I fit best."

"Because you can't change."

"Yes."

"It was a wise decision at the time."

She blinked. "I'm surprised to hear you say that."

"Why?"

A small smile graced her mouth. "Because you seemed to put a large store by tradition."

"Actually, I don't hold with a lot of it but sometimes"—he watched as Sarah Anne's smile grew—"I find it has its uses."

He got his wish. "So I noticed," Sarah said.

Pressure at the base of the skull tilted her head back. He let his thumb slide over the chin down the underside. Her throat muscles worked against his thumb as she swallowed hard. It was his turn to smile as the scent of her desire teased his nostrils. He let his thumb rest against the hollow of her throat. The increase in her pulse was as visible as the interest in her eyes. "So, is a love for tradition the reason you are not denying us today?"

"No. It's more understanding of what's real." He loved the way the little tiny flecks of gold sparkled like jewels in her eyes. "And I'm real."

Her fingers clenched in his shirt. "I think you're the most real thing I know."

Twenty-one

GARRETT leaned in, recrossing the distance that so often had stood between them, seeing the hope in her eyes, seeing the aching sense of loss for her son. Seeing the longing for his reassurance. He had no right to touch her as a mate when he was failing her so, but he couldn't stay away. That warmth drew him like a flame. That need prodded him forward. He wanted to be the man she saw him as. Wanted to be the only one that made her smile, gave her confidence, held her when the world turned black.

His heart, the one that had never missed a beat in its life, skipped a beat as she sighed and relaxed against him. The total acceptance in the gesture floored him.

"Be very sure, Sarah Anne."

He had to give her a warning. It was his duty as a mate to protect her, even if he had to protect her from himself. Her arms came up around his neck, sliding over his skin in a whispering promise.

"It's too late to make me doubt you."

"There'll be no going back after this."

She cocked her head to the side and smiled that witchy smile that shot straight to his cock and filled him with the need to possess. "I thought we established that wasn't an option."

There was an option. He hadn't bonded her life force to his. As long as he didn't do that, his death would end her commitment, but he couldn't bring himself to say it. Couldn't have the possibility between them. Didn't want to see the hope for freedom spring back into her eyes. Instead, he slid his hands down over her shoulder blades, making a small circle at the points before continuing down to the hollow of her spine. "So we did."

The moistness of her breath teased his lips. He pressed with his fingertips, encouraging her up onto her toes. As always, she came up on her tiptoes, willingly. Eagerly. The fire between them arced.

Mine.

The knowledge whispered through his mind, picking up the cadence of his pulse, riding it, growing stronger as he mated his mouth to hers. She was his. No one else's. The urge to protect her drowned under the need to own her. To have what had always been missing in his life. The softness. The heat. The belonging. He'd make sure she didn't regret it. He'd control the wild side inside him. He'd be the wolf she deserved rather than the one everyone expected.

She made a little moan as she cuddled her breasts against his chest. His shirt chafed his skin. He wanted to feel those swollen nipples pressed into his skin as the softness behind flowed around. His mouth watered with the need to take them in. This was his woman.

"You won't regret being mated to me," he told her.

Her fingers caressed his nape. "I know."

How could she know that? How could she know anything beyond the fire that burned between them? It blurred his mind to the point he felt senseless and drugged with the passion. The rightness. He would never give her up.

He must have spoken out loud, or maybe he just projected the thought into her head, because she jumped. He waited for the familiar sense of fear, but instead, behind her start came a sense of satisfaction. It was his turn to blink.

"I told you you'd get to liking my possession."

Her smile pressed her cheek against his. "So you did. But I think I need another lesson just to be sure."

He laughed as he remembered the time he told her he'd give her a lesson in loving him. The one who had been giving the lesson had been her all along. "You really have no sense of survival."

She rested her cheek on his shoulder as he carried her to the bedroom.

"I beg to differ. I think my sense of survival is just fine. I think you're the one who doesn't have a very good sense of survival."

"What do you mean?"

"I mean exactly what I said. You were a footloose and fancy-free bachelor. Now you're tied down with a mate, two half-human kids not of your bloodline. Face it, your plans for the future never included anything you expected to have."

"What do you think I expected?"

"A lot more than this."

He kicked the bedroom door open and shouldered his way in, not taking his gaze from hers. She was right. All of his plans were as nothing now. But in going after what he wanted, he'd gotten what he'd wanted. The woman who fit the other half of his soul. The one person who could accept him as he was. Who gave him not status but a sense of self. A grounding. He pretended to toss her. She squealed, wrapped her arm around his neck. He smiled, let her legs drop and pulled her against him. "You're right. I didn't get a goddamned thing I'd shot for."

He didn't let her wallow in that statement. Didn't want her to hurt even for one second. "Instead I got more than I ever dared dream of."

She tilted her head back and looked at him, confusion in her eyes.

"I never dreamed I'd belong, so when I thought what my life

with my mate would be"—he unbuttoned her shirt—"it was always in terms of the status she'd bring me, because I never dreamed she would want me. Not emotionally. I figured the mating heat would be there and I'd work with that. But I never thought that you'd want me, so I never dreamed big enough to hold someone like you."

"Oh, baby." Her hands curled around his. She removed them from her blouse. For once he couldn't read anything in her eyes. When she pulled his hands away, he accepted it. He watched as she brought his fingers to her lips. Kissing the backs of one and then the other. Softness against hardness. "I think you really need to learn to dream bigger."

"Then you'll have to teach me."

She nodded. She would, Sarah Anne understood. She would have to teach Garrett to see himself as others saw him, not how he thought they did. His view was so warped by all he'd suffered in his youth, the betrayals that had hit him so hard, he couldn't see the man for the pain of the child. "I'll have to work fast, though."

He studied her with that same cautious look in his eyes. "Well, you'll need to learn to dream big for our children," she said.

He shied away from the wild hope that statement engendered. "We don't have to have children."

She shook her head, her fingers working the remaining buttons on her shirt. Not to redo but to undo. "Of course we have to have children. It would be such a sad world if a little boy of yours wasn't running around in it. Or if a little girl of yours wasn't making some male's life hell."

His hand cupped her cheek, all callus and strength. She could feel the tremors running through it. Tremors he didn't want her to see. She'd been right. He did feel. He just kept all that buried deep where it couldn't be used against him. Inside, more hope blossomed. She was good with hope. And before her was a man that hoped for everything, but expected nothing. Even from herself. Through the connection she could feel him building his defenses, eradicating the moment between them. Because he wanted it so much. She was beginning to understand when he wanted something that badly, he quickly built a wall against the need. He wasn't going to shut her out.

She slid her hand up his forearm and circled her fingers around his wrist and held on. He could break her hold with a simple twist. He didn't. "I want your child, Garrett. I want us to have many children together." She wanted the promise the future held. "As many as we can squeeze into our lives."

She continued to unbutton the buttons he'd abandoned.

His eyes watched her fingers, and the smile that was never far when he was around tugged at her lips. And the material fell to the side. The flicker of his eyelashes made her smile even more. She glanced down, tracing the trajectory of his gaze with a smile that kept expanding with the emotion releasing inside. There could be more here than just a man and a woman drawn together by desire. There could be a relationship. If they had the courage to reach out and take it. In this case, Garrett didn't have the courage.

In this, she was the leader. In this, she was the one who knew which way to go. Instead of being unsure, confidence flew through her. She trailed her fingers from her throat down between her breasts, smiling as his gaze followed.

"Know what the nice thing about me deciding to keep you is?"

"You feel comfortable seducing me?"

"Well, there is that." She shrugged the shirt off her shoulder. It caught at her elbows. Her bra was functional with a minimum of lace. It didn't matter. She knew it didn't matter. What Garrett wanted from her didn't have anything to do with enticement. He wanted a partner. An anchor. He wanted what she wanted; he'd just gone about it in the wrong way. Granted, it was the typical Garrett logic. And that had thrown her for a while, but Garrett wasn't a typical werewolf. And what he wanted from his mate was more than obedience. She could work with that.

"What else is there?" His much larger, darker finger followed the trail hers had taken. She closed her eyes as the pleasure flowed through her, chased by a trail of goose bumps that caused the corners of his mouth to tip up in his own pleasure.

"The fact that I'm willing to lead."

"You are?"

She let the shirt fall to the floor, shaking it free as it caught on her wrists. Tucking her hands behind her back, she reached for the hooks on her bra. Only to find his were there ahead of hers.

"What if I don't want you to?"

There was a time when she would have taken that as criticism. But now that she knew him better, she heard the amusement tucked into the question. Amusement at himself because, as it was with her, she was beginning to understand his need went deeper than the physical, too.

She leaned into his chest and let his body heat seep into hers, breathing deep of his scent. He always smelled so good. Beneath her ear, his pleasure rumbled. "Then I wouldn't."

"Do I hear doubt?" The bra unfastened. His fingers traced outward across her shoulder blades, taking the straps with it.

"You never have before."

She couldn't help a small chuckle. He obviously hadn't thought this through. With a flick of her wrists, she liberated the bra and her spirit of adventure. "So you're going to discourage me now?"

There was the slightest hitch in his breathing as awareness hit. "Not a chance."

She went to work on the buttons of his shirt. "Good."

He stood as if mesmerized. Or maybe, she realized, as if completely unsure what he was supposed to do. Hadn't a woman ever taken the lead with him before? She glanced up at his face, finding him watching her with that control that told her he was assessing every move, and she had her answer. Apparently not, which wasn't surprising considering the dominant side of his nature, not to mention the natural caution he took with everything. Her knuckles brushed his abdomen as she undid his shirt. The sudden retraction of his muscles made her smile. It was on the tip of her tongue to tease that this wouldn't hurt a bit, but it occurred to her at the last second that would be a mistake. Garrett was putting his tremendous pride on the line, giving her control, trusting her. She leaned in, kissing the hair-roughened skin over his breastbone. He wouldn't regret it.

His hand cupped her head, not restricting her, not pulling her away. Just another connection, or maybe a precaution.

She shared her smile with him. "This is going to be fun."

If she didn't know him so well, she'd be upset at his grunt, but she did know him. And she knew what that tension in his muscles signified, what that narrowing of his eyes indicated. More than that, she knew what that stroke of his pinky down the side of her neck meant. Emotion. The kind she was afraid to put a name to in case of jinxing it. Goose bumps chased the caress, sending chills down her spine and tingles of heat to her core. Oh, yes, this was going to be fun. The last button of his shirt came undone. That didn't mean she stopped her hands' descent. There was equally interesting territory lower. Garrett's breath sucked in as she cupped his erection through his jeans. She didn't break with his gaze as she kissed her way down his stomach. Watching the flames heat in his eyes as she pressed her lips against his straining cock was something she would remember always.

"You don't have to do that."

The phrasing so at odds with his desire gave her pause.

"You don't like it?"

"It's not necessary."

Of course it wasn't necessary. Their love life to date proved that, but, watching the flames in his eyes be banked by that incredible control, she realized that didn't mean there wasn't a need. And Garrett needed in ways she doubted even he understood. He needed someone to love him, who could handle that intensity that was so naturally a part of him, who could accept his differences and could glory in the man that he was rather than fear him. There was only one way she knew to cure that. Reaching for his jeans, concentrating hard on the path from her mind to his, she closed her eyes and asked, *But what if I want to?*

The snap popped with his jerk back. She held on, letting his momentum take the zipper that first inch.

"I told you before you don't have to bargain. I'm going to get Josiah tomorrow."

That, she hadn't known. "I thought it wasn't safe for you to leave."

"Things change."

She hadn't noticed any more Protectors on the grounds, which could mean only one thing. The rasp of the zipper as it slid down grated alongside panic. "Josiah's in trouble."

His fingers stroked soothingly on her nape as he applied pressure to bring her to her feet.

"No reason to think that. Cur just didn't check in at his usual time."

She took a breath. It could be a disaster, or it could be that Rachel, thinking she was being pursued by an enemy, had given Cur the slip. It was likely the latter. Rachel was a resourceful woman. That Garrett hadn't left already was calming. She hoped. "If you were very worried—"

"I'd be gone already."

She placed her palms against his chest, feeling the comforting bulk of muscle. Garrett wasn't a weak human. "But you're going tomorrow because—"

"I wouldn't take chances with our son."

Our. The word came so naturally off his lips. When it shouldn't. She slid her hands up over his shoulders, palms tingling as the soft cotton gently abraded her palms.

"Don't take chances with yourself, either."

Daire

One

DYING was not an option. Daire would give his mate almost anything she wanted, but not that. Rage roared through him at the thought. Ancient, with more time behind him than in front, he'd long ago given up hope of a mate, but now there was one in his life. Abused, terrified and depressed, Teri might hate the sight of him and everything he represented, but dammit, she would live. He cleared the stairs to the porch in one leap. His hand touched the doorknob. It twisted under his fingers. The door opened. Sarah Anne stood on the other side. Behind her as always was Garrett, the set of his shoulders backing the challenge in Sarah Anne's eyes.

"She doesn't want to see you."

Daire could barely suppress the urge to snarl. "You are between me and my mate."

Her head tilted to the side. Despite her start of apprehension, she didn't move. "Do you see the concern in my eyes?"

He didn't see it in hers, but he could see it in Garrett's.

"I should."

"Why?" Sarah Anne's shoulders squared. Garrett took a step forward. "What are you going to do?"

Instinct said whatever it took, but Sarah Anne was a woman, and under his protection. And Garrett, dammit—he liked the pup. Touching Sarah would have the other Protector attacking, and killing Garrett would weigh heavily on Daire's conscience. Which meant . . .

He sighed and folded his arms across his chest. "You may speak your concerns."

Sarah bit her lips and blew out a breath, but she didn't question the permission, which was a good thing. He could hear Teri upstairs. She was crying. Each muffled sob ripped along his control, tearing shreds off it, making him not care about Sarah's concerns, Teri's notions of what she needed. All that mattered was what he wanted. And that was for Teri to thrive and be happy. Even if that had to happen miles away from him.

"Well?"

Sarah blew her bangs off her forehead. "Stop rushing me. I'm trying to find the right words."

Daire met Garrett's eyes over her shoulder. "You should teach her more respect."

The other Protector shrugged and that might just be a smile around his lips. "I kind of like her the way she is."

"There are werewolves with whom her attitude could bring her trouble."

Sarah took a step back as Garrett took one forward. "She knows whose buttons she can push."

Not if she thought it was safe to push his, Daire knew. The blackness was too close to the surface, the rage too strong lately. To the point there were days he wasn't sure it was safe for him to continue on.

Sarah planted her feet. "*She* is right here."

Daire didn't take his eyes from Garrett's. The other werewolf lacked the control of a fully trained Protector. Especially where his woman was concerned. Daire wondered if the rage he could feel emanating from the other would break through or if he had learned to control it. "Then she should exercise common sense."

Sarah blew her bangs off her forehead. "Teri's my friend, Daire."

He folded his arms across his chest. "And my mate."

"The two don't have to be mutually exclusive."

The waves of Garrett's anger surged and then whisked away behind a wall of normal energy. That was good. The Protector was maturing into his gifts. Soon Garrett would be able to mask his emotions completely. Sarah Anne was still looking at him. If she thought her friendship with Teri meant she could interfere with his care of her, Sarah had another think coming. "What do you want to say?"

Her lips shaped the caution he could feel within her. "She's just been so hurt."

"I am aware of this." And when the time was right, the Carmichaels subdued, he would take revenge for that.

"And you're so . . ." She motioned with her hand, filling the space around him with vague implications.

Daire drew himself to his full height, hiding his internal flinch. He was used to people seeing him as evil, dangerous. But it didn't always make it comfortable. "I am a Protector."

Garrett squeezed Sarah's shoulder. "More important, he's Teri's Protector."

Sarah's gaze skirted Daire's to lock on Garrett's. "But he's so ruthless and Teri's so . . ."

Daire let Sarah's doubt slide off him. "Human?"

Sarah snapped around, her irritation clear. "Yes, human, frail, soft, gentle, sentimental." She frowned. "Do you even know what sentimental is?"

"If I have to deal with it, I will learn."

Garrett's lips twitched. "You might have bitten off more than you could chew there."

"Whatever she requires to be happy, I will give her."

Sarah snorted and ran her gaze over Daire from head to toe and then back up. Her eyes lingered on his scars. "You have no idea what she needs."

"And you do?"

"Yes."

The hell she did. Wyatt had been specific about Teri's condition, the listless way she lay in the bed, her lack of care for herself, her refusal to eat. "Then why have I been called here? Why have you not given it to her?"

"Because—"

He was tired of standing here when he could feel Teri's distress so clearly. "Because it's not within your power, and you know it."

Her chin snapped up. "It's not within yours, either."

"Yes, it is, and"—he sniffed, smelling the fresh blending of life force of werewolves freshly mated—"were you not so recently bonded, you would understand this."

"Oh, my God—"

It amused him that Sarah Anne blushed. She'd spent too long among humans that she could be embarrassed by a wolf's plain speaking on something so natural as the blending of life essence that occurred at a bonding. He also saw something more: the perfection of mating acceptance in the way Sarah leaned into Garrett and his immediate, instinctive, sheltering response. Daire imagined Teri with her black hair and pale skin standing beside him, allowing him a mate's right to protect. And then he mentally snorted at his own nonsense. Such things were not for him. In a hundred years, Teri would not look at him like that. She had too much pain, too much hate, and he was too damned ugly. Looks mattered to humans.

Sarah Anne was nothing if not bold. "What has that got to do with anything?"

A lot. "Nothing at all. Do you wish to say more?"

Fabric rustled as Garrett's fingers tightened on Sarah's shoulder in warning. "No, she doesn't."

"Then step aside."

"There's no need to be rude."

"I wasn't trying to be rude." He cocked an eyebrow at her, enjoying her start of annoyance at the gesture. "But I'll let you know when I am."

Two

"YOU are so rude," Teri huffed as he carried her into the bathroom.

Daire smiled. The show of spirit was welcome after yesterday's apathy. "So your friend says."

Teri stared over his shoulder. "You could at least ask before manhandling me."

Daire glanced down at her. "Why, when you would only stubbornly say no?"

"Maybe I would be saying no because I don't want a bath."

"All women want baths."

This he knew. Didn't Sarah have Garrett put in a big fancy tub in place of the perfectly good shower as soon as they moved in?

"That's a terribly sexist thing to say."

"It seemed better than pointing out you stink."

"Go to hell."

He wasn't an ancient for nothing. He could tell when a woman was spoiling for a fight. He let a grunt serve as an answer. Predictably, Teri blew out her breath in another huff. Before she could build to a new tirade, he let her silkily clad body slide down his. Her nightgown, a loan from Heather, glided up her thighs, exposing soft white skin. He bit down hard on his back teeth. The neckline slid to the side, revealing the old scars. A growl escaped his control.

Immediately, the scent of Teri's fear fouled the small bath. He kept his voice calm. "I am not the one who hurt you."

She snatched the neck closed, staring at him with big green eyes the way she always did when he referred to her scars.

"You could."

He growled again, putting his hand over hers, drawing her fingers away, feeling her tremble. "No. I could not."

"That's a lie."

The hairs on the back of his neck raised as an emotion he couldn't name shot through his abdomen, settling in a hard knot in his stomach.

"I cannot lie to you."

She glared at him. "But you can bully me, make me do what you want."

"You wanted a bath; you were just being stubborn."

"You assumed."

"I scented your longing."

The correction was necessary. Too often she judged him by human standards. He was not human. He was Protector. Her Protector. And dammit, she would be happy. Even if she hated him for it.

"You scare me."

He opened his fingers over the ridges of scar tissue. "Maybe, but you need to trust me."

Her hand covered his, drawing it away. A hint of his talons showed. She eyed them nervously. "No."

She would someday. "My talons show because I'm angry."

Her tongue flicked over her lips in a pink flash of temptation. Everything about her tempted him, her scent, the softness of her hair, the paleness of her skin, the vulnerability in her eyes . . . Damn, that vulnerability.

"I know."

His fingers pressed ever so gently into the slash of scars over her breast, feeling how deeply the violence was scored, feeling her distrust just as keenly. "But not with you."

She needed to understand that.

She took a step back. Another and she'd be flat on her ass in the tub.

"I'm not so sure it matters what one of you is angry at."

He slid his hand over her shoulder, stopping her retreat. Against his fingertips, her ribs expanded on a startled breath. "By 'one of you,' I assume you mean werewolves?"

"Yes."

Every muscle tensed. He pointed out as casually as he could, "You're about to take a tumble."

Her eyes didn't leave his, as if through watching them she could see his intent. She wouldn't see anything he didn't allow, but she didn't know that. She kicked back with her heel. It thudded into the tub.

"Oh."

He smiled. She was both intelligent and resourceful. Good qualities to have in a mate, wolf or human.

The scent of lavender drifted up from the pass of the vibration through the water, masking most of her distress. He turned the hot water on, freshening the water.

She licked her lips. "The tub is full enough."

He could still smell the scent of her distress. He dumped another handful of bath salts in the water, reconsidered, and grabbed up the bottle.

Teri's hand fluttered in an aborted movement before he could dump the contents in. "That's too much."

"More can't hurt."

"My eyes are watering as it is."

A quick glance confirmed they were. "Oh."

So were his, come to think of it. He motioned to the tub with the jar. "Lavender is supposed to be soothing to humans."

"In small amounts it is."

He looked at the small apothecary jar. It was half empty. "No problem. We'll just start over."

"It's not necessary."

"Yes, it is." He didn't usually make mistakes. He didn't like that he was making them with his mate. If this had been the first, maybe it wouldn't be so bad, but starting with bonding her against her will, pretty much his hand had been forced in all their interactions. And today was going to be no different. She was going to eat. Whether she wanted to or not. He handed her the jar. He circled the prominent bones of her wrist with his fingers as she took the jar. There was plenty of grip left to go around. She froze, her gaze locked on his fingers.

Light played off her hair in a feeble attempt to shine. Her immune system was depleted, her body malnourished. That needed to be rectified. "Lunch will be waiting when you finish your bath."

Teri put the jar very precisely on the sink. Did she hope he wouldn't see the tremor in her fingers if she did it carefully enough? "I'm not hungry."

She needs someone sensitive. Sarah Anne's words came back to haunt him. With his free hand he touched the dull strands of her hair and ground his teeth down on the retort that it didn't matter what she wanted. He strove to keep his voice even. "Wait and see how you feel after your bath."

"Don't tell me what to do."

He wasn't that successful this time in keeping his voice even. "Do not argue with me."

"Why? Because you've got an overinflated sense of your own importance?"

"Because I'm your mate and my word is law."

Her eyes flew wide. The jar rattled when her hand bumped it. So much for sensitive. "Not for me."

Teri was an obstinate woman, even when terrified. He slipped the sleeve of her gown back up over her shoulder. The smoothness of her skin teased his fingertips. She was also a very feminine woman. He imagined he would be attracted to her whether she was his mate or not. It was hard to tell. She stood frozen under his touch. He forced himself to pull his hand away. He would have much rather pulled her to him. And if she had been wolf, he would've done just that, letting the bonding pull comfort her. But she was human, and all she felt at the draw of her soul to his was terror.

"What are you doing?"

He drew his hand away, and shook his head. "Being sensitive."

She blinked, a slow lowering of her eyelids that could have meant anything but, he'd come to realize over the time he'd cared for her, actually meant she was gathering her composure. It was a learned technique. He wondered what it was in her life before he met her that had taught it to her. He waited, wondering what she would say. All he got was a "Thank you."

He supposed he could work with that. "At least you're not running screaming for the hills."

Another blink and then, "Not yet."

The tiny flash of humor gave him pause. And hope. He reached down and turned off the water. For a brief second the smell of lavender covered the scent of her. He was grateful for the reprieve. He needed it to get his arousal under control. "Just let me know when you feel the urge."

As he hoped, her curiosity drove her to ask, "Why, so you can chase me down?"

From the acrid scent of fear that flooded over him when he straightened, he didn't think the same sexy urges were going through her mind as were going through his. He touched her cheek. The thought of her running from him in fear made him sick. "No. So I can open the door for you to run free."

So I can open the door for you to run free.

Teri sank deeper into the fragrant bathwater. The implication of

Daire's parting words rippled around her with the same frequency of the water. He wanted to set her free. From her fears? From the black hollow that was threatening to swallow her whole? From the all-encompassing hold he had on her? She flicked her fingers in the water, settling back against the tub. Her hand instinctively went to the scars running from her neck vertically down over her breast, remembering the heat with which he watched her. She'd seen enough of Sarah Anne's and Heather's men to understand that the latter was not an option. Werewolves were very possessive of their mates.

Her hand slipped below the water to cup her empty stomach. She'd often wondered if her child hadn't been killed, would his father have come for it? The need to procreate was very strong in a werewolf, but half-werewolf children were seen as a source of weakness, not pride. So why had those werewolves raped her? They'd been very clear that their intent was to impregnate her, but why, when their offspring would have been reviled by the pack whose opinion they valued so highly?

She closed her eyes against the memories clawing at the barriers she'd set up against them. That night didn't deserve to be relived, and she'd vowed it wouldn't own her, but the baby—dear God she'd wanted her baby. All her life she thought she'd been barren. All her life she'd thought for her there'd be no blood bond connecting her to anyone else in the world, and then out of the ugliest thing that had ever happened to her, there had come that miracle. And she'd wanted it. Her nails dug into her abdomen, everything in her reviling the flatness, the absence of life, the lack of hope. She wanted to cry, scream, rant, but she couldn't. All she could do was lie there in the soothing bath and feel the darkness grow deeper. Soon it would swallow her and there was nothing she could do to stop it.

"You will not do this."

There was a time when a man suddenly appearing beside her bath would've sent her into a splashing panic. But now, she couldn't even work up the emotion to cover her breasts. "You're the one who insisted I wanted a bath."

The smell of chicken soup teased her nostrils. There was an abstract sensation of hunger, but not enough to get her motivated. Eating required effort and she didn't have the energy to spare. "I'm not hungry."

"As I said, you will not do this."

She kept her eyes closed, not wanting to see Daire's scarred face that carried so much of his personality. Because if she did, she'd feel that strange need to hug him that threatened to pull her back into the pain of living. She couldn't go back there. "Just what is it you think I'm doing?"

"Crawling into the grave with your baby."

The bald truth cut deep.

"It's not your call."

Fingers closed under her chin. Pressure tilted her face up. There was nothing brutal in the move, but it was loaded with conviction. She let it slide off into the blackness that rose to meet the emotion. The darkness was not only strong enough to swallow her; it could also protect her. And if she just hid behind it long enough, she'd be safe forever.

"Open your eyes, Teri."

No, she wasn't doing that. There were things she didn't want to see, remember.

"Open your eyes."

This time the order echoed in her mind, stronger and more compelling, overwhelming the blackness, forcing her to comply. Oh, dear God, he was stronger than the darkness!

Teri shoved against Daire's hold. Nothing could be stronger than the darkness.

"I am."

Had he said that or thought it?

She clung to the obvious while she battled the subtle. "You're telepathic?"

"I'm an ancient. I'm many things."

Not an answer. Her stomach turned, her brow felt cold and clammy and she couldn't get her breath. A panic attack. She was having a panic attack.

I am here.

And he was. Suddenly, there was the kiss of cool air as she was lifted out of the tub and then the warmth of his body and the strength of his arms holding her as the fear grew. Daire settled back into the water with her, unmindful of his clothes and the overflowing tub.

"I need to go to bed," she whispered. Back to the only place in the world where she felt safe.

"No."

She dug her nails into his skin, almost laughing hysterically as she realized what she was doing. What threat were her puny human nails against a man who could grow claws big enough to disembowel another with a single swipe?

"I need to go to bed now." Before she lost her hold on the darkness. Before it could get angry and let her go. Before it left her to deal with everything she couldn't.

"You need to sit here with me and face your life."

She didn't have a life to face. She didn't have anything.

"You have me and the future I have given you."

Flashes of the night in the cave razed her mind, and through the kaleidoscope of fear and pain came a promise.

No one will ever touch you again.

Her scalp tickled from the kiss Daire pressed on her hair. He'd made her that promise. And he was the one breaking it.

"Except you," she whispered. She had no doubt Daire intended to touch her. He considered her his mate. It would be inconceivable to him to do anything else.

"Is that your fear? Is that why you hide within yourself gathering all the sadness around you like a shield? You fear you have to make love to me?"

How did he know her so well? She shook her head no, not wanting to admit the truth to a man who could read her mind. His hand slipped to her abdomen, covering hers. She hadn't even realized she'd still been holding herself there, sheltering a baby that no longer existed.

"I will never touch you without your consent."

"You are now." His strength was beneath her, around her. In her.

His hair tickled the back of her shoulders as he shook his head. The pressure in the top of her head from his kiss gently slid down her skull until it brushed her ear.

"No. Now I am just responding to that part of you screaming for help. Open your eyes and see the truth."

Her lids lifted whether she wanted them to or not. Was he forcing her or was she just that desperate? As her gaze met his, he said, "I mourn with you, seelie."

He couldn't. There was no way he could know what that tiny flutter of life meant to her.

"Don't lie to me."

"In order to save you, I had to lock my mind to yours. That takes an incredible bonding. I felt your daughter's life force."

She doubled over in pain from the blow. Unfair. Unfair that he could know it was a daughter, and he knew her daughter in a way that she couldn't. He went with her, sheltering with his big body as if there was anything that could take away the pain of the wound he'd just ripped open.

Think. She had to think. "All you would have felt at the touch of her life force was the urge to kill her," she rasped.

He snapped back mentally. Shock poured over her along with another emotion she didn't want to define. She practically threw herself out of the tub. Water sloshed over the side, drenching the floor. She grabbed a towel off the rack and held it in front of her like a shield. He sat there in the tub, staring at her with nothing particular in his expression, yet she knew he hurt. She'd hurt him, and she hated him for letting her know that.

"I know how werewolves are. You're a vicious, jealous, possessive lot. You never would've tolerated my daughter to live." She turned on her heel and left the room, her motions a discordant jangle. She needed to lie down, to find the embrace of the darkness. It hurt too much to live.

IT hurt too much to live.

That last, desperate thought that projected so much emotion struck Daire hard. There were times when the pain in his life, the loneliness, had made him wonder if moving on to the next world should be an option. But he hadn't taken it, never really seriously considered it. His duty was not to himself. It was to his pack. But Teri didn't have pack. Had never had pack, but her need to belong was as strong as any wolf's need. And her baby, no matter how it came about, had been the one thing she'd always wanted. Had been a start on creating a family. He stood and undressed, leaving his clothes beside the tub. He eyed the neglected soup. He'd have to make her eat soon.

Stepping out, he grabbed a towel and roughly dried himself before following Teri into the bedroom. She was lying on her side in the bed, the covers pulled high. The only thing visible was the top of her head. He walked around to the other side of the bed and lifted the covers. She didn't move as he slid beside her and spooned his much bigger body around hers. He settled his hand over hers as it pressed into her abdomen. He drew her back against him and rested his lips on the top of her head. She was wrong. He did understand.

Three

"TRYING out new cologne?" Wyatt asked, grimacing from where he sat behind his desk.

Daire didn't blink as he crossed the office, the scent of lavender traveling with him. "Yes."

Wyatt studied him for a second, his eyes narrowed, and then relaxed in that subtle way Daire was beginning to understand meant he'd seen what he wanted.

"Just a word of advice—it's a little too feminine for you."

"I'll keep that in mind." Daire sat in the big leather chair opposite. "You sent for me?"

Wyatt took the hint. "A problem has returned."

"Oh?"

"I need it taken care of."

"Why can't Kelon or Donovan handle it?"

"I need it handled quietly."

Daire sat a little straighter in his chair, his curiosity piqued. "I never knew either of them to lack discretion."

"I'm afraid in this case, discretion will be beyond their ability."

"What is it?"

"Buddy is back in town."

"The human who hurt Robin and tried to kill Lisa?"

"One and the same."

Daire smiled. At last, something he was good at. "I'll be happy to deliver Haven's justice."

Wyatt sighed. "I don't want him killed."

Daire sat forward. "The law is clear."

Death was the sentence for those that attacked a pack woman. Wyatt tossed his pen on the pile of papers on the big desk. "We can't afford the attention. It's bad enough the Carmichaels are grouping for war. If they attack, a pile of werewolf bodies is going to be hard enough to explain, but if the deaths spill over to humans . . ." He shrugged. "Hell, every branch of law enforcement in three states will be crawling all over here. If we want this pack to survive on the fringes of the human world, we need to blend."

Shit. "So what do you want me to do?"

"I want you to convince Buddy he needs to sell his holdings and leave."

He could do that. "No problem."

"I don't like the look of that smile."

"Just anticipating."

Wyatt leaned forward and met his gaze squarely. "When I say 'convince,' I don't mean through force."

Daire stilled.

"I want you to *influence* him."

"That is forbidden." The penalty for any wolf using persuasion against anyone's will was death by disembowelment, followed by beheading.

"I know what I'm asking."

"It would be bad for everyone if it were found out. Influence does not last forever."

"We'll cross that bridge when we get to it."

"It would be easier to kill him."

"Yes, it would." But Wyatt wasn't going to allow it. "Do you need to think about it?" the Alpha asked.

No. He didn't. His future was here. He couldn't live with Teri in any other pack but Haven. Haven had to survive and here was where they'd made their stand. "Where is he?"

"At his old haunts."

"The pool hall where Lisa taught him respect?"

There wasn't a werewolf around who hadn't heard the tale of how Donovan's mate had avenged the injury done her sister. She'd stormed into the pool hall, picked up a cue, marched into a group of men and made her point. She was legend among the werewolves for the sheer novelty of a woman, human or werewolf, having such courage. It helped the legend that Donovan had been there that day and liked to tell the tale.

"Yes."

He stood. "I'll pay him a visit."

Wyatt stood also. "The pack will be in your debt."

Yes, they would. "I'm going to ask a favor in return."

"Anything."

"That's a sweeping promise to make an ancient."

Wyatt smiled. "I'm feeling reckless."

"If word gets out about what I've done, you buy me time."

"For what?"

"To get to Teri and get her out. We're bonded."

Wyatt didn't look shocked. "I expected as much."

"You don't seem surprised."

"I saw the extent of her injuries. Nothing short of a life bond would be enough for you to keep her alive."

"She wasn't willing." The penalty for that was death.

"Then I guess before she has to come before me and accept your bond, you'll have to convince her."

Daire noticed Wyatt didn't give him a time frame in which the acceptance had to occur. It was strange having so much flexibility from an Alpha. Daire wasn't even sure it was good, but he would take advantage of it.

"I'll handle Buddy."

"Then I'll handle the rest."

Wyatt had to know that Daire could just as easily influence him as he could Buddy, but he didn't see any sign of worry. The Alpha trusted him. Damn.

"Thank you."

Wyatt smiled and held out his hand. It was a distinctly human gesture. At Daire's hesitation, Wyatt shrugged. "Heather says we need to incorporate some human traditions, one of them being accepting deals with a handshake."

Daire held out his hand. "Why?"

"For one, she says it will help us blend within human society."

"And two?"

Wyatt's hand met his. "She says the tradition of acknowledging the sacrifices inherent in a deal with the respect of a handshake creates a bond."

Daire let go of Wyatt's hand, the impression of his energy solid. Clean. "She has strange ideas."

Wyatt flexed his fingers. "But some of them are good."

Daire closed his in a fist. "So it would seem."

———

HE found Buddy in the local pool hall that served as a gathering area for the town. The door swept closed behind him, bathing him in a last breath of fresh air. There were no women in the hall. He could see why. In the thirty seconds he'd stood in the entryway, the scent of stale sweat, stale beer and stale cigarettes surrounded him in a gradual cloud. Under it all was the scent of testosterone. Men came here to play and to fight. He flexed his finger as his night vision flashed in and out with the rhythm of the neon signs in the window. He could accommodate the latter.

A few men looked up as he approached, their courage bolstered by the illusion that their numbers protected them from his wrath. He tried to imagine Donovan's mate, Lisa, walking this same path. Human, unprotected, intent on revenge, her anger might have carried her into the room on a foolish wave of courage, but the men here wouldn't have seen her as a threat. She'd just be an annoyance to some. A potential toy to others.

The bartender looked up as Daire reached the counter. He stopped rinsing a glass and set it in the sink. The scent of his nervousness reached Daire as the man reached under the bar. Catching his gaze, Daire shook his head. The man froze. Daire bared his teeth. The man brought his hands back up.

"Buddy?"

Indecision warred on the bartender's face. Fear tainted his scent. Then with a jerk of his head he indicated the back of the hall where the pool tables could be seen.

With a nod, Daire acknowledged the bartender's life-saving decision to give him the information he sought rather than pull a weapon. "Good choice."

Daire continued on, sorting through what Wyatt had told him about Buddy and comparing that to the faces of the four men laughing over a joke as the fifth lined up his shot. Six foot, dark hair, blue eyes, with the build of a football player going to seed and, more likely than not, wearing a ball cap. Daire's focus narrowed to the man in the green ball cap. He fit the description, and the way the others stood around him, close but slightly back, suggested deference. Daire's lip curled. Humans' concept of what constituted power was warped. Buddy's money wouldn't save them from Donovan's or Kelon's wrath. Neither Lisa nor Robin should have to suffer the shithead's presence in their town. Daire's fingertips tingled as his claws prodded him to action. Buddy didn't deserve the break Wyatt was willing to give him in the pursuit of peace. He deserved to have his guts ripped out for trying to force any woman, but a mate to a wolf? His lip curled back from his canines. There should be no mercy.

"Table's full up, friend," one of the bystanders said.

Daire let his snarl relax into a facsimile of a smile. "I wasn't looking to play."

The men straightened. From the strong scent of liquor seeping from their pores, they'd been drinking all day. With the economy of the area being so depressed, there was no work, and in the human or wolf world, indolence bred trouble. These four were trouble. The fifth . . . he stiffened inside. The fifth was more than trouble. The fifth was wolf. And he wasn't Haven. There was no good reason for a nonpack to be in Haven territory. Even less of a good reason for the wolf to be hanging around with Bobby and his friends. He had to be a Carmichael spy. The wolf leaned on his pool cue the same as the humans, blending in except for his energy and scent. Daire met his gaze. The wolf couldn't hold his for more than a second. Not an Alpha, then.

"Well, we're not putting on a show," another of the humans snapped, not looking up. From the way he was watching the game, Daire was willing to bet he was the biggest contributor to the pile of bills on the small round table behind them. Daire ignored him and focused on the wolf. "I was sent to collect on a debt."

The flicker of the wolf's brows indicated he understood the formal challenge of a Protector.

"Well, shit," the one he suspected was Buddy said, as he leaned over the table and lined up the cue ball. "There's no one in this town that's got a penny." He motioned with the tip of the cue. "Ten ball left pocket."

Daire bet he'd smirked just that way as he'd tried to force Kelon's mate, and likely when he'd thought he'd driven Lisa's car over the cliff. He bet the man smirked like that a lot in this small corner of his human world. The balls clacked together. Daire caught the ball before it dropped into the pocket. He gave it a little toss, drawing the men's gazes up. "That's fine. I'll take payment in blood."

It took a second for the threat to register. When it did, the four men straightened and hefted their cues. The wolf blended to the back. No loyalty there.

Buddy, his friends at his back, exuded confidence. "You've got balls, stranger. I'll give you that."

Daire tossed the ball again, aware of how he looked to the humans with his hair pulled back in a ponytail, emphasizing the harsh planes of his features and the scars that gouged through them. Big, dark and threatening, his wolf tweaking their instinct for self-preservation with a subconscious urge to flee. It would take very little effort for him to send the mental nudge he was supposed to, but Lisa's, Robin's, and lastly Teri's faces flashed into his mind. Women of Haven. Women for whom justice had been delayed. Women whose honor had been held hostage to politics.

I want you to influence him.

Daire didn't want to influence Buddy. He wanted him bleeding and pleading the way Robin had been. The way Teri had been. He wanted him helpless and begging for mercy. And then Daire wanted to deny it.

Teri's image flashed in his mind. The scars on her body speaking of the horror she'd endured at the hands of wolves. Rage welled. He should have been allowed to know her then. Should have been there when the rogues had come calling. Power rippled around him. He felt the start that signaled the other wolf's recognition of retribution looming. Felt the instinctive flinch of fear, the urge to retreat. Too late.

Stay. He sent the command deep into the wolf's mind. The wolf froze.

The humans gathered closer to one another. So easy. It would be so easy to deliver justice. The darkness swept over him, flashes from the past peppering the thick blackness with the faces of those who'd come before. Faces of those he'd arrived too late to spare, but had avenged. His claws extended, biting into his palms in a familiar prelude. Oh, yes, he'd avenged. Time and time again. Until the scent of blood was indistinguishable from the scent of the night. Until the rage was like a living creature inside him, hungry for release.

You scare me.

Teri's face flashed in his mind, as white as the shower wall behind it, her eyes huge in her face, cringing from his touch. Because she'd sensed his wolf, or because she'd sensed the centuries of rage that battled for dominance? The madness that threatened all ancients? The rage flared behind the wall of control, seeking a way out. A different energy flared out of nowhere. Softer, sweeter, but strong. Incredibly strong as it wrapped around the darkness and smothered it. Rage was replaced with hunger, equally primitive, equally uncontrollable. The sweet energy winked out on a blatant retreat, leaving no trail for him to follow. No imprint for him to recognize. But leaving him stable once again. What the hell?

"I believe you were saying something about a debt," Buddy cut in, tapping his cue stick against his palm.

Debt? The second it took Daire to remember his purpose was even more disconcerting than that invasive energy. He might rage, but he never lost focus. The wolf slipped out the back door. *Shit.* He must have broken free of Daire's control in that moment of distraction. Wyatt wasn't going to be happy. Daire curled his lip at Buddy.

"It was a poor choice to come back here, Buddy."

"I own this damn town."

"Technically, your mommy does."

"It's still mine."

"Consider it sold."

"Because you and that damned cult you belong to say so?"

Cult? The word unexpectedly pinged off Daire's sense of humor.

Buddy leaned forward, hands slapping down on the table. "Oh, yes, I know who sent you, and you can tell that arrogant bastard you work for that no fucking Satan worshipper is going to buy me out like he has everyone else. I can't be bought."

Imagining Wyatt's amusement at being told he headed a cult, Daire smiled as he pointed out, "But you can be killed."

"Are you threatening me?"

"Yes."

He looked to his companions. "You heard him, boys." The boys nodded. "You touch me, asshole, and the law will be on your ass so fast it will make your head spin."

Daire let a trickle of his power ease over the group. The men shifted positions. This time his smile was genuine. "One way or another, you *will* leave."

"What makes you so sure?"

Daire folded his arms across his chest. "Because you touched the women of Haven, and they sent me to settle the account."

Four

"A cult? They think we're a cult?"

Daire shrugged at Wyatt's outrage. "Beats the truth."

"Yeah, I suppose it does." Wyatt shook his head. "They really think we're a cult?"

Daire shrugged. "I didn't dissuade them. Figured it was better than the alternative."

"Yeah, the truth would blow their little minds. Does this mean our mission was accomplished?"

"Partly."

"What does 'partly' mean?"

" 'Partly' means I delivered enough bruises to make 'em think twice about staying."

"You were supposed to influence them."

Daire shrugged again, remembering the terror on Buddy's and his friends' faces when he flashed the nightmare in their mind.

"I kept my word."

"So they're leaving?"

"There'll be some bluster. You'll have to negotiate."

"By that you mean pay through the nose?"

"Yeah. A guy like Buddy is not going to just walk away. He'll need some sort of win for his ego so he feels he's walking away victorious."

"Did you promise him a number?"

"Our negotiations didn't get to that level."

"Should I expect him at any time?"

"I imagine he'll wait till his bruises heal."

"That gives us what? Two weeks?"

"Roughly."

"So why do I hear a 'but' in there?"

Daire leaned back in the chair. It was a comfortable chair, in a comfortable office, in what might be a comfortable pack. If it were allowed to survive. "We've got another problem."

"Just what I need, more problems." Wyatt sighed. "Give it to me."

"There was a wolf with Buddy and his friends."

"What pack?"

Daire shrugged. "I couldn't tell."

"You didn't question him?"

"I didn't get a chance. I was a bit distracted."

Wyatt grunted. "On his worst day, an ancient can handle a Beta."

"You would think."

"But you couldn't."

With a growl, Daire vowed, "It won't happen again."

"I don't imagine it will. But now we've had a wolf infiltrating our pack and no one knew about it. That worries me."

"Me, too."

"I think it's safe to say he was here to cause trouble or to spy."

Daire nodded. "That, too."

Wyatt swore. "I was hoping negotiations would settle this."

"The Carmichaels won't settle. In their eyes they'll only tolerate an allegiance with a strong pack. Your pack runs with human blood. To any wolf, any human is inherently weak."

"Yeah. I know."

Daire thought of Teri, of all she'd endured, the memories that had come from her to him. A lifetime of rejection, loss, and always she'd bounced back. Stronger than any wolf could. He wouldn't call her weak. Unbidden came the memory of that energy that had wrapped around his rage. Had it been her? Could a bond work that way? He thought of Megan and her powers, Garrett with his. Human/werewolf mixes were revealing surprising abilities. Ones usually reserved for the occasional ancient.

"They'll want Megan."

Wyatt's expression hardened. "They'll never get her."

"If the spy learned of her existence, got a whiff of her power—they won't stop."

"There aren't many wolves that believe in the old legend."

It was a false hope. The legend Wyatt referred to promised of the coming of a child who would start a new order. The legend guaranteed the pack that held the child would hold sovereign over all other packs.

"The Carmichaels are traditionalists. They'll hold the legend as truth. Half will want to kill her. The other to use her."

Wyatt spun his office chair around and dropped into it. Steepling his fingers, he looked out the window. "The wolf you saw, was he a Protector?"

Daire shook his head. "No, not an Alpha."

"So there's a chance he doesn't know?"

"Not one we can bank on."

Donovan stepped into the room. "You're going to need to alert Garrett."

"Shit." Wyatt ran his hand through his hair. "I promised both him and Sarah Anne she'd be safe here."

Donovan shrugged. "She'll be as safe here as she is anywhere."

"What are you saying?"

"I'm saying there had to be a reason the rogues killed Sarah

Anne's husband, chased her so hard. I'm guessing they already know about Megan. I'm guessing they made the link between her and the legend. As much as the rogues would like everyone to believe they're packless, they do have each other."

"Something no one considered when they tossed out the mixed-bloods," Wyatt added dryly.

Daire nodded. In the past the lost had disappeared into the human world where their werewolf attributes had given them an edge, but in the last century there'd been a shift. The lost still banded together, but their targets were becoming pack.

Donovan took a couple steps toward Daire. "Speaking of tossing out. On behalf of my mate, I thank you, Daire."

"Don't be thanking him," Wyatt snapped. "He went against my direct orders."

Donovan cocked a brow at Wyatt. "To avenge my mate. And I find it hard to believe that he disobeyed your direct orders. Ancient or not, he's a Protector."

"Who hasn't sworn allegiance to this pack."

"As far as I'm concerned he's displayed it; the words aren't necessary."

Wyatt's jaw set. "The words are always necessary."

There was more Carmichael in Wyatt than Daire had imagined. "I didn't break my vow. I promised you I'd influence them and I would not draw attention."

"A bar fight in the middle of town doesn't draw attention?"

"A bar fight in the pool hall is normal for a Saturday night. And it's not as if Buddy hasn't lost a fight before."

"True."

Daire could sense the anger and frustration emanating from Wyatt. He was trying to do the impossible. He wanted a bloodless coup. Slide the Haven pack into what had once been a lumber town using the economy as a cloak. But Buddy's family had a vested interest in this town.

Too much was at stake. His own frustration surged. He could

just kill the remaining residents, drive them out the old-fashioned way through fear and violence.

The immediate *no* that whipped through him surprised him. He needed this pack for Teri, for the union. He dug his claws into his palm. For his sanity. None of which he let show. An unstable ancient was nothing anybody wanted around.

"I need to go check on Teri if you're done."

"You're sure there's no indication what pack this wolf is from?"

"The one Daire lost?" Donovan asked, an edge to his voice.

Wyatt waved him quiet. "Let's not start warring with each other."

Daire bit back a retort and stood. "No, but it shouldn't be hard to find him. I'll get on it as soon as I check on Teri."

This time Donovan shook his head no. "Kelon and I will handle it."

Daire didn't ask how they'd know which one it was. It really didn't matter; this was Haven territory. Any wolf not Haven would be up to no good. Any wolf not Haven would need to be dealt with.

It went against his grain to delegate but on the edge of his consciousness he could feel Teri's distress rising. He'd been too long apart from her. He frowned. She shouldn't be needing him yet. Was her condition worsening? Was she relapsing?

He nodded. The "Thank you" came hard. He left the room, not realizing until he was on the porch that Donovan had had his hand out when he thanked him in the human way, offering him the handshake that forged bonds. He shook his head and stepped down into the yard, unsure how he felt about the offer, unsure how he felt about missing it.

———

TERI stood by the window, holding herself upright through sheer force of will. Her body ached with weariness, but at the same time, she was consumed with a restless, negative energy.

She couldn't shake the feeling that something was wrong. She pulled the curtains back. She could see a man stride out from under the porch roof and into the yard. Daire. A shiver went down her spine. The curtain crumpled in her grasp. He turned and looked up. She hated that ponytail. Even from here she could see the scars on his face. She brought her hands to her neck. The roughness of her own scars abraded her fingertips.

His eyes met hers. She wanted to drop the curtain back, to block his gaze. She couldn't. He stood there staring, as if he couldn't break the connection, either.

You need to sit here with me and face your life.

She didn't want to be alive. She didn't want to sit with him, be with him.

Liar.

His voice or hers? The answer when it came was shocking in its abruptness. Hers. She clutched the window jamb. She did want to be alive. She did want to be with Daire. Because he was so scary. Because he was so big. Because with him, there was no way anything bad could happen to her. Because he knew her in ways no one else did. Because he was telepathic. Because he'd touched her daughter's mind. Because her daughter had not died without knowing someone's touch. She sobbed, biting her knuckle. Her knees crumpled. She slid down the wall. Because she owed him for that.

The door creaked open. Arms came around her. She didn't need to ask whose. Only Daire could move that fast. Only Daire cared that much. Because he was wolf. Like the men who'd raped her.

He turned her into his chest as he knelt beside her. "Not like them."

His scent smoothed over her. Clean and earthy with a touch of musk. It'd been her talisman as the pain had raged. As she had raged, fighting for life and then fighting for death to be with her baby, but he hadn't let her go. She hit his shoulder as the sense of loss rolled over her again.

The sob caught in her throat, choked her.

"Why?" Why wouldn't he let her go? Why did he make her stay?

She felt the brush of his lips over her hair. "Because I need you."

"You don't know me."

"I know." His finger under her chin lifted her face. "But I've waited centuries for the chance."

"OH, God."

He was telling the truth. He saw her as his mate. "It can't be me." She was broken, scarred, incapable of loving, barely able to live.

His gaze didn't flinch from hers. "It can't be anyone else."

"Of course it can. They wouldn't have raped me if there can't be more than one; they wouldn't have come hunting me." There was a flicker in the energy blending with hers. "What?"

He didn't answer, just rubbed his thumb along her cheekbone. "Oh, my God, they didn't come for me."

"You would have been a bonus."

"Sarah Anne."

Again that fluctuation in his energy that she was recognizing meant a negation. That left only three others. She remembered the wolf that had gone after Megan. There had been such determination in his eyes. Such hatred.

Oh, no. "Megan. They want Megan."

"They won't get her."

"Why?"

"There's a legend among the wolves about a child who will be of two worlds. A child of power."

She shook her head. "Megan can't even change."

"Her power is not that of a wolf. That's what scares them."

"But they tried to kill her."

"Some believe the child can be used. Others believe she'll be the downfall of all pack. The legend is why wolves have no tolerance for telepaths."

"You're a telepath." It was strange to say that out loud.

"Yes."

It was stranger to hear him agree as if that had no import. But he'd just told her that wolves didn't tolerate telepaths, which meant he had not been tolerated. If anyone knew. "Did people try to kill you?"

"No one succeeded."

Which wasn't an answer. Teri rubbed her fingers across her scars. "It's just a legend."

"A very old legend."

"That some believe." She looked up. "Do you?"

His gaze didn't flinch from hers. "No."

There was no ripple in his energy.

"I believe you."

"I cannot lie to you."

"So you keep telling me."

The corners of his mouth twitched. "In the hope that you'll eventually believe."

Because he didn't want her to know he could? Her head began to ache. She leaned against his chest as the weariness rose with the pain. "Will I ever get better?"

"You almost are."

"It's only been a few days!"

His palm curved over her shoulder. "Then why are you complaining?"

"I'm not." But she was wondering. If he could do so much, why couldn't he have done the thing that mattered? Why couldn't he have saved her child? The question stuck in her throat.

"You're tired."

"Yes." She suddenly was.

"You shouldn't have gotten out of bed."

"I had to."

He lifted her. "Had to?"

There was no way to explain the waves of energy that had rolled over her, angry, relentless, chaos in need of order. How hard it had been to disassemble it. "Yes."

Her stomach rumbled as he laid her on the bed. She blushed. He smiled. "You're hungry."

She was a doctor for all that she'd been a patient of late. "More signs of healing."

His hand slid under her T-shirt, covering the scars. With his head tilted down she could see the beauty of his face without the distraction of the scars. He was a very handsome man. A tingle of awareness went down her spine. He went to lift her shirt. She caught it in her hands.

"What?"

What was she supposed to say? That she didn't want him to see how ugly they were after all this time? She let go. The hem rose. Her stomach sank. She closed her eyes. "Nothing."

His hands slid up her sides, encompassing her rib cage. He had such big hands.

"Are you shy, seelie?"

The question was followed by the touch of his lips. Since Teri didn't want to answer such a leading question, she opted for one of her own. "What's seelie mean?"

"The one who holds my heart."

She wished she'd kept her mouth shut. "Oh."

Another kiss. A tightening of his hands. "You don't think you hold my heart?"

"I think you don't know me well enough to even say I hold your big toe."

"That, my seelie, is the difference between human and wolf. A wolf is born with the knowledge he lives for his mate."

"Even when she's not there?"

"Yes."

She opened her eyes and looked down between her breasts to meet his gaze. "That's so sad."

"Until the mate is found, yes, but then"—he lifted her to the press of his mouth—"the waiting is as nothing compared to the joy of discovery."

"I don't feel that joy."

"I know." He kissed his way up the underside of her breast in light, airy caresses. It was purely a sexual gesture, so why did she feel so cherished?

"I may never," she gasped.

"You're my mate. There is no option for either of us."

"I'm human. Maybe I don't play by the same rules."

His tongue curled around the tip of her breast. Fire shot through her body.

"I'm adjusting to that."

He was adjusting? She leveraged her way up to her elbows. "I'm the one who's been shanghaied into a life I didn't ask for."

"And suffered for it." His lips brushed the upper curve of her breast in a kiss of fire.

How could she want him so when everything was so wrong? How could she want him when he wasn't even human?

"Is that what you want me to understand, Teri?" Another kiss, this time in the hollow of her throat. Her pulse took off. "That you have suffered for being my mate?"

Was it? "Yes." She wanted it to be yes, but he hadn't been the one who had hurt her. He'd been the one who'd held her, fought for her. Protected her. "No."

He loomed above her. "Which is it?"

She shook her head. "I don't know."

His face was so austere without the softness of his hair falling about it. He had beautiful hair, thick and wavy. Hair of which any woman would be jealous, and when it was loose it made him appear . . . human.

"If I could go back in time, I would have been there the night the rogues attacked."

She knew what the red lights seeming to burn in his eyes meant. Rage.

She remembered that night. How the door had splintered as if made of toothpicks, the noise, the chaos. She'd flicked on the light and the men had poured into the room with lazy grace that just enhanced the evil of their purpose. She hadn't known how to kill a werewolf then. She'd stalled, worried about conserving bullets rather than inflicting maximum damage. And they'd taken over. Been so strong. Tossed her about as if she were no more substantial than a cotton ball. She'd felt so helpless, then and after. Bits and pieces of their expressions flashed in her mind, falling over one another in such rapid succession, she wasn't sure she could identify any one of them.

Daire interrupted her thoughts. "You don't need to."

She blinked. "Yes, I do." Because one day, she would find them.

His hand cupped her cheek. "I have their faces now. I will find them."

And kill them.

The knowledge should have appalled her, but it didn't. Someone had to pay for that night. Someone had to make sure it didn't happen again to someone else. But it didn't have to be Daire. Those men had been so strong. And there were four while he was just one. She would die if she lost him. He was the one constant in her world now.

The knowledge came out of nowhere, shocking. Comforting? Oh, God, she didn't know who she was anymore. Reaching up, she yanked the rawhide tie from Daire's hair, removing the warrior. He didn't flinch, just stared at her as his hair fell forward, covering her, shielding her in darkness, but not from him. She would never escape from him.

She bit her lips. It didn't help. She couldn't suppress the sobs.

They pushed up and out. Daire leaned down. The darkness grew deeper. "What is it, seelie?

What did it matter if she told him? "I used to love the night, the sounds, the scents."

A sob broke off the rest.

"But?" he prodded.

"But I hate it now. It reeks of *them*."

There was a long pause. The tips of his fingers pressed delicately along her cheekbones. She felt the warmth of his lips on her temple, the probe of his energy at the edge of her consciousness.

"I could give you back the night."

She shook her head. "Sex with you won't make me forget."

His body jerked along hers. Had she finally succeeded in shocking him? Before all this she'd been a confident, outspoken woman. Nothing like the coward she was now. She looped her arms around his neck. He smelled so good. She buried her face in his throat. "But I wish it were possible."

His fingers pressed just a little bit harder. Her mind felt full, too full. She lost her train of thought.

"I can take away the memory."

She blinked. She could just make out that fiery glow that transformed his eyes when he was angry or under stress.

"It will be as if it never happened. No rape. No attack. No losing of the night."

It was so tempting. "Can you really do that?"

His lips moved to her forehead. "Yes."

The warmth of the kiss sank through the coldness, spreading through the chill, replacing it with heat. Sexual yet . . . healing.

It got harder to concentrate. A haze slipped over the past, taking away the pain, the knowledge. Taking away—

She grabbed his wrist. "Stop it."

"Shh."

"No! You can't."

"There's no need for you to have the pain of memories better forgotten."

She held his wrist. "I don't want to forget *her*."

He froze. The haze wavered. "Her?"

"My daughter." Tears wet her lashes. "I can't forget without forgetting her."

"No."

That was a very cautious no. "She deserves to be remembered."

"I will hold her for you."

It wasn't enough. If she couldn't forget, then there was something she needed to know to heal. "Could you share her with me? I need to know what she was like."

"It will only build your sense of loss."

She doubled her hands into fists and pressed them against his chest. If he couldn't give her this, she didn't want anything. The spot between her neck and shoulder burned. "She was my daughter. No one should know more about her than me. No one."

Such a soft whisper to hold such fierceness, Daire thought. But his little human was very passionate about everything she cared about, and she was right. No one should know more about her child than she.

"Open your mind."

She blinked. "I don't know how."

He could do it for her. Stroking the hair off her face, he brushed his lips over her lashes. Instinct closed her eyes. A mother's need kept them closed. He could feel her struggle to open her mind, wanting it so desperately she was blocking success. Emotion poured from her to him. His heart twisted in his chest. So much pain in his seelie's life. So much unfulfilled want.

"Just relax and let yourself float. This is my gift to you. You don't have to do anything but let me give it to you."

Her lower lip slipped between her teeth. He shook his head and smiled. She was a stubborn woman, thinking she could control everything. He brushed his mind over hers, once, twice, letting her get used to the feel, getting used to it himself. He'd never touched another's mind with anything other than a need to extract information, but this time he was going to merge, linger, share. With his mate. A shudder shook him from head to toe. He savored the sensations as his mind entered hers, that first tiny bit and energy, delicate and strong, wrapped around his. Oddly familiar. Addictively feminine. He reached deep into his memory for that moment he'd touched the life force of her child. Try as he might, he couldn't eliminate all the other memories wrapped within; her terror and pain rode the link, taking her back to that moment she'd lain on the cave floor bleeding out from the werewolf's attack. Her terror flooded over her.

"Don't see that; see what's within."

"What?"

He did his best to mute the violence. He tried to focus on how the little girl had felt. She'd felt like . . . a bright spot in the middle of hell. "Look for the light in the darkness."

"I don't understand."

"Just keep looking."

He knew the minute Teri found it. She drew in her breath, held it. Her hand reached up. He caught it in his. Linked as they were, he saw what she saw, felt what she felt, knew what she knew. That vibrant touch of new life. Pure emotion. Scared. Even at that tiny age, the child had known on an instinctive level that something was wrong.

Teri's nails dug into the back of his hand. "Daire."

"Yes."

"She's so sweet."

"Yes." The only thing he'd ever touched with his mind that had been sweeter was her.

"And scared." A sob ripped from her throat. "I told myself at least she'd been too young to know but, oh, God!"

He didn't know what to say. The infant's understanding had

been primitive, but— Teri's grip tightened on his arm. Wonder and something else pushed the sadness out of her voice.

"Daire . . ."

"What?"

"Thank you."

Their minds were linked and he didn't understand her. How did nontelepathic werewolves manage their mates? "For what?"

She tugged. He leaned down. Her arms came around his neck. Her tears saturated his shirt, heated his skin. "You gave her love."

Yes, he had. As best he could, everything inside him surrounding that tiny bit of life in a surge of protectiveness.

"I tried." He wasn't sure he even understood what that was, so much of his life had been empty of anything other than duty and justice. Teri held him tighter. "She knew she was loved by you and"—her frown pressed her tears into his skin—"and someone else?"

Ah, she'd felt that. "Megan."

"She's that strong a telepath?"

"Yes."

Her hands cupped his cheeks as her eyes opened. The connection to the past lessened. "Thank you."

She was throwing too much emotion at him. He shifted uncomfortably. "It's just a memory."

She didn't lessen her mental grip, didn't let him go. He felt the calm spread over her as her green eyes darkened to emerald with gratitude and something else. "It was everything I needed."

Five

THE next day Teri was ready to rejoin the living. It was amazing what a night with a werewolf could do for a woman. Even if all that wolf did was hold her close and soothe her fears. If Daire wasn't careful, she could love him.

Teri kicked the covers off her legs and stood. The lack of dizziness verified what she felt, and she definitely felt stronger today. Daire was right—she was healing quickly. The doctor in her couldn't resist appreciating the miracle of that along with wondering how and why.

Her clothes . . . well, not *her* clothes but the clothes somebody had lent her—the mysterious Heather, Wyatt's wife, she thought—were folded on the chair. Daire hadn't let anybody up in the room while she'd been recovering except Sarah Anne, and then only a couple times, which was ludicrous. What did he think the other women were going to do? Contaminate her with humanness? Too late; she'd been born human and no late-in-life conversion was likely to change everything. She looked around the room. Every variation in the paint, every shadow on the wall was too familiar. She definitely needed to change her environment.

Downstairs she could hear the murmur of feminine voices interspersed with quickly hushed laughter. No doubt Daire had left strict instructions that she not be disturbed, but considering Daire was out with Kelon and Donovan hunting the wolf that had gotten away yesterday, this was a perfect opportunity to explore her surroundings.

She picked up the jeans. They were two sizes too small, but with the eternal hope that all women have when faced with their ideal size, she tried them on. She blinked. They fit. Jeans this size never fit. Not outside her daydreams. She tested the waistband. Not tight at all. She really had lost a lot of weight. Part of her wanted to look in the mirror; part of her didn't dare. Was she a scarecrow? The bra was a little small. Well, at least she had fat where it counted. She pulled a T-shirt on over it with a shrug. She was just going to pretend she looked gorgeous. It would give her more confidence.

Her strength didn't last as long as she'd hoped. She felt like an old woman descending the stairs, holding on to the railing, not sure if her legs were going to support her the entire distance. By the time she got to the landing, she was shaking. She leaned against the wall, taking a moment to regulate her breathing.

She could hear the women in the den. She had a now-or-never feeling about this moment. A small plump woman with brown hair came around the corner. She had a very gentle aura about her and a very winning smile.

"Well, hello."

Teri smiled and tried to steady her breath. "Hi."

"Decided to join the living, did you?"

"Yes."

Two more women came out of the room. They all had the same brown hair, smooth skin, blue eyes. One had her hair pulled back in a ponytail and flashed an easy smile. The other was thinner and had an intensity about her that made a body want to stand up straight.

"I'm not sure if she decided to join the living or leave her jailer."

The thinner woman came forward and held out her hand. "I'm Heather and this is our sister Lisa."

Teri let go of the wall and took Heather's hand. "Teri."

There was no way she could hide the trembling in her hand. Heather's eyes narrowed. This close, Teri could see they were more hazel than blue.

"Do you want to sit?" Heather asked.

"Yes, please."

"Upstairs or down?"

"Definitely down." If Teri never saw that bed again, it'd be too soon.

"I'm glad you came down to join us." The woman with the ponytail came forward and took her arm, supporting her. "It saves us the trouble of breaking you out."

Teri blinked. "You were going to break me out?"

Heather nodded and smiled. "Yeah, we talked about it last night. Robin and I decided it was time you got to join the rest of us. Daire seems to be a little overprotective."

"A little?" Robin snorted. "He makes Kelon look like an amateur."

Teri remembered how Garrett had been with Sarah Anne.

"Are all werewolves so protective?"

Heather put a hand under Teri's elbow and helped her the last step to the floor.

"You get used to it," Heather assured her.

"Or find ways around it." Lisa grinned.

Teri had a feeling she was going to like her.

Robin smiled. "That is always plan B."

"We try not to use it too often, though," Heather cautioned as she steadied her. "Otherwise, they'll catch on to us."

Teri decided she was going to like them all. The laughter seemed to carry her in to the living room, give her the strength her shaky legs needed. It felt good to be back among women. Daire meant well but he was always so serious, so intense. She missed laughter.

Lisa stopped at an array of snacks set out on a table. "Since you made it all the way down those stairs, what's your pleasure? We have . . ." She looked at an assortment of things. "We have tea, we have soda, we have water—"

"Milk shakes," Robin piped up, nudging Teri with her elbow. "I'm pushing for milk shakes."

Lisa rolled her eyes. "Ever since she realized that a werewolf's metabolism is always on high, there's no stopping her."

"Hey." Robin shrugged. "You've got to celebrate the upside."

Heather snorted at her sister. "As if Kelon isn't upside enough."

Robin shrugged again. "You pick your upside. I'll pick mine."

Teri blinked. "We don't gain weight as wolves?"

"Not an ounce after the conversion is complete"—Lisa grinned—"but then again, we don't lose it, either." She slapped her voluptuous hips. "We just stick where we were bitten."

Teri touched the waistband of her jeans. "Wow."

"What?"

"I just realized I get to spend eternity at my goal size."

Lisa laughed as Teri took a seat in the overstuffed chair. "Lucky you."

"So I should put you down for a milk shake?" Robin asked.

"Why not?"

"Chocolate?"

"Fine."

"Great. I can never make it right if it's just for one." Robin opened the door of the small fridge beneath the table and pulled out a carton of ice cream.

"We're not really wolves, you know," Heather cut in, taking a seat on the couch across.

"We're not?" Teri got the impression Heather might be the one who kept the other two grounded.

"It's more a bonding than a conversion."

"Oh."

Lisa popped the top on a can of soda before sitting beside Heather. "And we don't actually get to live forever."

"How long do we live?"

"Well, if you're life bonded, you'll live as long as your mate does. But when you die, he dies."

Teri blinked. That, she hadn't known. "How do you know if you've been bonded?"

"You're bonded," Sarah Anne said, walking in the door. "It was the only way Daire could keep you alive."

Sarah looked as good as always. Better, even. Her skin seemed more lustrous, and there was a calmness about her that was new. She leaned down and hugged Teri. Teri held her hand, as she would have stepped back.

"You mean I had a choice?"

The calm slipped. "If you'd been conscious, maybe."

"I didn't have to be a wolf?"

"Uh-oh," Lisa whispered.

Robin hit the button on the mixer. The noise wasn't loud enough to obscure Sarah's answer.

"I gave him permission."

"Who?"

"Daire. I told him I wanted you to live no matter what and he did what he needed to do."

"And he agreed?"

"He didn't have much choice. I told him you were pack and that no matter what, I wanted you to live."

So Daire had done what a Protector always did: he put pack first. Great, she hadn't even been his choice and now he was bonded to her. Forever.

"The bond can't be broken?"

"No, there's no breaking it."

"And if he wants someone else?" Like his real mate.

"He won't want anyone else," Robin said, bringing the milk shake over. "He's bonded to you."

Teri took the glass. The chill traveled from her hand to her soul. Daire had given everything up for her, not because he'd wanted her, not because it was meant to be, but because she'd been a duty he hadn't been able to avoid.

Once again in her life, she was second best.

Six

TWENTY minutes later, Heather, Lisa and Robin declared they had to get home and get supper ready. Amid laughter and jokes about stepping back into the dark ages, they left.

"They're happy," Teri observed, standing by the couch as the women left the room.

"Their mates are some of the strongest werewolves living today."

"Yet they married humans."

"Most wolves don't have a choice where they mate."

"I can't imagine anyone forcing Daire to do anything."

"The mating bond is more powerful than any force a human could apply."

An image of Daire's scars flashed in her mind. At some point someone or something had applied a lot of force to Daire. Had they succeeded in getting what they wanted? She touched her own scars, running her fingers along the grooves, hating the thought of anyone hurting Daire, hating the thought of him being humbled. "I'm trying to understand it."

Sarah Anne stepped in and hugged her. "I haven't even had a

chance to have a real hug." It felt good to hug her friend. So much had changed in the past week, but this was familiar. Blessedly normal. "How are you?"

"If you'd stop hugging me so tightly, I'd let you know."

"Oh, my God!" Immediately, Sarah let Teri go. "Did I hurt you?"

"Don't be silly. I'm wolf now. If I get hurt, I just heal."

Sarah cocked her head to the side. "Not all wounds heal."

She was talking about losing the baby, the attack.

"I haven't given up hope."

Sarah frowned. "I'm so sorry—"

Teri shook her head. "Why? You didn't order those rogues to attack me."

"But if you weren't with me, they wouldn't have found you."

"We've been over this before. They were just bad apples. Period. And I had the damned bad luck to be standing by their basket."

The analogy didn't make Sarah Anne smile like she expected.

"In the old days, that never would have happened. Protectors would never have let rogues get close, let alone live."

"But these aren't the good old days."

Sarah licked her lips and looked out the window. "No, they're not."

Standing this close, there was no missing the lines of tension at the corners of her mouth and eyes.

"Have Josiah and Rachel been found?"

"No."

The hairs on the back of Teri's neck stood on end. "Oh, my God." She looked around "Where's Megan?"

"She's napping."

"You left her alone?"

It came out harsher than she wanted. Sarah Anne's eyes narrowed. "Garrett's with her. Why?"

Teri rubbed her arms. "I just don't like the thought of her being alone. What if one of those lone rogues gets in here?"

Sarah Anne turned and met her gaze. "They'd never get past the guards."

"That spy didn't have any trouble getting in here."

Sarah Anne's gaze didn't waver. "They wouldn't get past Garrett."

"You have a lot of faith in him."

There was the faintest of smiles. "I discovered there's more to him than arrogance."

Sarah's hand went to her neck. It was the same place where Daire had bitten her, Teri realized. The place that heated up on Teri whenever Daire was near. She put her hand over the spot on her own neck. The mating mark. "You've bonded to him?"

Sarah Anne shifted uncomfortably. "Not a life bond, not yet."

"Why not?"

"Apparently"—her lips quirked in a grin—"Garrett thinks I need to be courted first."

"Courted?" Werewolves courted their women?

Sarah Anne didn't meet her gaze. "I know it's only been a couple years since John died. . . ."

Teri ran her hand through her hair. It was longer now, shaggy. She didn't like the way it stuck to the back of her neck. It was getting long enough to need to style. Long enough for someone to wrap their fingers in, hold her. A cold chill raced over her skin. "Just tell me one thing."

"What?"

"Are you happy?"

"You know"—the grin blossomed into a smile—"despite everything that's going on, despite how it came about, I really am. I used to mock the old myths that talked about the beauty of mating with your true mate."

"But you've had a change of heart?"

"Yeah. Garrett makes me very happy. Way down inside where it matters."

"Good." Teri hated to knock that small smile off Sarah's lips, but she had to know what'd been going on while she'd been laid up. "What news has there been of Rachel and Josiah?"

Sarah Anne bit her lip. She folded her arms across her chest. The way her fingers dug into her arms was a bad sign.

"It's not good news, is it?"

"What makes you say that?" Sarah Anne asked.

Teri motioned with her hand. "The way you're gripping your arms. You only do that when you're nervous."

Sarah Anne looked down, and sighed. "I guess before I work on my poker face I need to work on that."

"We've known each other a long time."

Sarah Anne's gaze dropped to Teri's scars. Teri's went to Sarah Anne's bare ring finger. "And been through some tough times together." Her attack, John's death. The struggle to rebuild their lives. "And we've always come out on top."

"I'm not sure we can this time."

That didn't sound good. Teri sat back on the couch. "Shoot."

"I'm sorry." Sarah sat beside her. "You're tired."

She was tired, but not weak. This werewolf metabolism was an amazing thing. "It's more I'm bracing for the worst. Daire wouldn't tell me a darned thing."

Sarah didn't immediately respond. It had to be worse than Teri thought. "No matter what you tell me, I'm not going to fall apart," Teri said as she sat on the sofa. "I think the one thing to come out of all this is there's not much that's going to shock me and not much I can't handle."

"Maybe I should let Daire—"

"If you do, I'll go to my grave ignorant, and that's unacceptable."

Sarah's lips twitched. "Finding him a bit protective?"

"Yes and if you laugh, I'll hide all the chocolate."

"He's a very traditional wolf."

"Then he's going to have to modernize fast, because I am not the little-woman type."

The twitch spread to a grin. "No, you're not." Sarah Anne

leaned over. Her arms came around her shoulders. She hugged her tightly as her voice choked with emotion. "Thank you so much for saving my daughter."

"You're welcome."

"You paid an awful price."

Teri closed her eyes, tears burning behind her lids, clinging to the memory of that bright light that had been her own daughter, hearing again Megan's terror as the wolf had lunged for her. "Some things weren't meant to be."

Sarah Anne stepped back and wiped at her cheeks. "Your daughter—"

Daire must have told her it was a daughter.

"I meant Megan," Teri said, cutting her off. She couldn't talk of the baby she'd lost without breaking down. "She was never meant to die like that. And if I had to do the same thing all over again, I would."

As she said the words, Teri realized she meant it. It wasn't a matter of what-ifs. She would make the same choice again. It was like a weight lifted from her shoulders. No matter what the consequences, she'd made the right choice that night.

"I can never thank you enough."

"You would have done the same."

"I wish I had been close enough."

"But I was and it all worked out."

Sarah Anne opened her mouth. Teri cut her off. She might have made the right decision, but that didn't make it hurt less. "Now, tell me what's going on with Josiah and Rachel."

Sarah perched on the edge of the couch, fingers digging into the cushion. "They didn't show up at the meeting place."

Meeting the next morning had been an absolute. Only something horrible happening would have kept Rachel away. Fear shot up Teri's spine as she contemplated all the horrible things that could happen to a woman and a child with werewolves on their trail.

"They're not dead?"

"Oh, no. We just don't know where they are."

She said it as if that was a small thing. No doubt so Teri wouldn't stress. Too late. Little Josiah with his too-brave moments and his little-boy smile? Rachel with her soothing manner, missing? Teri grabbed Sarah Anne's hand and squeezed, prepared for the worst, hoping for the best. "They were captured?"

Sarah Anne shook her head. "No. This Protector, Cur—"

"That's an awful name."

"Yes." Sarah folded her arms back across her chest. "This Cur seems to think Rachel doesn't want to be found."

Teri let out her breath. They were alive. "Our Rachel?"

"Yes."

"Then she must have a damn good reason."

Was it her imagination, or did Sarah Anne seem relieved? "That's what I said."

"I hear a 'but.'"

"Garrett and the others think she's being deliberately evasive."

"Well, why wouldn't she be? She probably thinks she's being chased by rogues."

As if the words snapped an inner coil of tension, Sarah Anne collapsed against the back of the couch, closed her eyes and smiled. "I'm so glad you're feeling better."

"Missed me?"

"You and your logic." She glanced at Teri out of the corner of her eye. "I'd forgotten how obsessive wolves can be when they get an idea in their head."

Teri looked out the window at the bright sunshine dappling the shaded front yard. "And they think Rachel stole Josiah?"

"Yes."

A squirrel hopped across the yard, his tail gracefully flowing behind him. Just hopping across the yard as if he didn't have a care in the world. As if the cat crouched behind the bushes wasn't a threat. As if he had forever. "Because of Megan." As soon as the words left her mouth, Teri wished she'd bitten her tongue.

Sarah Anne sat up. "What about Megan?"

"I don't fully understand the whys—"

"You're a lousy liar."

"Well, it's your legend."

"Legend?"

"Yes. The one about the child with powers."

Sarah sat back. "Oh, my God."

"You didn't know, did you?"

"No. It never occurred to me." From the look on her face she thought it should have. Now. "She was just my daughter," she whispered. "I worried about people knowing she was telepathic, but the child from the legend?" Sarah Anne shook her head. "That's just a myth."

"The healthy reaction of a sane person. So refreshing to see."

The joke went over Sarah's head. Where a minute before she was relaxed, now she was so tense she looked as if she'd snap. "Does Daire think she's the child of the legend?"

"No, but he's not dismissing others' assumptions."

Sarah Anne licked her lips. "But does he . . . fear her?"

There had been nothing of fear in the emotion she'd felt between Daire and Megan. "I got the impression he thinks she's an amazing little girl."

Blowing her hair off her forehead, she whispered, "Thank God."

So much relief made Teri suspicious. "What about Garrett?"

"Believe it or not, he loves her."

Teri half turned and tucked her foot beneath her. "And what's not to love? She's a wonderful child."

"Garrett's wolf. They see things differently."

"Half wolf," Teri corrected. "And obviously it's his human half that has a hefty dose of common sense."

"Because he loves Megan?"

"Because he loves you both."

"You don't know that."

"I can tell from the tone of your voice when you speak of him. You've got that warm fuzzy thing going on."

"That sounds awful."

"I think it sounds nice."

"You would."

Teri couldn't resist. "Too bad he's wolf. Otherwise, he'd be about perfect. "

Sarah managed a weak chuckle. Teri was surprised she managed anything at all with her daughter threatened and her son missing, but Sarah Anne had always been a resilient woman. "Wolves aren't that bad."

"Neither are humans, and I think you werewolves do yourselves a disservice by dismissing any human influence as inferior."

"Purity of bloodline is important to werewolf culture."

Teri shook her head. "I don't know why you cling to that belief when everyone knows mutts are the hardiest."

"It's not the same."

"I bet it is. Genetics are genetics, no matter what the species."

"Wolves are stronger."

Teri traced the furrow in her neck until it crossed her collarbone, skimming the two inches to the side until her fingertip touched the mark Daire had left during the bonding ceremony she didn't even remember. The spot was cool, barely discernible. When a werewolf mated for love, was the mark different? Deeper? More significant?

"I wouldn't be so quick to count us humans out."

And if Daire was smart, he wouldn't be so quick to count her out, either. She could be one hell of a right mate if she wanted to be.

Seven

THERE wasn't a sign of the spy anywhere. Daire cast his senses wide. Beside him, Donovan and Kelon stood shoulders back, heads up, listening. He felt the flinch of discomfort at so obviously using his powers in front of Protectors. In any other pack they would be sworn to kill him upon the revelation. Even now it was a risk. He reined in a bit of his energy. All Wyatt had to do was rescind his permission and a death sentence would be carried out.

Kelon looked over at him. "Giving up?"

"No."

Donovan didn't take his gaze away from the direction they were assuming the wolf was going. "Then why did you pull back?"

Interesting that the twins could sense the fluctuations in his power so easily. "A momentary aberration."

"I assume you're not feeling nervous?" Kelon asked with a lift of his brow.

Daire kept his energy focused first north and then south. There was nothing. It was as if the wolf had disappeared into thin air. "Do I have cause to be?"

"With any other Alpha but Wyatt, I'd say yes."

Daire glanced over at Kelon. "I was just thinking the same thing."

"And probably wondering where this is all heading," Donovan added.

Daire cast his senses to the east. "It doesn't matter where it's headed. I mated a human."

"Which means you're pretty much along for the ride, right?" Donovan inserted smoothly.

Kelon pushed his hair back from his face. "And if you think we believe that, you're not the ancient we were told you were."

There was no trace of the wolf to the east, no lingering threat of energy, no trail of scent. There wasn't even an odor of petroleum to suggest he left in a vehicle. "The old ways are changing."

Donovan cocked an eyebrow at him. "And you're changing right along with them?"

"It's always been an adapt-or-die world."

Kelon shared a glance with Donovan. "Which explains why he gets along so well with Wyatt."

Daire smiled. "And what I said grates on your nerves so much. I heard right up until the moment you met your pretty little mate there was no way you'd sanction a human/werewolf mating."

Daire had the pleasure of feeling Kelon's internal flinch. The man was quick to rally. Daire liked the way he didn't make excuses, just laid out the truth. "There are some women that make a man rethink everything, including his devotion to duty."

And it had been a huge moral conflict for Kelon to make the choice to mate with Robin. As a Protector, he had been born to put pack first. Mating with Robin meant he'd become one of the packless lost, given up being Protector. Given up his identity. But he'd done it.

Over the years Daire had wondered if there was anything that he would ever be able to put above his sense of honor, and his devotion to pack. As a pup, he'd believed in the power of a true mating, listened to the stories with a sense of hope that for him there would come that one perfect moment when the woman made for him would touch his soul. But then the years had passed, his powers had grown, and calluses had grown over his optimism. And gradually, reality had pushed back fairy tales. Like Kelon, he'd backed tradition, not seeing any point in diluting the blood of their dwindling numbers. He'd also given up seeing the world in black and white.

The latter was why he had no pack affiliation. While he didn't see the value in diluting wolf blood with human, he no longer saw it as cause for destroying lives. The bottom line was, werewolf numbers were too few, and their years in existence too short to deny any pack member whatever happiness they could find.

Being packless had freed him from orders with which he didn't agree, but it had done nothing to fuel his need to have a purpose. Which was why when he heard about Pack Haven, his curiosity had been piqued. And after he met Wyatt, he decided to stay on awhile. If there was any hope for wolves to go on into the future, Haven represented it. Of that he was convinced.

"Lately, I've begun to see your point," Daire told Kelon before turning his attention to the west.

Donovan glanced at him out of the corner of his eye. "Speaking of that, how go things with Teri?"

"I haven't heard her screaming at you to get out lately," Kelon added.

There was a trickle of something to the west. Not a scent, not exactly a vibration, but a certain offense to the natural order that spoke of a disturbance. He straightened. "I'm growing on her."

"What is it?" Kelon asked.

Daire turned toward the disturbance, frowning. "I'm not sure."

Donovan scanned the horizon. "Shit."

Kelon growled. "Yeah. If an ancient doesn't know what he's dealing with, it can't be good."

Daire crouched down and touched the ground. The vibration

didn't increase, so it hadn't come from the earth. Which meant it was likely man-made. Or wolf-made. He stood. "There's something wrong with the energy to the west. I think it's safe to assume that whatever caused a disturbance was left by the werewolf we're chasing. Either that or he can teleport from place to place."

"That would make him an alien, not a wolf," Donovan cut in, "and my imagination can't stretch that far."

Neither could Daire's.

"In your best guess, what are we dealing with?"

"Someone or something that knows how to cover the energy trail normally left by living creatures."

Kelon put his hands on his hips. "Ah, hell, that doesn't seem so bad."

Donovan nodded. "I've got to agree that doesn't get my tail in a twist."

Daire growled in his throat. "As long as that's all they know how to do, we can probably rest easy."

"That's right, just rain on my parade," Kelon growled. "I've got a pretty little wife at home just waiting to show me how much she's missed me, and you've got to hand me a mystery."

"It's not like I'm heading home to an empty bed." Not anymore. The knowledge spread through Daire in a building warmth that ended in anticipation.

Donovan tossed Daire a pack. "Funny how fast change can come, isn't it?"

Both Kelon and Donovan watched him as they picked up their own packs, weighing his response. He didn't hide his satisfaction from them as he answered, "Yes, it is."

Eight

TERI was waiting for him in the parlor with Wyatt. Kelon and Donovan took one look at her face, and made their excuses. Wyatt stood as he entered the room.

"Evening, Daire."

Daire nodded his head as if Wyatt hadn't given that greeting like a man looking for an escape. "Evening."

It wasn't hard to see that everybody was bolting as if a tiger had been set loose in the room. The energy coming off Teri was restless and charged with . . . anger? He'd been gone for all of twenty-four hours. What on earth could have made her so angry?

Wyatt clapped him on the shoulder as he left the room. Speaking too low to carry, he whispered, "Good luck."

Sensation lingered after the Alpha left. Daire reached up and touched his shoulder. A lot of things were apparently going to be different in Pack Haven, including the unwritten rule that one didn't get friendly with Protectors or ancients. He wasn't sure how he felt about that.

"It's about time you got home."

"You knew I was hunting."

"You make it sound like deer season and you're out for a lark with the boys to see if you can catch yourself one."

"Same technique, different prey."

The increase in Teri's agitation was obvious. She paced by the window. One, two, three steps, a turn and then three steps more. With every step, her fingers tapped a rhythm on her thighs. There was a settled pattern to her behavior. "Do you always pace when you're angry?"

She glanced at him over her shoulder, flipping her bangs out of her eyes with the force of the gesture. "Does it matter?"

He leaned against the doorjamb and folded his arms across his chest. "Nope. Just getting a feel for what's normal."

That had her snapping around and instead of pacing back and forth she came straight at him, green eyes dark with fury, hands fisted at her hips. The scent of her anger caught on the edge of his passion, brought it forward. He accepted the challenge in her eyes with the crook of his finger.

She came, teeth set in a grimace. She drew her arm back. He expected her to hit him, was prepared for the blow, but instead she poked him in his chest with her finger. "It's not fair."

He blinked. "What's not fair?"

"I won't let you do this."

He didn't have a clue as to what she was talking about so he just stood there and let her poke him in the chest again. "What do you think I'm doing?"

"I won't let you make me second best."

Her hand went to her mark and she took a step back. She still wasn't used to her mark's reaction to his presence. The heat she felt from her mark translated to the heating of his blood and the pounding in his cock. If she were werewolf, he'd be wearing her mark and her burn would be his. But she wasn't werewolf; she was human. And she thought he found her lacking. "Who said you were second best?"

He knew damn well it wasn't Wyatt.

She folded her arms across her chest. Anger fueled the red in her cheeks, which deepened the green of her eyes. Her short haircut spiked all around her head. Likely she'd been running her hands through it. She should have looked ridiculous. Instead she just looked adorable. Sexy. Perfect.

"I may be human, but that doesn't make me inferior."

"I don't remember saying it did."

"And I'm not some duty you pick up and discard as it pleases you while you lament your bad luck."

He pushed away from the door. She took a step back. Reaching out, he snagged her arm, hauling her against him. "And I'm not someone you fear."

"Why not? You're so angry all the time. I can feel the rage in you. You're also werewolf. Any human with a lick of common sense would be terrified of you."

The rage she spoke of seethed within, triggered by her unreasonable fear. Immediately, he felt a soft touch of that energy from before wrapping around the angry mass, soothing it, mellowing it, replacing it with desire. It had been her. Somehow she'd reached across the distance during that bar fight, found his rage and calmed it. Damn.

"You're not afraid of me."

Her gaze didn't duck the challenge of his. "I should be."

But she wasn't. He didn't know if it was because he'd told her not to be or if it was because she was so darn pissed at whatever slight she imagined he'd done, but she came up on her tiptoes and grabbed his shirt and shoved her face in his, hissing, "And I'm as good as any werewolf woman."

Where had she gotten the idea that she wasn't? He cupped his hand behind her head and tilted her face to the side. His gaze locked on her mouth. That beautiful mouth that would look so sexy plumped from his kiss, wet with their passion. "You're better."

"Why?"

"You're mine."

He felt the leap of her pulse against his thumb as he wrapped his fingers in the tendrils of hair at the base of her neck. Fear tainted her scent. An image shot into his mind. A male werewolf's gloating grin as his fingers wrapped in her long hair, holding her still for the descent of his mouth. He felt Teri's icy fear, saw the gleam of the man's canines. He cut off the memory before Teri could relive the bite. He had no doubt the werewolf had bitten. Easing his fingers out of her hair, Daire pulled her face against his chest and wrapped his arms around her. He didn't know what to do except hold her tight. "I'm sorry, seelie."

"I'm not a baby."

"No, you're not." He brushed his lips across the top of her head, inhaling her scent. Warm, feminine and familiar. He knew he'd gone centuries without breathing her in, but he honestly couldn't conceive how he'd managed it. "But you're hurting and I need to understand why."

She took a slow, deep breath and blew it out just as slowly. It eased through the opening of his shirt in the softest of caresses, joining them for a brief moment. He cherished the moment. Committed it to memory. He had a few memories now. Teri turning to him for the first time. Teri letting him hold her while she slept the other night, the moment of understanding binding them. Teri sharing his memory of her daughter and her tears in the aftermath. And now this. Her letting him comfort her even though he was the one that caused pain. All precious memories he never expected to have as an ancient who hadn't found his mate and was reaching the end of his endurance. There was nothing more precious to him than her. Not pack, not duty, not even, he realized, his honor.

"You're stuck with me," Teri said.

He massaged the nape of her neck, replacing the sensation of being held with another, hopefully more welcome one. "I like being stuck with you."

"But you'd love being stuck with someone else better."

Ah. That was the crux of her issue. He tilted her face up. He could see the pulse pounding in her throat. The hormones in his bite worked like wildfire on her human system. She licked her lips nervously. He bent down and kissed her moist lips, rubbing his against hers until they parted on a little gasp.

"There's no one else for me."

Her hands pressed against his chest. Slowly they closed into small fists. He wanted to kiss them both and then ease them open. Tenderness was such a foreign notion to him, it took him a minute to recognize it. Once he did, he paused to experience it. This was what Donovan and Kelon felt when they touched their women. What the mating myth was about. This overwhelming rightness, combined with the pleasure of caring for her. This was what had taken Garrett from an angry man to a contented Protector. This was what was going to change him.

"Because Sarah Anne forced your hand."

Daire touched the tip of his tongue to Teri's lower lip, indulging his senses as he sorted through the best responses.

"Sarah Anne is not my Alpha; she can't command me to do anything."

"But she put you in a position where you couldn't say no."

He stroked his thumb over her cheek, noting the healthier color with satisfaction. "I knew who you were the instant I saw you. Knew what I was losing. Sarah Anne was the closest thing to pack you had. Asking her permission was a formality. I would not have let you die."

"That was so reckless. What if you couldn't have kept me alive?"

He kissed her lips. "Then you would not have crossed alone."

"That's crazy."

"Maybe to a human."

Her lips moved against his in a tentative caress. "Don't lie to me, Daire. I've spent my whole life being second best. I don't want to spend the rest of my life trying to measure up."

"You are the only one I have ever wanted. The only one I will ever want."

"What if some sexy lady werewolf prances by?"

He couldn't help it. He laughed. "I'm centuries old. Many a sexy lady werewolf has pranced by."

"And you didn't want to bond with them?"

"Not a one. Why are you asking me this?"

She bit her lip. "I had a thought last night. . . ." She didn't finish.

"Yes?"

He nibbled his way across her cheek, kissing the curve of her jaw before he found the sweet spot below her ear. She shivered and moaned the way he liked. Pleasuring a mate was so much more than technique. "You were saying?"

She grabbed the front of his shirt and hung on for dear life as if she feared he would disappear before she finished confessing. "I couldn't bear to be second best with you."

He slid his hand down her back until he could cup her rear and lifted her to him. His cock fit naturally between her legs. He waited, expecting her to flinch back. She didn't, but she didn't lean in, either, just rested against him. "I am always here for you, seelie. Always yours."

A smile touched her lips. "Mine to command?"

The laughter inside grew. He hefted her a bit higher, held her a bit closer. "You can try."

"And when I do?"

"I'll handle it." The sweet scent of feminine desire rose.

"How?"

"The way any Protector does when challenged by his mate."

"You'll go all masterful on me?"

From another woman he might have taken that flirtatious statement delivered with a coy bat of an eyelash as an invitation. From Teri, it was a dare. Not to "go all masterful," as she put it, but to prove to her she could trust him. "Yes."

She flinched and stiffened. He smiled and kissed her gently on the side of her neck, nibbling his way down to her mark. She held her breath as he neared. He knew how good it felt when he kissed her there. He knew how much she wanted this, but while this was about feeling good, it wasn't about sex.

"Daire?"

He nibbled around the faint shadowing beneath the surface of her skin. *His* mark. The sense of satisfaction roughened his voice. "Yes."

"I'm afraid."

The truth hung starkly between them. He breathed deeply of her scent. So good. Turning, he sat down on the chair, swinging her legs to the side. "I know."

"It's not like I don't know this can be good. I've had lovers. There haven't been rockets, but I know it can be more than rape, so . . ."

The growl rumbled past his control. "Seelie?"

"What?"

"I've told you you are more important to me than my life. I've told you you are the one who holds my heart."

"I know, but—"

He pushed her hair out of her face with his fingers. Her bones were so fragile. Her spirit so strong. Her pulse throbbed in her temple. "If you know, then you will trust me to show you what you mean to me."

"Would you be offended if I told you I'd settle for a handshake?"

"Yes."

"Rats."

"We do not have to do this. I can wait."

"That's not what Heather said."

"Heather is not an authority on me."

"She's as close as I have to an authority on wolves."

Daire hooked his hand under Teri's thigh and pulled her up so she was curled in his lap. "You have a higher source."

Her hand came up and curled around his shoulder. "You?"

"Yes."

"But you wouldn't tell me the truth."

Interesting. "How do you think I could lie to you?"

"If you thought it would make me unhappy, you'd lie." She cocked her head to the side. "You would, wouldn't you?"

He brought her hand to his lips. "*If* I could lie to you and *if* the lie would not put you in danger, yes."

"Those are big ifs."

"Starting with the first." He pressed a kiss to the back of her hand. His woman, his seelie. And she thought he could lie to her. "You have only to touch my mind to know all answers."

Her eyes were very big and very hungry as they studied his face, revealing many things she probably didn't want him to know. There was desire, yes, but there was emotion. Not immediately identifiable. And he discovered what fear felt like. What if her human heart couldn't love the way he needed?

She chose that moment to touch his mind. It was awkward, unskilled, but she made the effort. He braced himself for her revulsion but he didn't shield. He was Protector, not human. There was a difference. She needed to understand that.

Her gaze softened as her fingertips touched his jaw. "You were scared."

He clenched his teeth.

She blinked and then smiled. "I wasn't talking about just now."

Did she have any idea what that touch did to him? What it made him want to do to her? It was the first time she'd touched him with the tenderness of a mate. He wanted to turn his head, catch her fingers between his teeth. He wanted to nip, kiss and love on her until she didn't see them as anything but one. Wanted to bind her to him in every way. "Then what were you referring to?"

"When you bonded to me, you really were afraid I'd die before you could get to know me."

"That makes you smile?"

"That makes me smile, because it tells me"—she kissed his chin—"I really wasn't second best."

Nine

DAIRE shook his head and tilted his mouth so her lips brushed over his. "I already told you this."

She wrapped her arms around his neck, her fingers going to the leather strip holding his hair back. "Sometimes a woman needs to be convinced."

He frowned at her, putting more depth into the scowl than he felt. "My word should be enough to convince you, woman."

"Sorry."

She didn't look at all repentant. As a matter of fact, the way her eyes crinkled in the corner on a repressed smile made her look completely sexy, sassy and intriguingly human. "You're not sorry."

"No. I'm not." One tug, two, and his hair fell free. She was always doing that. "You don't like my hair?"

"I love your hair. I don't like the way you wear it all scary like that."

"Scary? The tie keeps it out of my eyes."

"It makes you look mean."

He couldn't help a chuckle. "I am mean."

She drew his hair around his face, letting it trail through her fingers as it draped over her shoulder. "Not to me."

"No." Never to her. "To you I'm going to be very sweet."

Her smile slipped. "Daire, about that thought I had."

"Yes."

"If I ever decide to love you."

He cocked an eyebrow at her. "Decide?"

"I'm human. It will be my choice."

And, apparently, choice was important to her. He lifted her up, turning her so she could straddle his lap. "And if you decide to love me?"

Her arms draped across his shoulders. "You'll have to love me back."

"You're my mate."

"No." She shook her head, letting him tug up the hem of her T-shirt. "Not like that."

He tugged the shirt up. She caught it when it got face high, staring at him over the red material. He sighed. Clearly, the brief glimpse he was getting now of her torso was all he was going to get until this got settled.

"How, then?"

"You need to love me because you want to."

"Agreed." He tugged again, but she didn't let go of the shirt.

"I mean it, Daire. I don't want you saying you love me because of some hormonal clicking. You have a choice."

He had no idea what she was talking about. "I'm wolf, Teri. The choice was made before I was born."

She pushed out of his arms, tugging her shirt down. "No, it wasn't." She turned on her heel and stomped out of the room. He watched her go, desire, anger and frustration churning his gut. The door slammed shut behind her. *Shit.*

The door opened. He knew from the scent it wasn't Teri, but his pulse still leapt. "You're not going to win her that way."

Robin stood in the door. It was easy to see what attracted Kelon to her. She had a very sweet touch to her energy. If he wasn't so damned pissed, he'd probably appreciate it. A growl rumbled in his chest.

"Do you always eavesdrop?"

As if his warning growl had no effect, she strolled into the room. "Oh, please, if I was eavesdropping, you'd never know I was here." She walked over to the end table and picked up her book and held it up. "Unfortunately, I abandoned Lady Mary and the Earl in the middle of a steamy love scene. They have a marriage of convenience that could fail or succeed based on how well he interprets Lady Mary's needs in this crucial moment."

Daire looked at the brightly rendered cover of a male and female embracing. With a wave of his hand he dismissed her excuse. "Let me save you the trouble. She comes. He comes. They live happily ever after."

Robin gave him a pitying smile. "Ah, but it's not that easy. Lady Mary is an intelligent, discerning woman. It's going to take more than the Earl's conviction that she belongs with him to get her to see him as husband material. And until that happens, the happily ever after is in question."

He had a feeling they weren't talking about the book anymore. "Their marriage means they don't have a choice."

Robin tucked the book under her arm. "Yes, the Earl does seem to be relying on that belief."

"It's a safe bet."

To his surprise, Robin patted his shoulder. He didn't like the smile she gave him. He'd never been pitied before.

"It's only safe as long as Lady Mary feels the same. Being an intelligent woman, however, she knows she has options."

"What the hell does that mean?"

Robin laughed and walked out the door. "That, I think, you'd better figure out for yourself."

They definitely weren't talking about the book. What the hell did she mean 'options'? Teri was mated to him. There were no options, no other man, no believing, no nothing. There was just him and her.

Ten

DAIRE took the stairs two at a time. He felt Teri's mental start as he hit the landing. By the time he opened the door to her room, she had her response under control. She was standing by the vanity. In the mirror behind her, he could see the lace edge of her low-cut nightgown as it framed the delicate line up her spine, the curve of her ribs and the tempting curl of her hair at the nape of her neck. He remembered her fear when he'd curled his fingers in her hair.

She has options.

No, she didn't. But that didn't mean being human Teri didn't feel she had a few. And it didn't mean that she might need a few. A lot had happened to her in a very short time. Then Daire remembered the feel of her hands against his chest. Mind to mind. Skin to skin. Heartbeat. Her first initiative. If he wanted more of that, he was going to have to make it happen.

"What is it?"

Teri couldn't wrestle his pinky into submission, but she stood there, arms folded across her chest, chin lifted, daring an angry wolf. Damn, he loved her. "You're challenging me?"

"I'm asking you what you stormed up here for."

He took two steps into the room. "I came to tell you you don't have options."

"Yes, I do, and where did that come from anyway?"

He pushed the door with his foot. "No, you don't. And it was Robin."

The door clicked shut. She frowned, eyeing it nervously. "Robin was here?"

"She forgot her book."

"Oh." She licked her lips. "And that made you mad?"

"Yes."

Rolling her eyes, she mourned, "Just when I was beginning to like you, you have to go insane."

He took another step forward. In the mirror, he could see the muscles of her back tense. His seelie. Hurt so much, but still swinging. He ran his fingertips down her cheek. She watched him, blinking slowly.

"We have unfinished business between us."

"What kind of business?"

"The kind that answers your questions."

"Which questions?"

He pulled her in. She took the step, reluctantly, but she took it. "The ones which ask, can he really want to be with me? Can I please him? Can he please me?" The next step brought her body flush against his. He lowered his cheek to hers, pressing with his thumb against her temple, holding her there as he kissed her cheek. "Will he hurt me?"

"Will you?"

He caught her earlobe between his teeth and nipped lightly. "Never, my seelie." The scent of her desire teased his senses. So did the scent of her fear.

"Why should I believe you?"

"Because your heart says to."

"My heart has never had any sense."

She sounded so grumpy, he couldn't help a chuckle. His tension melted away. "Because you were telling it what to do rather than letting it lead you."

"And you think my heart was trying to lead me to you."

He curved his hand over her shoulder, holding her to him. "Didn't you?"

Silence.

"I asked a question."

"That doesn't mean I have to answer."

A "yes" sat on the tip of his tongue. He squashed it. If Teri needed to think she had options, then he wanted to be a viable one. It was inconceivable to him that anyone could resist a bond, but humans didn't think like wolves, and in his lifetime, he'd seen how perception was everything. Hell, there'd been battles he should have lost when he'd just started out in his role that he'd won on the other side's belief that as a Protector he couldn't be defeated. He looked into Teri's green eyes. They didn't flinch from his. Humans had an endless capacity to believe.

"Fair enough. So what did you believe?"

Her throat muscles worked as she swallowed. Her energy flicked away from his. A shadow chased across the surface of her gaze. "That I was doing everything right."

And not getting rewarded. She didn't need to tell him that. A woman didn't long as hard for a place as Teri did if she was content.

"And what did you want?"

She blinked. "I wanted to belong somewhere, to someone." Tears gathered in the corners of her eyes. "And I wanted . . ." She shook her head. The tears hovered. "It doesn't matter."

It did. Daire pressed his thumb to the outer corner of her right eye. The tear spread over the surface. Her mind spread across his with the same even glide, filling the empty places with her touch. He wanted to close his eyes and absorb the bliss of having her there, but he couldn't. She needed him to hold her together in this moment when she was so vulnerable. "You wanted someone to belong to you," he finished for her.

Another swallow. Another tear. "I thought it was going to be my baby."

"I want it to be me."

Her hand came up and encircled his wrist. Her other covered the scars on her chest. "Want?"

How could she not know? "Want. Need. Desire. Hunger. Crave." Her lower lip quivered.

Love?

The question she wouldn't speak snuck past her guard. He considered what he felt. Was it love? He'd always considered love a paltry human word for the power of what a werewolf could feel. But the emotions that always came at him from Teri were as strong as any wolf's.

"I don't know what that is."

She blinked the next tear away. "If you felt it, you'd know."

"But I may not define it the way you do."

"Are you always so logical?"

"Yes. Except . . ."

As much as he wanted her to, she didn't look away.

"Except what?"

He slid his fingers down to the nape of her neck and drew her up onto her tiptoes. "Apparently, I'm not at all logical when it comes to you."

She went willingly, her gaze searching his, her body tense. She needed answers. He wasn't sure he had the ones she needed. "How do you feel when you're with me?"

"Like I'm supposed to."

The hope in her eyes faded on her exhale.

"Damn it, seelie," he growled against her lips. "Tell me what you need to hear."

"Nothing," she whispered back. "I don't have to hear anything."

He wanted to shake her for the lie. He could feel her need, the desperate want. "If I knew what it was, I would tell you I love you."

"Thank you."

He could feel her pulling back. He wouldn't allow it. Not when for a moment, they'd been so close. Tugging her closer, he slanted his mouth over hers, knowing the hormones in his saliva would bring the passion back, and through that desire he could bring her back.

Her hands pressed against his chest. He prolonged the kiss. She moaned. The scent of her desire increased, but her mind didn't touch his.

He allowed a breath of air between them. "Don't you hold back from me. Rant, rage, but don't hold back."

Her hands cupped his cheeks. Soft, delicate. Hands that held his world without even knowing it. He caught one and brought it to his mouth, pressing a kiss deep into the palm. "That scares the hell out of me."

"What?" she asked.

He squeezed her fingers. "You hold my world in your hands, yet you worry about meaningless words like 'love' when I've proven there's nothing I won't do for you, nothing more important to me than your well-being."

She frowned up at him. Her calf slid up the outside of his. "You have?"

"I bonded my life to yours." He placed his palm over her mark, the moment vivid in his memory. Pure potential. Pure emotion. Pure perfection. He wouldn't take it back. "My soul to yours, in this life and the next. We are bound."

She shivered and then froze. "Heather said that means you die when I die. And vice versa."

"Yes."

"Yet you bonded to me when I was dying."

He slid his hand under the edge of her gown. The hollow of her back beckoned. "Yes."

"Because there was no choice?"

"Because after feeling the touch of your energy, seeing your face, I couldn't go back to nothing."

It was a statement of fact every werewolf understood. A mate was light, hope, a gift from God. Precious. Teri reacted as if he'd given her a prize. Her energy surged over his; her mind thrust into his. Her scent spiked with excitement.

"You wanted me."

He lifted her up. Her legs went around his waist. Her groin pressed against the ridge of his cock. He growled in frustration as the long skirt of the nightgown bunched between them. There was too much keeping him from her. "I've waited centuries for you."

She smiled and tugged his tie out from his hair. The sting in his scalp only added to the excitement of holding her. "You're an old man."

Did that matter? "I am closer to the end of my life than the beginning."

She kissed his chin. The darkness pressing in on him lightened. "You're just ancient."

"Yes."

She smiled. "We have to work on your literal interpretation of everything. I was joking."

"I was not. I offer you less time than Garrett offers Sarah Anne."

"I was only looking forward to another sixty years anyway."

He brushed his lip over her eyelids. He could probably give her a hundred and fifty. "Then maybe you won't be disappointed."

"I think you were the one who was more likely to be disappointed. You didn't know what I looked like."

"But I knew how I would feel when I was with you. I knew I'd no longer be alone. There could be nothing more beautiful to me than you."

"And when you met me?"

"You were more than I ever dreamed would be mine."

And he'd almost lost her in the same moment. There was no other word to describe the pain of that moment other than anguish. He carried them to the chair and a half in the corner of the room and sat, needing to hold her to abolish the memory of the feel of her slipping away to the darkness he couldn't see into. . . .

"Daire!"

He winced as her gasp blew past her ear. He was holding her too tightly. "I'm sorry."

Her arms wrapped around his neck. "It's all right."

"I forgot myself."

Because he loved her, Teri realized, reading his mind. It wasn't an emotion that came to Daire slowly. It was the equivalent of love at first sight, something she believed in. But more. So much more. She'd been in his mind when he'd recalled the first time he saw her face. She'd felt his shock and wonder. His despair when he'd recognized her condition. The fierceness with which he'd fought for her life.

My soul to yours, in this life and the next. We are bound.

The words welled out of memory, hoarsely growled, ripe with emotion, the one clear recall she had amid the chaos of that night. The spot on her shoulder burned hotter, as if it absorbed the energy of his emotion. She touched it. "Will you really die if I do?"

"Yes."

"And if you die, I die."

"Yes. I'm sorry."

She waved the apology away. He had nothing to be sorry for. She hadn't been any more ready to die then than she was now. He'd given her back her life. "And there's no way out?"

"Do you want one?" He was always doing that. Answering her questions with another.

"I don't know." There was certainly a lot to admire about Daire, but there was that one little sticking point she couldn't get past. "I don't like that I didn't make the choice."

"You did."

"When?"

"When my energy touched yours, you could have pushed me away or let go anytime afterward."

"And if I had?"

"You would have died."

He said it without inflection, despite the instinctive lash of denial she felt from his energy.

"You couldn't force me to stay?"

"The will to live is a primal emotion. Too individual to force." He pushed the hair back from her cheek. His fingertips lingered against her jaw. "The best I could do was try to persuade you you had something to live for."

Him. The price for her life was a future with him. Handsome, sexy Daire with the will of iron, the core of honor that went soul deep, and the ability to love that was as deep anything she could have wished for. And he claimed it was for her.

"For the record, it freaks me out that you can pop in and out of my mind at will."

"I know."

Again that emotionless statement of fact. "I'm also jealous that you can be so certain about us."

That gave him pause. It might be small of her, but she liked that she could do something to shake his confidence.

She started unbuttoning his shirt. "It's grossly unfair and leaves me feeling like I'm missing out on something."

"Werewolves are born with the knowledge that they will have instant recognition of their mate."

"News flash." The third button gave her trouble. "I'm not werewolf."

"I'm aware of that."

She imagined he was. She imagined that, since he was born with this knowledge, he'd made quite a few plans on what he'd do when he found his mate, imagined a few passionate scenarios that all led to happily ever after the wolfie way. And she probably wasn't living up to any of them.

The button didn't give. "This whole finding your mate thing didn't go like you imagined, did it?"

He smiled ruefully. "I did think it would go smoother."

She considered just popping the button off. "That's because you're a control freak."

In the familiar way that heated her from the inside out, his fingers slid around the back of her neck and pressed. Such a sexy way to demand his kiss. Such a sexy man period.

"I think you're sexy, too."

If her smile was a little shaky, tough. What she was contemplating was scary for her. "A good place to start, don't you think?"

His gaze searched hers, but to his credit, he didn't probe her mind. She appreciated that. "What are you saying, seelie?"

She took a steadying breath. The button popped off in her hand. She closed her fingers around it, unsure if it was a good sign or bad. "I'm saying I'd like to start there and see where it takes us."

Eleven

TERI held her breath. Daire didn't. He smiled, his expression softening. Tenderness infused his touch as he took her hand away from her mark and replaced it with his lips. Heat suffused her body until she was burning.

"Thank you."

"For what?" she managed.

His smile spread against her skin. "For giving me the chance you need."

His lips slipped lower. Her pulse throbbed. Her breath caught. A squeak destroyed her knee-jerk "You're welcome" as her breast swelled with anticipation.

"You won't regret it. Please." She arched her back, offering him her breast, offering him everything. "Please, don't let me regret it."

His lips closed over her pouting nipple, pressed . . .

"Daire!"

"I'm here."

For now. The thought popped into her head, a legacy from the past where she'd never been the one wanted for keeps.

The pressure released. Cool air wafted over her skin as the bodice tore under the pass of his claw.

Forever.

The correction was immediate. She watched as he separated the edges of her blouse, letting gravity dictate the speed of its descent. Those deadly claws grazed her skin as he slid the delicate lace to the side. She should have been terrified. She wasn't. Being touched by Daire was exciting, wonderful, different from anything else she'd ever experienced. He touched her with a reverence that was so much deeper than passion, but the passion was a close second. She closed her eyes and let it roll over her, absorbing the wonder of the connection, the perfection of his mouth closing over her nipple. Hot. Wet. Burning.

"Oh."

Daire's laugh vibrated down the sensitive nerve endings as she arched up. "Yes, give to me."

She couldn't help but give. Whatever he wanted. No lover had ever made her feel like this before. As if she was the most desirable woman on the earth. The only woman who could sate his passion. The only woman he wanted.

"You are."

A curl of his tongue around the hard nipple jolted her forward. He was ready for her, taking more of her breast in his mouth, kneading the plump firmness with his hand as he sucked hard. Lightning shot down her spine. She cried out, twisting away. It was too much.

"Stay," he growled.

That low rumble just excited her more. Everything about him was exciting, the brush of his hair on her skin, the addicting fragrance of his natural scent, the flavor of his kiss. Oh, his kiss. Tugging on Daire's hair, Teri tilted his head back. From there it was only a slight shift to have his mouth on hers. He tasted so good. Like an exotic spice made just for her.

"Seelie."

Another warning growl that excited her more. She scooted down on the chair, needing to be closer. Her knees hit the back. She tugged his hair again, this time in frustration.

He shifted down on the chair until she was riding his cock. Even through his jeans it was impressive. She moaned and rocked on him. He moaned and pressed up.

"Do you want me, Teri?"

"Yes. God, yes." Her pussy spasmed; her womb clenched. She needed every inch of that thick cock buried deep within her. And the longer he kissed her, the more she needed. The more she wanted. Damn, she loved his kiss.

"Then take me." He lifted, the ridge of his cock pressed into her clit. She cried out, bearing down, needing to be closer.

"Mine." The claim welled out of nowhere. Primitive, possessive, hungry. So unlike her but now so right. Daire was hers. She'd waited her whole life for him to show up, and now he was here and the waiting was over.

"Always."

Yes. He'd always been hers; she just hadn't understood. But it was so clear now, with his energy wrapping around hers, his mind blending with hers. His body pressing into hers through the layers of clothing. The clothing. She reached down and unzipped his pants. He jumped and laughed, his lips biting into hers. "Careful."

She noticed he didn't pull away. "I'll be very careful."

She had to swing off his lap to work his cock free. When she tugged, he lifted and his jeans slid down. Looking at his boots, she decided that was good enough. She couldn't wait until he got his boots off to touch him.

His cock was beautiful. Long and thick. She licked her lips. Maybe too thick. Unwelcome memories intruded. The pain of her rape. The devastation.

Oh, hell, no, Daire thought. Catching Teri's face in his hands, for the first time since Teri had come awake, he overrode her mind, blocking out the memories.

"There's no one here but us, baby."

He looked around. There was a chair; no wonder she was having flashbacks. He couldn't even keep his mind straight long enough to get her to the bed. Kicking off his right boot and then the left, he stood her by the bed, holding her with his mind while he shucked his pants. Releasing his mental hold, Daire scooped Teri up in his arms. She bit her lip and curled against his chest. When he laid her on the bed, her hands lingered on his shoulder, sliding down his chest. He came over her before they could drop away.

"It's just us, baby, and we're beautiful."

Her fingers spread wide. "It's just that you're so big."

He pushed the hair out of her face. "And you couldn't help but remember."

"Yes."

"They will never be a threat to you again."

"You can't know."

Yes, he could, because as soon as the Carmichaels were under control, he was going hunting. "Trust me."

Her eyes were big as she stared at him. Her lips slid between her teeth, and there was that pause that said she was thinking on things. He pressed his advantage. "Just for tonight. Twelve hours, that's all. You just have to trust me for twelve hours."

"And then what?"

"And then you can make a decision whether you want to stay or go."

"You're giving me a choice?"

"Yes."

"Why?"

"Because you're right. Every woman should have one."

"What happens if I want to go?"

Sliding his hand under her nightgown, he cupped her hip in his hand. She was so delicate compared to him. His world, and he'd promised her the opportunity to leave him. He needed his head examined. "We'll deal with that if it happens."

"But you don't think it's going to happen."

"No." He tugged her gown over her head. "I have faith."

"In what?"

He could see her pussy, the pink inner lips unfurling in wanton invitation. "Your common sense."

"You're relying on sex to hold me."

She was sharp as a tack. Smiling, he circled her ankle with his palm and moved her leg to the side, improving his view. His tongue tingled as he crawled up her body, kissing her hard. He told her, "Yes, I am."

On the way back down, he stopped at her breasts, kissing one hard peak and then the other before moving his mouth to the hollow between, breathing deeply of her scent. Feeling drunk on the pleasure, he ordered, "So just lie back and enjoy it."

"Is that an order?"

Nibbling and kissing his way down her belly, he laughed at the bite of indignation. "Of course."

The next kiss landed on the top of her mound. She arched up. "I should rebel on principle."

"You should." The crevice beckoned. He probed lightly with his tongue. The inner lips were silky smooth, fragrant with her juices. Delicious. She moaned and gasped. Her fingers knotted in his hair. Another invitation. He didn't hesitate, just settled, sampling lightly at first, lapping gently at the delicate folds until she was pulling him in rather than holding him away. With the next flick he found her clit. Hard and distended, it accepted his caress with a little flex of joy. Teri cried out. He settled in to enjoy, cupping her buttocks in his palms as he propped her up for his pleasure, loving the taste of her on his tongue, her scent in his nostrils, her cries in his ears. Tension in her thighs told him she was close. He held her balanced on the edge, resting his tongue flat against her straining clit while she twisted and bucked, striving for the pressure she needed.

"Daire, please."

It was what he'd been waiting for. Closing his lips around the tender bud, he bit down and drew it out, shaking his head as he did, letting the vibrations spread the tension, biting harder when she screamed, licking and lapping as she came, prolonging the moment until she moaned and dropped back onto the bed, thighs quivering.

His cock full to bursting, he rasped, "I love giving you that."

Her "what" held only a shadow of her previous vehemence. She was only half with him, which was fine. He wanted her in a haze of pleasure when he took her. He'd rather have her focused on the pleasure he'd just given her than on the past.

Walling his hands up the mattress on either side of her body, he confessed, "I love making you come. You make such sweet sounds."

"Oh, God!" She covered her face with her hands.

Her nipples were berry red and distended, too tempting to pass up. The right received the first nip, the left the second. While she soothed the sting with her hands, he kissed her mouth. "You are a very sexy woman, Teri."

Her lips parted at the pressure of his. "I have to be to keep up with you."

He liked the thought of that, the two of them feeding each other's desires. "Good."

He moved between her legs. His cock fell heavy and hungry against her clit. He watched closely, looking for distaste. Instead, he felt the bolt of pure lust that went through her. With small pulses, he made love to her center, letting her juices ease the friction, increasing the pressure gradually until her heels dug into the mattress and she arched up. "Daire, please. I need you."

He needed her, too. Needed his cock in her body, needed to feel her pussy clasp him hard as his aching balls gave her what they both needed. An end to the uncertainty.

Tucking his cock along her clit, he rubbed it back and forth as he ordered, "Put your arm around me, Teri."

As soon as she did, he pulled back, letting his cock slide down the slick channel until it tucked into the well of her vagina. So hot, so wet. He wasn't going to last long. Replacing his cock with his thumb, he rubbed her clit in slow circles as his cock pressed in, parting her tender muscles. He went slowly because she was right—he was big, thick, too, and she wasn't going to take him easily. She twisted and cried out. He pumped and rubbed. Her muscles gave and his cock slid in. He felt the shock wave go through her as her muscles spread over the head of his cock. Felt the bite of pain with her pleasure. His claws dug into the mattress as the urge to thrust, to claim, welled.

"Easy."

"You're so big."

"And you're going to enjoy every inch."

She shook her head. He didn't know whether it was in denial of his size or her ability to take the pleasure he intended to deliver. In the end, it didn't matter. He was past the point of stopping. His balls were full, his patience shot. She was his. Only his.

He pushed in. Her pussy clenched around his cock in a velvet fist rippling with the impact on her senses, drawing him further into the maelstrom of her passion.

More. The order, feminine and strong, slid along his desire.

Yes, he needed more. Pulling out, he thrust back in, winning another inch, another cry. The hot sting of Teri's nails on his back drove him on, thrust after thrust, always deeper, always harder, seeking that perfect point where it would all come together. Teri leaned up and sank her teeth into his shoulder. The pain rode the fine edge of lust, driving deep to his core, and suddenly he was there. Grabbing Teri's hips, he arched her up, driving into her, grinding his groin against hers until she had all of him, groaning as her climax slammed through her mind, her body. Her channel milked his cock, taking his seed from him in a mind-blowing explosion that left him mentally limp, but physically ready to go again.

Pumping slowly, Daire dragged out both their pleasure, kissing her eyes, her nose, her chin and finally her mouth before asking, "Think you might want to stay?"

Her right eyelid cracked open. He could see the glitter of her iris behind. God, she was beautiful with her swollen lips and passion-heavy eyes. "Maybe."

"Damn, woman, what's it going to take to convince you?"

"A repeat performance?"

Peace flowed over him. "I can probably manage that."

Her other eye opened. Tenderness infused her expression. "Maybe more than one."

"You've got me confused with Superman."

Her hands cupped his cheeks as her thumbs stroked over the ridge of his cheekbones. "Then I guess you'll have to work up your stamina."

"How long are you giving me?"

"How about the next sixty years?" Her calf slid up his thigh. "We'll renegotiate then."

"Renegotiate."

She shrugged. "If necessary."

His breath caught in his lungs. "What are you saying?"

Her thumbs tucked into the corner of his mouth in an imitation of the pre-kiss caress he'd given her. "You want me to spell it out?"

He turned his head, catching her thumb between his teeth. Yes, he did. This was too important to leave to chance. "Yes."

Her fingers pressed into the back of his neck, pulling his mouth to hers, his heart to hers. For the rest of his life he'd remember how she looked in that moment as she put her mark on his soul with four little words.

"I've made my choice."

Curran

One

HE was out there.

The superhuman someone that had cut through her evasive tactics with the smooth slide of a hot knife through butter. The someone that had dogged their footsteps with tireless determination. The someone who chased them, defended them, wouldn't give up on them.

Rachel grabbed Josiah and shoved him behind the boxes in the corner of the small storeroom in which they were hiding. It was a dead end, nowhere to hide. *He* never would have found her if she hadn't overslept. But she was so tired and her dreams were so vivid, portraying the inevitability of this moment in staccato bursts of events, not telling her if it was good or bad, not letting her see the ending, just telling her he was coming.

Rachel glanced at the door, feeling the stranger's energy as tangible as any touch. He knew they were there. He was playing with them. A devilish game of cat and mouse. She slipped into the small space behind the boxes.

Josiah's eyes gleamed up at her. As her night vision kicked in in response to the darkness, she could see the stress on his face, the quiver in his lips, but he didn't cry out. She put her hand on his shoulder, smiling at him with a confidence she didn't feel. As silly as it was to think that hiding behind boxes in the corner of a storeroom was going to fool whatever had been tracking them for the last two weeks, she had to try. She couldn't give Josiah up without a fight.

"It'll be okay," she mouthed.

Josiah's lips firmed and he nodded at her.

She wanted to cry right there. He believed in her, trusted her, and she couldn't tell him that it was over. She couldn't look away from the door, watching the handle with a morbid fascination, waiting for the slight rattle that would tell her that his hand was upon it, that the moment was here. She hated her gift, part prophecy, part torment. Her dreams last night had revealed to her that this dead end would come. And they told her that whatever came through that door was going to be big, bigger than anything she had met to date. But they didn't say it was good and they didn't say it was evil. She just knew, the minute that door opened, nothing was going to be the same again.

Josiah opened his mouth. She slipped her hand over his lips, sealing off any whisper of noise. She heard, or maybe she just sensed, the footfall outside the door. Whoever had been chasing them, he wasn't one of the rogues. The rogues had been easy to evade. This man was something else, something more, and he scared the hell out of her. The doorknob rattled as *he* tested it to see if it was locked. It was. She'd done that when she walked in. She motioned to Josiah to turn his head a little bit.

He did.

She leaned down and put her lips against his ear. "If I tell you to run," she whispered, "you run and you don't look back."

His eyes flashed to hers in the dark, wide, terrified. A five-year-old was too young for the burden they were putting on him. But he had a Protector's instincts, and after that flash of fear, his shoulders squared. He mouthed, "What about you?"

She shook her head and put her lips back to his ear. "Don't worry about me. You run," she ordered in a voice barely above the whisper. "You find Haven. Travel by day; hide at night."

The door rattled again, harder this time.

She looked around. In her normal frame of mind, she never would have chosen a dead end as a place to rest, but her dreams had led her here. Dreams that promised safety until last night, when they'd changed after it was too late to move. Then they'd turned into nightmares. That delay had been happening more and more often of late. She bit her lip as she acknowledged the reality. Her gift was out of control. When she'd moved to the humans because she couldn't hide it from the wolves anymore, she'd been able to control it. But every year it had grown stronger, calling to her, driving her down paths she didn't want to go, evolving into a curse. She'd thought when she'd found Sarah Anne that she'd been where she was supposed to be. But that promise had turned out to be false, too.

Closing her eyes, Rachel felt along her inner mind, trying to find the remnant of a dream, looking for a sign that Josiah would be all right, if his wild bolt in the few seconds she'd be able to buy him would get him anywhere. But the dreams weren't talking and the remnants were empty. The same couldn't be said for her instincts. There was a wolf's cry of danger. Of futility. She pushed Josiah a little farther back in the corner. No. She wouldn't let that be the truth. When the time came, she'd come up with something. She always did.

Hearing the slide of a foot across the floor, knowing without a doubt whatever was on the other side of the door was about to kick it open, Rachel knew the moment was at hand. She caught Josiah's head in her hands, gave a little press in lieu of a hug, kissed his temple and whispered, "I love you."

This time the tears hovered in his eyes.

She shook her head at him. "You're Protector. Remember that."

He nodded. "And a Stone?" he murmured.

It was unwise to talk—they could give away their location within the room—but how could she send him out in the world alone without hope? "Yes. Josiah Stone, Protector of Pack Haven."

In reality, she didn't know if the pack would accept him. A Protector—half wolf, half human? There would be prejudice. But, if anyone with any gift touched his energy, they would know the truth. In Josiah's case, the mixing of blood had enhanced his Protector abilities, rather than diluting them. He was going to grow up big, he was going to grow up strong and he was going to grow up scary. If Haven's Alpha had any sense, he'd want that truth on his side.

She didn't want him to turn rogue, so she gave him the only thing she could—a pack of his own. "Josiah Stone of Pack Haven," she repeated. "You remember who you protect."

He nodded.

The door crashed open.

She absorbed his start into her palms, holding him still through pressure from her hands and the force of her will.

Don't move. Don't move.

He didn't. Had he heard her or was he just too terrified to twitch? Glancing through the slit between two of the boxes, she could just make out the door and what was coming through it. Her imagination had built him up to be a monster, but it was a man who stepped through the entry. She could tell from his broad-shouldered, lean-hipped build. And judging from the force of the heavy metal door's slam against the wall, he was werewolf. Hopefully Protector and not rogue.

Dear God. Help me buy Josiah time.

Desperation elevated the thought to prayer. The backlighting from the hall caused her night vision to flick on and off, creating the strobe effect as the man took one step, two steps, into the room. The farther into the room he came, the less distraction there was from the hall light, allowing her to see more than his silhouette, letting her see the muscles that filled out his frame beneath his clothes. Protector or rogue, she couldn't defeat either. She had no magic. No strength. She was a werewolf with a witch's gift. What use was it?

"Come on out now." The man's voice was deep, more rumble than drawl.

His voice stroked along her nerve endings. Where she should be feeling terror, she felt pleasure. She blinked. Josiah shook his head and tugged at her hand.

On another blink, she realized she was standing. What the hell?

"You ran me a merry chase, but there's nowhere else to run."

She knew that. It didn't mean she had to give up without a fight. And if the only fight she could muster was to make him look for her, well, that was what she would do.

He took two more steps into the room, leaving her line of sight. His scent came to her from the other side of the boxes. Masculine. Earthy, with a hint of musk.

Again, her mind said run, but her instincts said stay, take another breath, inhale a bit more, savor it. *Oh, my God.* She rubbed her hand across her forehead. She was losing her mind. Too many days running too hard with too little sleep. It had all caught up with her. She braced her hands against the boxes.

Josiah followed suit. She nodded. Once, twice, with any luck the stranger would be just on the other side and the tumbling boxes would distract him long enough, or maybe even injure him enough so Josiah could get away. She gave the third nod of her head.

She pushed. He pushed.

The stacks were heavier than she expected, teetering forward, giving the stranger a warning. Dammit. Before she could get the curse out, they rocked backward, teetering threateningly before they rocked toward the wall. The top hit, and held. The middle bulged inward. There was a thump, and then the whole stack came tumbling down.

Rachel screamed and grabbed Josiah, pulling him under her, trying to prevent him from being crushed. There was a curse, a crash, and then a hand locked around her upper arm like a vise, hauling her out from beneath the danger, tossing her back.

She stumbled backward, reaching for Josiah, but he was gone. The hand jerked her around. She stopped but for a split second the room kept moving. She blinked. When everything righted, she was standing in the middle of the floor, half dangling from the stranger's grip on her arm while Josiah dangled two feet off the ground by his shirt from the stranger's other grip. The little boy's lips were pulled back in a snarl, his small canines flashing, white in her night vision. His claws reached out and raked down the man's arm.

The stranger swore, and then, unbelievably, laughed. "Got a bit of fight in you, I see."

"Let my aunt go."

"In a minute."

"Now!"

Josiah lashed out again. The fresh scent of blood swirled over the smell of sweat and fear. The stranger shook him harder. "Settle down."

Josiah did no such thing. The stranger growled. *Oh, damn.* Rachel realized he could kill the child with just a flex of his muscles.

Her own claws extending, she gathered her strength, aiming for the man's throat. He caught her eye. The small shake of his head froze her midpreparation.

"I wouldn't."

She hesitated. The flash of his teeth in the shadow indicated he was smiling again, but Rachel couldn't see his face; the lighting was too uncertain, hovering between dark and bright, faking out her night vision, frustrating her day vision.

"Good choice." He hefted Josiah, giving him a little shake and swearing as the boy snarled and clawed him again. "If you'd clawed me, I'd be forced to drop him."

She licked her lips. Drop or kill? She couldn't take a chance it would be the latter.

She retracted her claws. The man nodded approvingly.

"Good to know you have some common sense." He jerked his chin in Josiah's direction, never taking his eyes off her. "Now, tell him to settle down."

She licked her lips. "Josiah, stop." There was a time to fight and a time to surrender and they definitely needed to surrender for the moment.

He did.

The man set Josiah on his feet. "Now, don't go turning tail on me."

The boy's shoulders squared. "I am Protector," he said with all the dignity a five-year-old could muster.

"Good. Then you know better than to run and leave a woman alone and unprotected."

In the middle of capturing them, the man was giving protocol lessons? Rachel blinked and tried to steady her heartbeat. "Who are you?"

The stranger smiled and took a step forward into the darkness of the room. Her night vision kicked in, throwing the handsome planes of his face into perfect symmetry. Her breath caught in her throat.

"Cur Beck, the man set on taking you home."

She sagged in his arms, her breath freezing in her lungs. She recognized him.

Two

RACHEL stared at that face, her mind reeling, her senses in chaos. Every dream she'd ever had, good or bad, she'd seen that face swirling out of the darkness, laughing, frowning, bloody, clean, always there, never good, never evil, just there. She reached up. Was she hallucinating? Was this just one more time when she was caught in a dream so vivid she couldn't tell real from fake? She reached up, hesitating before her fingers touched his cheek, afraid to know the truth.

Cur stared down at her, the same dumbstruck look on his face that was on hers.

She shook her head and whispered, "You're in my dreams."

It was a stupid thing to say.

He blinked. "Was I any good?"

She tried to remember but there wasn't any more. Just those brief flashes of recognition. "You weren't . . . anything."

He snorted. "Figures."

"Aunt Rachel?"

Ignoring Josiah's question, needing to know if he was real, she forced her fingers that last quarter inch and felt bristle. Not a dream, then. She snatched her hand back as an electric shock shot up her fingertips. She snapped her hand closed. "Who are you?"

"The man sent to bring you back to Haven."

He was lying. She could sense the lie under his skin. She jerked at her arm. "Why didn't you identify yourself?"

His grip loosened on her arm. She took a step back. A tug on her shirt had her spinning around. He held up his hands. In the left was her gun.

She snarled at him before shifting her position so she inched that much more between him and Josiah. He watched but didn't comment.

"You never let me close enough, and quite frankly, we weren't sure what your intentions were."

"We?"

"Haven's Alpha and myself."

"You questioned my intentions?"

"Lady, you take off after a rogue attack, you don't show up at the meeting place as scheduled, but instead you take off over hither and dale with a kid that's not your own. Any way you look at it, that's kidnapping."

"I was supposed to meet Sarah Anne. You took her."

"Haven took her. She's back at the pack now."

Rachel hadn't been born yesterday. "How do I know that?"

He started tossing boxes out of the way. He glanced at her out of the corners of his eyes as he snagged her pack from under the pile. "Well, as soon as I get you out of here and in a safe place, I'll let you chat with her on the phone."

"How do I know that she won't be forced to respond? To say what you want her to say? How do I know she's not a captive?"

His head tilted to the side as if he were listening to things she couldn't hear. His nostrils flared as if scenting things she couldn't smell. "Lady, knowing right now whether she's worrying about a phone call that's a good five hours away is the least of your worries."

She felt it then, the presence of others. Rogues. She grabbed Josiah's hand and pulled him to her. "Do something."

Cur smiled and said, "I am."

He wasn't doing anything except standing there, looking impossibly arrogant, a lock of his hair falling across his forehead, giving him a devil-may-care aura when she knew darn well the man was a born predator.

"You're Protector. You have to protect us."

To her surprise, he handed her her pack, before repeating, "I am."

"What are you doing?"

"I'm waiting."

"For what?"

There was a huge explosion. The building shook; boxes tumbled. He grabbed her and Josiah and threw them against the wall before covering them both with his body. His shoulders were broad enough that he sheltered both of them. This close she couldn't mistake his scent. She breathed deeply, over and over, as bits of cement and debris rained down around them.

Oh, my God, this is crazy. The building was collapsing and all she could worry about was how good he smelled. For the last time, she asked again, a sinking feeling welling in her chest, "Who are you?"

Curran's head descended and the softness of his lips pressed against her ear. A growl rumbled against her hands.

"Your mate."

Three

HER mate. For a minute Rachel just stood there, stunned by the knowledge. Josiah tugged on her hand.

"He said we needed to duck down."

She looked around. Cur was gone and Josiah was coming out of his skin. She followed him back behind the boxes.

Rachel shook her head. She had to make a decision. Trust a stranger who claimed to be her mate, or take her chances running. The noise from the hall was fierce. There were growls and cries of agony. The hall was the only exit. To get away she would have to get Josiah passed the rogues and Cur.

Josiah tugged her hand again. She knelt beside him, behind the boxes, pulling him close. She could feel his heart beating against his chest as he leaned his head on her shoulder. He was tired. She was tired. They'd never make it. Their only chance was to hope that Cur meant what he said. That his plan was to bring them to Haven. From the hall there came a roar and then silence.

"Is it over?" Josiah whispered.

"I think so."

"Did our guy win?"

She hoped to hell Cur had. She reached behind her back for her gun, forgetting he'd taken it from her. Dammit. Even though she'd run out of bullets days ago, it was still handy as a club. Her canines ached. Her muscles tightened to knots of readiness. Her claws extended. She shifted silently to the left away from Josiah. Any attack she made would still be hampered by the boxes, but this was the best compromise.

Barely audible footsteps came down the hall. Beside her, Josiah growled. She held her finger to her lips. Lips still pulled back in a snarl, he nodded. She took a breath and held it. Fear and anger writhed for dominance inside her. She wanted to run. She wanted to kill. More than anything, she wanted this over.

"The coast is clear. You can come out."

There was no mistaking that deep rumble. Rachel sat back against the wall. It was over. Cur had won. Her breath escaped in a shaky gasp. She brought her hand up to her forehead, pushing her hair back, as shaky as her breath. Josiah didn't seem to have the same reaction. With a whoop he leapt over her. His foot knocked her hand.

"You got them?"

The Protector didn't seem at all put off by Josiah's bloodthirsty question. He came into her field of vision just as Josiah reached him. He ruffled the boy's hair. "Rogues don't stand a chance against a Protector."

Josiah straightened and stuck his thumb to his chest. "I'm Protector."

Could the stranger see the insecurity beneath the bravado? She got to her feet. She needn't have worried.

Cur nodded as if he'd known all along, which he had, since this was the second time Josiah had mentioned it. "So you said."

This was the first time outside of family Josiah had had a chance to make his claim and with a five-year-old's need to be accepted, he pushed for more. "You believe me?"

The man nodded. "I've been following you and your aunt for a while now. I noticed how you protected her."

Josiah frowned. "You hurt my aunt and I'll kill you."

Despite the fierceness of the words, which Rachel had no doubt the little boy meant, his heart wasn't in it. Cur seemed to understand. Dammit. She didn't want to like him.

"Understood." He dropped his hand back to his side. "It wasn't just the way you protected your aunt that clued me in. You have a way of carrying yourself that another Protector recognizes."

Josiah leaned around a box in front of him, obviously trying to get a look at the carnage in the hall. "Did you kill them all?"

"Yes."

Short and to the point. Scrambling to her feet, Rachel grabbed Josiah before he could dart down the hall to see for himself. There were some things a five-year-old didn't need to see and one of them was the carnage a Protector left behind when he went on a rampage. And she had no doubt that this man had just gone on a rampage. The evidence was in the way Cur's eyes still glowed red and the shadow of wolf that lay across his features. It was in the energy radiating off him, the tension in his muscles. It was in the threat he still presented. Mixed-blood Protectors were reputed to be very unstable post-battle.

She took a breath and the scent of gunpowder, dust, rubble and blood all blended together in a confusing mix. And yet, despite all that, she could still make out his scent. It was soothing when she shouldn't be soothed.

"Thank you for your help."

She took another step back, but to the left. Her goal, the door. Too late she realized she should have just run past him with Josiah rather than grabbing Josiah and pulling him back. In worrying about the child's sensibilities she'd overlooked the opportunity. She always made mistakes like that, but then again, she wasn't a warrior; she wasn't a Protector; she was just a woman with a gift that would set her outside a pack if it was known.

"Aunt Rachel?"

"Quiet, Josiah." She turned to Cur. "Are you really from Haven?" she asked.

"Yes."

She noted his hazel eyes, not full-blood were, yet Protector. She didn't know whether to be soothed or panicked. Everyone knew mixed-bloods were unstable. But Protector mixed-bloods were the worst, especially when it came to meeting their mates. It was as if their human emotions often overwhelmed or fed their were possessiveness. Of all the women she knew who had been killed by their mates, and they were not many, their mates had always had human blood.

"You're not pure blood."

"Nope." He cocked an eyebrow at her. "You going to have a problem with that?"

Not that she'd mention out loud. "No." She held out her hand. "Rachel Dern."

He took her hand, but not to shake it. Holding her gaze, he brought it to his lips, grazing his teeth over the back. Before she jerked free, Rachel felt the touch of his tongue. Electricity shot up her arm, lodging in her chest, shattering her next breath into a staccato series of gasps.

He smiled. "Nice to meet you."

She could feel Josiah watching them, too young to understand the tension, but feeling it. She rubbed her hand against her thigh and concentrated on making her next breath normal. The tingling didn't stop and in her heightened state, she became aware of many things about Cur, including how handsome he was with the dark brown hair streaked with lighter shades falling over his brow, and the mobile expressions of his face, and that perpetual, irritating, goading smile that seemed to hover on his lips.

She took another step to the left. The door was so close, yet so far.

"You'll never make it."

Rachel's gaze whipped up to Cur's.

"I'll run you down before you get five steps."

She glanced down at his thighs. Even through the jeans the muscles were evident. And considering he wasn't even breathing hard after defeating six rogues, he was probably right.

But she had to try. Josiah was under her care and she had only Cur's word that he was from Haven. All she really knew was that he'd been following her since they'd escaped the cave, staying on her trail when others had been thrown off, until they reached this place, this time.

She licked her lips, remembering the knowledge she'd woken up with this morning that when the door opened, her world would change.

She looked Cur over again, seeing him as a man in his prime. Her womb clenched; her pulse picked up. Mate. This time her dreams hadn't lied. Nothing was ever going to be the same again.

Four

CUR watched as Rachel absorbed the knowledge that her running was over. Her soft brown eyes narrowed as her brain raced. Her teeth bit into her lower lip, causing tiny pinpoints of white within the lush red. He wanted to lean down and pull that lip from her teeth with his, suck it between his lips, kiss her, hold her, know the softness of her hair, the softness of her body, feel the lean muscle of her legs against his.

She was wolf. She should have formally recognized his claim, but she hadn't and he didn't kid himself as to why. He was mixed blood and in her book likely an uncertainty as a mate. But he was her only option and she was going to take it whether she wanted to or not.

"Do you have any proof you're Pack Haven?" she asked.

"Beyond the fact you'd know if I lied?"

"Yes."

"No."

She blinked, apparently the notion never occurring to her. Probably part of her overall rejection of the thought of him as a mate. Her next statement confirmed it.

"The mating laws may not apply to half wolves."

"That's a cop-out and you know it. It might not apply on my side if my human instincts were stronger, but between us, Rachel, there's no human, no ambiguity. We're all wolf. And if I were to kiss you right now, your arguments would end in a heartbeat."

She took a step back as if he'd threatened her. Son of a bitch.

Josiah stepped in front of her, his canines bared. Son of a bitch. Even the kid's hero worship was fading.

"Stand down, cub. I'm not going to hurt your aunt."

Josiah just widened his stance and squared his little shoulders. All it would take was a flick of Cur's hand and the boy would go flying. It didn't make any difference to the kid; he was making his stand. Cur had to admire that reckless courage.

"Your mother told me you were a brave kid."

The reference to his mother created the slightest break in the kid's composure.

Cur fed into it. "She's been very worried about you."

Rachel snarled and yanked Josiah back. "Don't believe him. He's lying."

"Are you?" Josiah asked.

Cur had to smile at the irony of that. "Yes, I am. I haven't really spoken to your mother. I've spoken to her mate."

Rachel blinked. "Sarah Anne doesn't have a mate."

"Yes, she does. My best friend, Garrett."

"Is he a mixed-blood, too?" she asked.

Enough was enough. "He is what he is—a good man. Protector. And he's already almost given his life twice protecting her. So the next time you speak his name, you can take the sneer out of your voice."

She had the grace to look ashamed.

Josiah looked between them, not sure what to do.

Cur didn't have time for this. Unclenching his fist, he pushed his hair back with one hand and with the other he motioned to the door. "We need to be going. Those six were scouting. There are more behind."

Rachel sighed wearily. "There's always more behind."

He nodded. "Yep, you two seem to be quite the prize."

"Why?"

He admired the way she was still gathering information just in case he gave her the opportunity to run. She wouldn't get the chance to run, but he'd feed her all the information she needed to stay alive. "The best we can tell is leverage."

"For what?" Josiah voiced the question on Rachel's lips.

Megan. The answer sprang to Cur's mind, but he didn't voice it. There's only so much terror a little boy should know. And Protector or not, the kid just seemed too young to handle the knowledge that not only was his sister gifted and different, but she was hunted.

Rachel met his gaze, gave a small shake of her head. He didn't know whether she knew the reason or just suspected from his hesitation it wasn't something that should be spoken out loud. But he didn't say anything, letting Rachel fill the gap with, "I upset some men and I think they're after me."

She had upset quite a few men. On his surveillance trips around rogue camps, Cur had often heard the venting of frustration how one woman could evade them so long. The ego that was damaged. The revenge they planned on taking.

"Yes, you have." And there was one thing he wanted to know as much as they did.

"Now why don't you tell me how you did it?"

Five

THEY were never going to talk about that. A half-human werewolf trying to fit into the wolf world would not want a mate who was more witch than wolf. After what Cur revealed, there was no way she could risk him dumping them now, and no way she would let him go off with Josiah alone. On top of that, she still wasn't convinced he came from Haven. It was a little too convenient that her best friend was now the mate of his and she was now his. Things happened fast in the wolf world, but this was too fast even for her to believe.

"I have no idea what you're talking about."

Cur nodded, turning Josiah so he could open his pack, checking the small stash of food and survival tools inside. "Anybody ask you that but me, and that's exactly what I want you to answer." Turning Josiah again, he tucked his hands under his arms and swung Josiah up onto his shoulders. "But when I ask you again, I'm expecting the truth."

He patted her rear. "Let's get moving."

It was clever of him to grab up Josiah. He knew she'd have to follow. Rachel ground her teeth and fell into step behind him. "Where are we going?"

"I already told you. Haven."

"Is my mommy waiting for me there?" Josiah asked.

Cur gave his thigh a squeeze. "Yes, she is."

"And Aunt Teri and my sister, Megan?"

"Yep, and a whole lot of other people eager to meet you."

"Other kids?"

"I believe we got a new family coming in any day now."

"Boys or girls?"

Rachel rolled her eyes. Josiah was insistent about having a playmate that was male. "I don't really know," Cur answered. "But I imagine you'll have fun with whomever they turn out to be."

"I guess."

Cur turned slightly and looked at Rachel over his shoulder. She didn't want to smile back at him but it was hard to resist. The man had charm for all he was an aggravation. She might even like him if he wasn't claiming to be her mate. But he was, and she wanted to live in denial of that a little longer, even if her own instincts recognized his claim.

Cur held up his hand as they reached the bend in the hall. The scent of blood was strong here. He stopped, handing Josiah down to her. She settled him on her hip. Josiah opened his mouth to protest. She shook her head. One thing Josiah had learned over the last few days was when to keep quiet. He did so now.

"Company," Cur mouthed silently.

Rachel dropped her forehead against Josiah's. Dear God. Was it ever going to end? She was as tired of running as she was tired of being afraid.

For ten minutes they stood there. Rachel strained. She could barely make out the sound of footsteps. Cur was only half wolf. How had he heard them at all? After another minute Cur whispered, "Close your eyes, Josiah. Don't open them until I tell you to."

"Why?"

"Because I told you to," came the absolute response.

And that was that. Rachel held his head against her shoulder. "Just do as he says."

Right now Cur was their best chance of getting out of this alive.

Cur looked at her with approval. "Do you have a weak stomach?"

She shook her head. His mouth twisted. "Well, if you decide to barf, do it on the move."

She nodded again. As soon as they rounded the corner, she knew why he'd told Josiah to hide his eyes and why he'd asked if she had a weak stomach. The hall looked like a war zone from a news broadcast with all the blurred-out parts exposed. She could see body parts protruding from rubble and as she stepped gingerly through the debris, her foot inadvertently landed in a pool of blood, and her stomach did heave. She'd never been so close to violence. She'd grown up the pampered daughter of a late-in-life mated couple. They'd loved her unconditionally, despite her odd moments. They'd sheltered and protected her and, when they'd died, left her woefully unprepared to navigate within a pack that had no tolerance for the curse her parents had told her was a gift. And the gift had just gotten stronger.

She took another step. The cloying scent of blood blocked out all others. She took a breath and then another. With every one her gorge rose.

"Aunt Rachel."

"It's okay, Josiah."

Cur looked back. "Keep up."

As if she wasn't trying. She made a face at his back. Josiah giggled.

"You're not supposed to be looking," she whispered.

"I'm just looking at you."

"Well, stop." She pushed his head back down.

Up ahead there was another pile of rubble of jagged beams and broken cement blocks. It was going to be difficult to get across.

"Did you have to blow up the whole building?" she asked Cur as he turned and waited for her.

"I like to do things big."

She bet. Balancing on a broken block of cement, she teetered. Immediately his hand was under her elbow, and immediately sparks skittered up her arm, lighting her nerve endings with pleasure.

Who are you?

Your mate.

Dear God, maybe he really was. What on earth was she going to do with that? "Well, next time, think smaller."

He didn't laugh. Just watched her. She stared right back, sick of feeling like a bug under his microscope.

"It gets a bit rough ahead."

"Of course."

No way it could be easy. She let him lead her across the pile, falling behind him when he let her hand go, telling herself she didn't miss the contact. She watched her step carefully as she descended. When her sneakered foot touched the concrete floor, she looked up.

It gets a bit rough. She'd thought he meant the passage, not the visual evidence of his battle. At first glance it appeared there was nothing but bodies, blood and entrails.

"Damn."

Josiah's head popped up. "What?"

She pressed it back down. "Nothing."

"What's that smell?"

She glared at Cur. He shrugged.

"The sewer backed up."

"What's a sewer?"

"The gross place toilets flush to."

"Yuck!"

It was yuck. She stepped between the bodies, actually only three. Her first impressions of blood and gore was accurate, but now that she was closer, she could see the bodies, and these men hadn't been weaklings. They were werewolves in their prime. And Cur had taken them out. Single-handedly. She glanced over. Without receiving a major injury. That would be a feat for a full-blood werewolf to pull off, but for a mixed-blood, it was amazing.

I'll run you down before you get five steps.

The threat took on new meaning.

"What are we doing, Josiah?" she whispered.

Josiah snuggled against her with a weary sigh. "We're going home."

Six

"ARE you taking us home?" Rachel asked Cur later that night, after Josiah had fallen asleep in one of the queen beds in the hotel room Cur had rented with cash. It wasn't much of a room, but it beat the streets and it beat the hard ground and the bed felt like heaven under her. Cur turned away from the window.

"I'm bringing you to Haven."

"You don't sound happy about it."

"I'm not."

"Why?"

"Because with the exception of Sarah Anne and Teri, there isn't a damn soul at Haven that doesn't think you kidnapped that boy."

"Why would I do that?"

"That's what we're going to talk about."

"You were chasing me." And the dreams were chasing her. Telling her of the threat that was coming. All she knew to do in the face of that kind of information was to run.

"That will work for a reason at first, but I know you saw Daire and me take out that first set of rogues."

"Just because you killed the men chasing us didn't make you good. It just made you a bigger threat."

She expected him to look shocked, not more relaxed. He let the curtain drop. "I can see that."

She had his undivided attention. Just what she didn't want.

"But it doesn't fit. You knew Haven was coming for you. You knew we were Haven."

"I knew what you said. That didn't make it true." And it hadn't stilled the voice inside her that had said to run. Of course, it didn't make any more sense to stop running in a storeroom in the back of an abandoned factory, but that was where her dream had led her. And abandoned her with only a sense of the inevitable to keep her company.

"No, it didn't."

He unbuttoned the cuffs of his shirt.

"What are you doing?"

His response was to pull the shirt over his head. "Getting ready for bed."

"Don't you want to take a shower?"

He tossed the shirt on the chair. "Why? You planning on joining me?"

"Not hardly." Though looking at the way his broad shoulders were set above his well-developed pecs and six-pack abs, the idea wasn't totally without merit. It was all too easy to imagine water pouring over his skin, tangling in the light growth of hair on his chest, following the point down over his washboard stomach, gathering in the dent of his navel before following that thin strip of hair down until . . . She jerked her gaze away from the sizable erection pressing against the fly of his jeans.

"Change your mind?"

"No."

His smile would have tempted a saint to commit murder. "Then I guess I'll settle for the washup I had at the sink."

Her fingers clenched to fists. "You're a big boy. You could shower alone."

"But it wouldn't be nearly as much fun as showering with my mate."

"Stop saying that."

He arched an eyebrow at her. "Still hoping it's not true?"

"Yes."

His smile didn't budge. "Tough."

"Does nothing ever get to you?"

"Peanuts."

"What?"

He shrugged. "I'm allergic to peanuts. They definitely get to me."

That had to be a legacy of his human half. "What happens when you eat peanuts?"

"I die for a bit."

"Good God, Gertie!"

"Not a pleasant experience, but not to worry." He grinned. "I bounce back."

His werewolf side. She walked over to the side table where a half-used pad of hotel stationery sat.

"What are you doing?"

She bared her teeth at him. "Making a grocery list."

She held it up. On it was one item: peanuts.

At his bark of laughter, Josiah mumbled and turned over.

"Keep your voice down," she hissed.

"Watch your respect."

It was on the tip of her tongue to mention she'd give it when he'd earned it, but truth was, he had. Which just irritated her more. "Oh, go take a shower."

"We already covered that."

Yes, they had, and she wasn't letting her imagination go there again. "Then go to bed."

He cocked an eyebrow at her. "You're awfully fond of giving orders."

"I find it saves time."

"Interesting."

"What?"

He smiled that irritating smile. "Just that."

He reached for his fly. She took a step back and forbid her gaze to drop. "What are you doing?"

"Getting ready for bed."

"You don't need to get undressed for that!"

"This is the first time in two weeks I'm getting to sleep in a bed. I'm getting comfortable."

She turned her back to the tempting sight. "What if the rogues find us?"

"They won't tonight. They'll be searching the woods and caves west of here, I imagine, since it hasn't been your pattern to frequent hotels. That should buy us one night of rest."

Something hit the floor with a slight plop. His jeans? It was all too easy to imagine what he'd look like standing there with nothing but underwear. Broad shoulders, lean hips and heavy muscle sculpted to perfection, made for a woman's hands.

My mate.

Her hands. She licked her lips. Did he wear boxers or briefs?

"Well, at least keep your underwear on. Josiah tends to wake up at night."

He laughed.

"Please tell me you wear underwear."

"You know as well as I do I can't lie to my mate."

He was standing there naked? Clenching her hands into fists, Rachel counted to ten, willing her pulse to slow, her desire to wane, the incredible urge to turn and ogle to die. "Oh, for Pete's sake."

"Come to bed, Rachel."

Come, not go. "I'm not sleeping with you."

She nearly jumped out of her skin when his hands slid over her shoulders. How had he snuck up on her?

"Yes, you are."

She didn't have any choice but to turn when he urged, didn't have any choice but to rest her body against his, as he pulled her close. Didn't have any choice but to look up when his finger tilted her chin.

"Tonight and every night from here on out, you sleep in my arms."

The thought was terrifying. She dreamed at night. "Have you never heard of courting?"

Again that smile. His head lowered. "What makes you think I'm not?"

Her lips parted. So did his. "This is not courting."

"It's not?"

"No." His lips were so close, she could feel their heat.

"Then what is it?"

She wanted to moan, rise up on her toes, anything but stand there balanced on the razor edge of anticipation. "Seduction."

"Hmm."

The fingers under her chin weighed on her skin like a pending decision. Why didn't he just kiss her?

"Then I'm doing something right."

He was doing too much right. And she had too much to lose.

"Josiah—"

"Is asleep."

A sense of inevitability weighed her lids down. Her senses picked up the slack left by her lack of vision, adding to the appeal of his scent, his touch, his energy.

"Oh, God."

"What?"

The syllable whispered across her lips in a prelude to the kiss everything in her needed. Desired. Craved.

She couldn't wait any longer.

"Damn you!"

Rising up on her toes, she fitted her mouth to his. Lightning arced through her body, followed by a complete sense of bliss as his big hand cupped her rear and pulled her to him.

"About damn time," he growled.

"Yes." She'd waited a lifetime for this, and even if it couldn't last, she needed to know what it felt like to have his mouth on hers, to feel his body against hers. She arched against his cock, catching it between her legs, her moan echoing his as he ground his cock against her clit. So good. Wrapping her arms around his neck, she pulled, needing to be closer, needing more of the fire, the perfection.

Four sharp pricks of slight pain in her buttock alerted to the reality of the moment. He was going to rip off her clothing. A shudder took her from head to toe. *Yes!*

She shook her head. "No."

His mouth bit at hers. "Yes."

Material began to give. His claws drew across her flesh in hot enticement. She shivered again. His mouth bit at hers again, his canines lightly scraping her lower lip as he sucked on it. She dug her claws into his shoulder and hung on.

"I don't have anything else to wear."

His big body went still against her. "Shit."

Her sentiments exactly.

His hand left her buttock.

She moaned at the loss.

He kissed her hard. "Yeah."

The hand that had been cupping her buttock slid around her hip. He turned slightly, enabling him to cup her pussy. His thumb dragged backward over her clit, centered through her jeans. Her knees buckled as the sharp point of his claw pierced her clothing.

"Oh!"

"Goddamn," he groaned into her ear. "I want to make love to you."

"Josiah," she gasped.

"I know, but son of a bitch, I will have this."

This was the press of his finger against her pussy while his claw raked lightly across her clit in a perfect symphony of pleasure. *This* was the mercurial rise of passion; *this* was the graze of his teeth on her neck, her shoulder, the curve between. *This* was the pleasure of a mate's touch, a mate's bite. . . .

Fire poured through her bloodstream. A scream rose in her throat at the exquisite pain. His hand at the back of her head pressed her face into his shoulder muffling the primal scream.

The swipe of his tongue over the wound burned in a hot culmination. Her breasts swelled and ached. Her womb clenched. And her knees buckled.

Cur laughed and swung her up in his arms. "You, my sweet, are going to be very fun to have as a mate."

Burying her face in his neck, she muttered, "If you're laughing at me, I'm going to kill you."

The mattress gave under her weight, shifting left and then right as he came over her. He smoothed the hair off her face with his palms before anchoring his fingers in the thick mass. His smile became softer, more encompassing, as he accepted the threat. "I'll keep that in mind."

Seven

THERE were a lot of things he should be keeping in mind, including the fact that the woman who was his mate was not to be trusted. Cur watched as Rachel helped Josiah over a log. The boy stumbled. Cur sighed. The boy was tired. So was Rachel. One night of rest couldn't make up for two weeks of running, but neither was giving up. They had grit. And determination. He'd admire both if the latter wasn't geared with how best to ditch his ass. He didn't know how Rachel could on one hand acknowledge he was her mate, and on the other contemplate leaving him, but she did. Maybe her mind always worked that way. It would certainly explain her erratic behavior after fleeing the cave. Josiah smiled up at her. She smiled back and ruffled his hair. Cur just couldn't believe it. Which meant there had to be another reason. One she wasn't telling him. He growled under his breath. She should tell him everything.

"Step it up. We're losing daylight."

"I don't understand why we're not traveling at night," Rachel pointed out for the third time, pulling her shirt away from her chest.

Cur admired the way it clung to her curves when she dropped it back. "We will be, but"—he pointed to the ridge—"I want to reach the top by the time it gets dark."

Rachel followed the point of his fingers. "Up there?"

"Yes."

"It'd be faster in a car."

"There isn't a road," he countered for the third time.

"A dirt bike, then."

"Aunt Rachel hates up," Josiah interrupted.

"Josiah!"

His chin jutted out. "That's what Momma says."

Cur grinned. The kid was giving away all her secrets. "A werewolf female with a dislike of exercise? I think I'm getting gypped."

Rachel glared at him. "Gypped is the least of what you're getting if you don't stop grinning."

"It's just up she doesn't like," Josiah was quick to put in, coming up beside him. "She likes down."

"Then we'll have to find her some down."

Josiah glanced at his aunt's expression. "That might be best."

The kid had a point. As much fun as it was to tweak Rachel, her mood was definitely going south.

"She'd probably like 'up' more if she slept more."

"Aunt Rachel never sleeps."

"Why not?"

"She says it's because she talks too much."

Interesting. "What do you think?"

Another look over his shoulder at his aunt before he whispered, "I think she's afraid of dream bandits."

"Dream bandits?"

"They make her scream."

"As her mate I'll have to help her with that."

"Good." Josiah skipped to keep up, looked down and then back up. "Is it true? Does my mom have a new mate?"

Cur shortened his stride. "Yes."

"Oh."

It wasn't hard to tell where the kid's mind had wandered. "Garrett is looking forward to meeting you."

"Is that his name?"

"Yes."

They continued for a few more steps. "He won't like me."

"What makes you say that?"

"I'm not his."

"A lot of men love children not their own."

"Not wolves."

Cur glanced back at Rachel. Had she been poisoning the boy's mind so he wouldn't want to go back home? "Where'd you hear that?"

"Mom."

Shit. "Your mom told you that?"

Josiah marched along, chin down, shoulders set. "I hear stuff."

"Overheard" might be a better term. "Well, I think you ought to wait and see what happens rather than make up your mind ahead of time."

No response for five steps, then, "I'm going to live with Aunt Rachel if I don't like him."

Ah. And now the crux of the matter. The kid was staking his claim. Just in case. Cur's lips twitched as he fought back a smile. "I see."

Another quick glance. "And you won't have any say about it."

The kid dropped back before he could counter. As a strategist, Josiah had potential. As a werewolf he had a lot to learn. When it came to Rachel, Cur intended to have all the say.

"Don't bet on it."

JOSIAH hadn't been kidding. By the time they got to the top of the ridge, Rachel was frowning and muttering under her breath, cursing him, the hill and then him again. Cur reached back to help her over a rocky streambed. She pushed his hand aside. From his perch on Cur's shoulder, Josiah said, "Told you."

"So you did."

He soothed his irritation by watching the sway of Rachel's ass as she strode ahead. She had a cute ass. Well-rounded for her size with just that touch of plumpness that invited a man to cup. His fingers twitched. And squeeze. Definitely squeeze.

He stopped by a large rock. Rachel kept going and that ass kept swaying.

"Aunt Rachel!"

Rachel turned at Josiah's cry. Cur motioned her back before swinging Josiah down.

"We're here."

She stopped in front of him. "Where's here?"

Pulling the brush away from the rock, he revealed the opening to a cave. Inside sat two dirt bikes.

"You couldn't have left them at the bottom of the mountain?"

"Nope." They were too likely to have been discovered. And once they got on these, the race would be on. The sound of motors carried, and the only thing between them and home was Carmichael land and rogues. If he were alone, he'd have enjoyed the challenge. Burdened by his mate and a child, all he could do was grit his teeth.

"Do you know how to ride?"

He could have saved his breath. Rachel was in the cave, backing one of the bright red bikes out. She put on a helmet with a sense of familiarity. "Yes."

She handed the child's helmet to Josiah. He put the helmet on with the same sense of familiarity.

"You know how to ride."

Josiah smiled. "My daddy was the best."

The kid's father had died more than two years ago. "Let's hope you inherited his genes."

With a kid's literalness, Josiah nodded. "My mom says I look just like him and Aunt Rachel says I have his coordination."

"Good, because some of the hardest riding you're ever going to do is coming up tomorrow."

Rachel paused, buckling her helmet. "Tomorrow?"

"We've got eighty miles between us and Haven. The quickest shot is straight through Carmichael territory, and in case you didn't know, they're a bit pissed at Haven right now."

"Why?"

"According to them, they don't like upstarts."

"And according to you?"

"I think they're annoyed their best Protectors jumped ship to marry humans and form a new pack."

She took off her helmet and shook her hair out. "So why are we going through their territory?"

"There's only so much gas we can carry and the rogues aren't letting up. They want Megan, and you two are their leverage to make that happen."

"Sarah Anne will never give them Megan."

"I imagine Garrett will have something to say about it, too, but that won't stop the rogues from trying." And maybe succeeding.

Josiah was over at the other bike, checking it out.

Rachel whispered, "Even if they capture him, what can they hope to gain? No mother would trade one child for another."

"No, but any mother would try to get him back, which could create an opportunity. And there's always the possibility they think Josiah shares Megan's gifts."

Still watching Josiah, she pushed her long brown hair off her face, yanking her fingers through a snarl. "I hate this."

He turned her into his arms, feeling like a lifetime had passed since he'd held her against him. "I know."

That she didn't fight him was more telling than her muttered, "Hate it, hate it, hate it."

Threading his fingers through her hair, he massaged her scalp.

He wished he had better answers for her, but the reality was what it was. "Haven's a start on change."

"Only if they allow it to stay."

"It'll stay."

"Because you will it?"

"Because we'll fight for it. I may be a mixed-blood, Rachel, but when it comes to loyalty, I'm wolf through and through. You don't need to worry about that."

"As if that was one of my worries."

Hmm. "If that wasn't one of your worries, what was?"

She pushed against his chest. "That."

He didn't let her go. "You're lying."

"I don't care. I'm hungry, tired and irritated. In other words, not in the mood for fifty questions."

He tipped her head back, seeing the truth in her expression. Yes, she was. And she was dependent on him to take care of all her needs. Not just the sexual ones. Satisfaction spread through him. Damn, he liked knowing that.

"I'm hungry, too," Josiah piped up, coming back over.

"Then I guess we'd better get to work. Josiah, put that helmet back on the bike. Rachel, put that bike back in the cave."

"And what are you going to do?"

He shrugged his pack off his shoulder. "I'm going to fix supper."

"What are we having?" Josiah asked.

"Roast beef?" Rachel asked hopefully, pushing the bike back into the cave.

"Mashed potatoes?" Josiah added, hooking his helmet on the bike.

"Green bean casserole?"

"Yuck!"

Cur laughed at Josiah's disgust. "How about corn on the cob instead?"

Josiah came scampering back. "You have corn on the cob?"

Cur almost felt guilty, the kid sounded so excited. He handed him a granola bar. "You can pretend that's corn on the cob."

Josiah took the bar, looked at the picture on the wrapper and sighed. "Maybe."

Rachel finished covering the entrance to the cave. "Say, 'Thank you.'"

The boy mumbled a thank-you and went to sit on a rock ten feet away. Cur handed Rachel a bar. She took it with the same lack of enthusiasm. "His world revolves around food. A few times I was sure we'd get caught because of his need to eat."

"It wouldn't have hurt him to miss a meal or two. That stop at that burger joint almost cost you." If he'd been a minute later arriving on the scene, the rogue tailing her would have completed the call reporting her location.

"I know. Except he gets so hungry."

Cur could remember going days with his stomach gnawing at his backbone without anyone caring. "It wouldn't have killed him."

She cocked her head to the side as she unwrapped her dinner. "I suppose I owe you a thank-you that we didn't get caught."

"It wouldn't go amiss."

She smiled. The first one he'd seen up close. She sat on the ground, bracing her back against the stone. The smile took her face from beauty to earthy charm and captivated him just as completely. He loved the way the left side of her mouth tilted just a touch higher than the right, the way it revealed her bottom front teeth were just the slightest bit crooked, the glimpse it provided of the real woman behind the guarded mask. "Thank you."

"You're welcome."

She waved her hand. "You can sit, you know."

He was still standing there holding the pack, staring at her like a lovesick pup in the throes of his first crush. He scanned with his senses. No danger. Dropping the pack, he sat beside her so his knee was touching hers. She scooted over a bit. He smiled at the betrayal of awareness. She'd been as nervous as a cat since that kiss last night. Though all he'd done afterward was hold her through the night, she seemed to be waiting for him to pounce. It was amusing, irritating and, well, too tempting a target to resist.

"Soon as I finish my supper, I'll get right on that."

She eyed him suspiciously. "On what?"

He jerked his chin in her direction. "Your ravishment."

She choked on the granola bar. He was obliged to pound her back. As soon as she caught her breath, she snapped, "Are you never serious?"

"I have my moments."

For a second she stared at him, her eyes bright in her red face, and then she groaned. "I seriously don't want to like you."

"I know. It's a mystery to me, seeing as we're going to spend our lives together."

The laughter left her face. "Yeah."

One of these days she was going to prick his temper with that question mark she kept attaching to their union. "Are you thinking because I'm a mixed-blood I can't bond?"

"Not at all." She took the last bite of her dinner and crumpled the wrapper. He had to wait until she finished chewing for more, and what he got wasn't what he wanted. "Is Sarah Anne happy with her mate?"

"So Garrett says."

"Garrett being her mate?"

"Yup."

Grabbing his pack, she pulled it toward her. "Well, that makes it a questionable source."

"Garrett doesn't lie."

"He sounds like a real paragon."

"He's as good a man as you'll ever meet."

"As good as you?" She raised her eyebrows at him.

He debated telling her about Teri, but since he didn't know if she'd survived, he decided against it. "Better."

That got another lift of her brow. "If you'll look in the front pocket, you'll find some chocolate."

Her entire face lit up. "Chocolate?"

"Yeah." In two seconds she found the candy. It was double-sealed in plastic so as not to give off a scent. "Don't rip the bags."

"I'm not an idiot."

"Never thought you were. You just seem to be in a bit of a hurry."

"Well, duh. It's chocolate."

He chuckled as Josiah came trotting over. "Uncle Cur has chocolate?"

"Don't call him that."

The boy paused, his lip pushing out pugnaciously.

"It's fine," Cur said. "I don't mind."

"Well, I do. Cur is an awful appellation."

"It's been my nickname for years."

"But not the name you were given at birth."

"This bothers you?"

"Yes."

He didn't know how to feel about that. Glad that she was watching out for his feelings or annoyed she had to make a big deal out of something he'd long since put to rest. In the end it was the way she looked at him that made up his mind for him.

"Curran."

"That's your name?"

"Yes."

Josiah repeated it. "Uncle Curran." He nodded. "That does sound better."

Hell, even the kid was on his case. "Whatever."

Rachel was back to rummaging in the pack. "What's this?" She pulled out a double-wrapped jar of peanut butter.

"What does it look like?"

"Peanut butter, which you said you're allergic to."

"I am."

"Then why do you have it?"

"It has its uses."

Rachel opened the bag. "Looks like we've got dipping sauce for our chocolate, Josiah."

The kid whooped. Rachel met Cur's gaze with a smug smile and dipped her fingers in the jar.

He swore under his breath and took another bite of his granola bar.

So much for his plans to kiss the sass from her.

Eight

SOMETHING was wrong.

Rachel kept her eyes closed and absorbed the silence around her within the small cave. She could smell the gas for the motorbikes, the rubber of the tires, Cur, Josiah, and . . . others! Cur's hand came over her mouth. His lips brushed her ear.

"We've got company."

She nodded to let him know she understood.

"Don't panic, but I want you to take Josiah and slip into that hidden alcove in the back of the cave. No matter what, you stay there."

"What about you?"

He reached into the pack. "Don't worry about me."

"Of course I'm worried about you."

"We're not bonded." Shifting up on his elbow, he dragged a whiskey bottle clear of the pack. "You've got nothing to lose."

Except him.

"That's a lousy thing to say."

"It's the truth. Now, very quietly, take Josiah to the alcove."

Josiah nodded as soon as she got near. He'd heard. It was eerie sometimes how easily the boy accepted danger. She knew for a fact with the exception of his father's death, no violence had ever touched his life. Sarah Anne had seen to that, but still, when faced with danger, he possessed an eerie calm. Maybe he really was a Protector. Maybe they were all like this. Maybe Curran had been like this. She didn't know. Protectors were identified early in life, and as soon as they were, they were taken into training. They didn't grow up mingling with the pack. They didn't form attachments. Their loyalty was to the pack first. Everything else second, and they were raised to ensure it. Another thing Sarah Anne didn't want for her children. God help Haven if they tried to enforce tradition with Josiah. And God help Sarah Anne if Josiah decided he wanted it. The boy at five was more single-minded than many an adult.

Josiah slid out of his sleeping bag. Taking her hand, he led her to the alcove. Curran's eyebrow rose at the boy leading her rather than the other way around, but she'd long since gotten used to it. Josiah protected all the women in his life.

Curran grabbed his sleeping bag and handed it to her. She pulled it on top of them into the tiny crevice that barely fit them both. She jerked in surprise when he poured alcohol on it. The stench burned her nostrils, drowning out all others. Snaking his hand behind her neck, he pulled her to him, kissing her hard and deep, his tongue thrusting past her lips, sliding along hers. Before she could do anything more than gasp in shock, he stepped back. His thumb stroked over her lips as his gaze met hers. She expected to see regret, sadness, but instead she saw . . . satisfaction?

"Keep her quiet, Josiah. And don't let her come out, no matter what."

She felt Josiah's nod against her arm. His hand grabbed hers.

"I'll see you in a few hours."

Hours? He expected them to stay here for a few hours? She leaned out. "Curran."

He stepped away, pouring some whiskey on himself, staggering around the area where Josiah's sleeping bag had been, his feet blurring signs that anything else had been there. The stench of alcohol obliterated anything else. He couldn't think pretending to be drunk was going to accomplish anything.

With a wave of his hand he motioned her back. Josiah tugged at her hand. "You're ruining his plan."

Curran had a plan? How the hell could he have a plan? His plan had been for them to ride those bikes tomorrow. Nonetheless, she folded herself back into the crevice, grimacing when the rock bruised her skin through her clothes.

She heard a noise. A thump followed by a series of smaller ones that came faster and faster until they were like a vibration in her head. Her breath caught in her throat. Everything in her cried out for Curran. She lunged for the opening. Little hands pushed her back. Josiah shook his head at her. His eyes glowed red in the dark. The pressure on her hip was incredibly strong. Josiah was calling on his wolf, following Curran's order to keep her there. She didn't care. Curran was in trouble.

Other scents spread through the cave. Male. Werewolf. Unfamiliar. Rogues. Too late. It was too late. Grabbing Josiah, Rachel pulled him to her, a silent wail of agony welling from inside. Josiah squeezed her hand.

"What do we have here?"

There was the sound of boots scraping over dirt. "A drunk wolf."

"If he's drunk, ass, he has to be a mix," another said.

"Of course he's a mix," another scoffed. "Look at the hair. No wolf has hair that color."

There was a pause. More footsteps entered the cave. How many did that make? Seven? eight?

"So, who is it?"

"Could be one of Haven's mongrels."

"Damn, it stinks in here."

"Get up."

There was the sound of something hard hitting something soft.

"Did the damn fool drink himself to death?"

"If he did, I've got dibs on those bikes."

The betraying thump came again. "The hell you do."

"Check his pulse."

Curran. They had to be talking about Curran. She held her breath. When the answer came she sagged.

"Nothing."

Oh, God.

"Stupid breeds. All the benefits they get from our blood and they throw it away on drugs or alcohol."

Rachel wanted to leap out of her hiding place and rip out the speaker's throat. Josiah pressed against her thigh. He shook his head. He was right, but not for the reasons he thought. If she left the crevice, the rogues would be compelled to search the cave to see who else they had missed. And they'd find Josiah. She didn't know what had happened to Curran, but she couldn't afford to fail Sarah Anne. She'd promised to keep Josiah safe, and she would.

Someone spat. "And Haven wants to welcome them all."

"Leave them to the Carmichaels."

"Except for the girl. The girl is ours."

"What do we do with him?"

"Leave him for the bugs."

"And the bikes?"

"Mark the cave. We'll pick them up on the way back."

"You think the Carmichaels will keep their word?"

"Who cares? We just need them to believe we're going to keep ours."

The deeper voice laughed. "Until we don't."

A couple of grunts and then, "And then we'll have it all."

"You think Haven is going to put up that much of a fight?"

"I think the McGowans can command enough respect to keep the Carmichaels busy long enough."

Long enough for what? Rachel memorized the wording. It might be important later.

Again the sound of someone spitting. "There isn't enough respect in the world to make a traditional pack like the Carmichaels accept a mongrel pack like Haven."

"It was Wyatt Carmichael's dad who sanctioned Haven."

"On his death bed. No one can hold a pack to that kind of sanction."

"I still think you're underestimating the Carmichaels."

"Think what you want. You're not in charge. Unless you've worked up the courage to challenge?"

The cave filled with tension. Rachel could easily envision the scene. Two males facing off, shoulders squared, hands open, legs slightly bent in a crouch, ready to fight to the death unless one backed down. One always backed down. It was the wolf way. Hierarchy was set by birth. Rarely was it upset by battle.

"That's what I thought."

"C'mon. Let's get moving."

"Remember, the bikes are mine."

"Yeah, we all heard you."

Yes, they had to move. Dear God, *move*. The need to get to Curran clawed at Rachel like a living creature. The urge to dart out grew by the moment, threatening to override her good sense. Rachel closed her eyes and built a mental image of Curran, focusing on his broad forehead with the lock of hair that tended to fall over it, the arch of his dark brows over his hazel eyes, and that mobile, perpetually-on-the-edge-of-humor mouth set above his square chin. He had to be all right. And they had to leave.

Josiah tugged at her leg. She looked down, the image dissolving away, leaving her with only a sense of panic and Curran's name screaming in her mind. Josiah motioned her to follow. Quick as a wink, he was out of their hiding place. Before she'd even ascertained it was safe.

"Josiah," she hissed.

She came around the corner to find him kneeling beside Curran's body, holding on to his hand as if it was a lifeline. Rachel couldn't look away from that hand. That big, capable hand that had seemed to command the world since the moment she'd met him. Had it been only forty-eight hours ago? How had he become so important to her in forty-eight hours?

Mate. And he lay dying.

Don't worry. We're not bonded.

"What kind of reassurance was that?" she whispered, dropping to her knees beside him. "Telling me we're not even going to have a chance."

Josiah sobbed, looking like what he was for once, a lost little boy. "What happened?"

She touched Curran's cheek, held her hand over his mouth, her finger under his nose. "I don't know."

"He's not breathing?"

"No." No. No. No.

Nine

FOR a moment Rachel couldn't get past the denial that ripped through her soul. Beneath her hand she could feel the warmth of his skin, the illusion of life.

I'll see you in a few hours.

He'd lied. Damn him. "He lied."

"Mates can't lie to each other," Josiah said with a desperation echoing her own.

They weren't supposed to. "I know."

It was so hard to talk with pain clawing at her soul. Loss like she'd never known before crashed over her in a tidal wave of knowledge. Why hadn't she seen this? She'd seen so much, why not this?

"He said he'd see us in a few hours," Josiah whispered, as if repeating what had happened could change anything. "I wasn't supposed to let you out, no matter what."

"You didn't."

"I just wanted to see," he whispered, the break in his voice catching on her awareness. "I didn't mean to disobey."

Oh, God. "This isn't your fault, Josiah." She pushed the hair off Curran's face. With her other hand, she pulled Josiah to her. Curran looked so alive, she couldn't stop touching him. With her sleeve she wiped the spittle from the corner of his mouth. "Whatever happened, it happened before the rogues got here."

Josiah looked hopeful. "Maybe it was part of his plan?"

"Maybe." She didn't know what else to say.

She ran her hands over his side, seeing a dirty smear over his ribs, remembering the thumps she'd heard. A snarl rumbled in her throat. Kicks. They'd kicked him when he'd lain helpless like this.

"What?"

"They kicked him."

Josiah's snarl followed her own. "I'll kill them."

No, he wouldn't, but she would. One at a time. She'd hunt them down and make them pay. Stroking her hands over Cur's chest, she had a flash of insight. Curran standing here, waiting. For what? The vision strengthened, replacing reality with prophecy. No, not prophecy. Truth. Curran trying to swallow, failing, a calm acceptance in his expression underlying the instinctive grab for his throat. Curran falling, feet kicking, convulsing. Curran lying still.

She blinked.

"What did you see?" Josiah asked with a child's acceptance of things he couldn't understand.

"Curran." She couldn't stop touching him, running her hands from his shoulders to his hips, over and over, as if she could stroke the life back into him.

Licking her lips, she imagined she could taste his kiss under the faint hint of peanut butter. Damn him. Peanut butter.

"He's allergic to peanut butter."

Josiah didn't question the statement, just stayed with her. "He didn't have any."

But she had, and he'd kissed her. As if he meant it. But maybe she'd mistaken his purpose for something else. Maybe this had really been part of his plan. Curran as Protector. He had to know he couldn't fight off eight rogues, but suicide? He'd never do that, even if he wasn't claiming her as his mate because it would leave a woman and child alone and unprotected in enemy territory.

What effect do peanuts have on you?

I die for a bit.

"Damn you." He was both were and human. Werewolves didn't die from allergic reactions. She scooted around until she could lift his head in her lap. Tracing the arc of his brows with her fingertips, she whispered, "I'll never forgive you if I'm wrong."

Josiah scrambled to his feet, his fists clenched ready to defend his hero. "It's not his fault."

Yes, it was. Every moment of it. "He's not dead."

Josiah faltered. "He's not breathing."

Running her fingertips down the sides of his neck, she squeezed his shoulders. The man was all muscle and bone. Wonderfully warm.

"I know, but he's not dead."

She slid her hands back up the sides of his neck, over his cheeks, his forehead.

"What are you doing?"

"Bringing him back to life."

"Wow! You can do that?"

"I have to."

"Why?"

"So I can kill him."

RACHEL was pissed. Cur didn't have to scent her anger to know it existed. It radiated from her in waves of aggression, emphasized by her narrowed eyes, clenched fists and tense muscles. Even Josiah, whom she adored, was keeping his distance.

She stood in front of him, right fist slightly drawn back. Was she planning on taking a swing at him?

"How could you do something so stupid?"

"I never do anything stupid."

"You're deathly allergic to peanuts!"

He reached for her. She dodged his hand, dancing back out of reach. She wasn't the only one whose anger was rising. She was upset and it was his duty to calm her.

"Yes, and I know precisely the effect it has on me."

"How can you know anything? You go into a coma."

"Garrett told me."

"Garrett participated in this lunacy with you? The same Garrett with whom you told me Sarah Anne is safe? With whom I'm supposed to trust Josiah?"

He ground his teeth, studying her carefully, glancing at Josiah, who was taking this all in. "Yes."

"Well, let me tell you, that's not much of a recommendation."

"So I gather."

When she darted to the right, he was ready for her, catching her in the crook of his arm, pulling her kicking and squirming into his side. Josiah snarled.

"I'm not going to hurt her." Christ, now he was justifying his actions to children. "She's upset. She needs to be calmed."

Josiah nodded. Rachel swore.

"I'm not a damn horse."

Threading his fingers through her hair, Cur held Rachel so she couldn't head butt him should she get the notion. "I know. You're my sweet mate."

Even Josiah snorted at that.

"And you've had a scare."

"I thought you were dead!"

"I told you not to come out."

"What difference does that make?"

"If you'd done as you were told, you wouldn't be upset now."

The logic of that flew over her head.

"Those rogues could have shot you!"

"No soldier, rogue or not, would waste a bullet on a dead man."

"They could have slit your throat."

It didn't seem worth pointing out they thought he was dead already, so he settled for a simple, "They didn't."

"But they could have."

Agreement might be the way to go. "Yes."

"And then what good would you have been to anyone?"

There was only one person he was wanting to be good to. He brushed his lips over her hair. "No one at all."

Her fists slammed against his shoulders. "I thought you were dead."

She kept coming back to that. "I know."

She sniffed. Once. Twice.

"Are you crying?" He didn't like the thought of her crying.

"Not over the likes of you!"

The hell she wasn't. He tugged her head back. Tears hovered in her beautiful brown eyes. Splotches of red spread across her face and a frown made up the majority of her expression. "Yes, you are." He kissed the tight line of her mouth, running his tongue over the seam. "I like it."

She hit him again, albeit not so hard. "Ass."

He chuckled, kissing her once more. "I've never had anyone care enough to cry over me, so fair warning, there's not much you can do to ruin this for me."

He felt her knee flex, and adjusted his position, just in case she got the notion to knee him in the balls. Despite his words, that would ruin the moment.

"I hate you."

"I know," he whispered against her mouth, feeling her surrender in the softening of her lips. "Now, kiss me back."

He felt the press of her claws, the graze of her canines; then with a sob, she collapsed against him. "I hate you."

He took possession of her mouth with the slow thrust of his tongue. Her moan of surrender was sweet to his ears. Fire blended with pleasure as her thighs cradled his cock, and her breasts flattened against his chest. His woman. His mate. His. He kissed her until she panted against him and he couldn't breathe for the need thundering along with his pulse, kissed her until the only thing left was to thrust deep within her tight sheath and complete the claiming he'd begun two days ago. Movement to his left reminded him they weren't alone. Josiah. They'd probably already given the kid enough of a sex education to scar him for life. Shit. He backed off the kiss, easing Rachel back to awareness. When she blinked at him, her lips parted and swollen from his attentions, he whispered, "It was a good plan."

As awareness returned to her gaze, he patted her rear and turned her toward the motorbikes. "Not only that, it worked."

Ten

IT worked. Rachel ground her teeth as she took the motorbike over the next hill, glaring at Curran's back. Who did he think he was kidding? It was only sheer luck that had that reckless plan working. A thousand and one things could have interfered with its success from the simple possibility that his reaction to the peanut butter could have been more severe than he'd anticipated to the rogues' frustration level being high enough to overcome the were-wolves' innate revulsion at disturbing the dead. And if she hadn't had the vision, she might have taken Josiah and left. It would have served him right if she had.

Curran pulled to the side ahead. She throttled down and came up beside him. Unlike her and Josiah, he didn't wear a helmet. Ostensibly because he needed to be able to hear and fight if necessary, but after last night, she knew it was just another example of his reckless nature on display.

The machine came to a stop. She braced her feet on the ground, balancing her and Josiah's weight. Her arms vibrated with the engine.

"How are you holding up?"

Not that well, if truth were known. It always looked so easy to ride a bike on TV. But to ride a bike through the mountains was a far cry from going around a dirt track. The strain was telling on her arms and legs. Fatigue was wearing on her brain. "I think it's time for Josiah to ride with you."

He frowned. "Are you going to make it?"

There was the temptation to lie, but aside from the fact that she couldn't lie to her mate, there was Josiah's safety. She was getting tired, her riding sloppy. He'd be safer with Curran.

"Its not that much farther." He swung his leg over the back of the bike and stood. "About another twenty miles." He untied the gas can from the back. "Hop off and walk around while I fill the tanks." Josiah was already off. Curran handed him a pack.

"There's peanut butter and crackers in the front pocket. Think you can make your aunt and yourself a snack?"

"Yep."

"Good, then get to it. We're not going to be here long."

Rachel got off the bike. The muscles in her legs were stiff and she could barely walk.

Curran chuckled. "Feels a bit like you're still riding, doesn't it?"

"Yes."

"Going down will be tougher than going up."

Naturally. Nothing could go easy. Rachel looked down the mountain. They were above the tree line. The path was steep and strewn with rocks. She couldn't see what happened to the trail once it disappeared into the trees, but she had a fair idea she could add mud to the list of obstacles. The thought of taking the bike down there scared the crap out of her.

"Maybe I should just walk mine down."

"Not an option." He pointed to the right. "See that valley over there?"

"Yes."

"That's the Carmichael strength stronghold. Sound carries up here. Someone will come investigating who's riding motorcycles up here."

The Carmichaels. "The rogues mentioned something about them."

Curran unscrewed the cap to the gas tank and poured the gas in. "I bet."

"I don't think they're in cahoots."

Curran looked up. "What makes you say that?"

"From what they said, I got the impression they don't have loyalty to either side."

Cur screwed the cap back on with an outward impression of nonchalance, but she could feel the tension within him.

"Be specific."

She couldn't. As hard as she tried to remember what she'd heard that night, all she remembered clearly was panic over Curran's state.

"It's important."

"I know." She closed her eyes, trying to remember the words spoken. "I remember hearing you fall down. The first couple men coming in made comments about you being drunk. Someone made a comment about leaving the mixes to Haven. Someone else mentioned about letting the Carmichaels take care of Haven. There were comments about the Carmichaels being a traditional pack. About them cooperating long enough."

"Long enough for what?"

"I don't know." She opened her eyes. "They didn't say."

"You sure?"

She closed her eyes again, trying to remember. The blackness at the edges of her vision began to blur to a gray. A vision. Oh, God, she didn't need a vision now, here. But as usual it didn't matter what she needed. The visions came when they did, taking over, ruining her life. Josiah's hands slid into hers. Reality blurred away as the dream spread from the center of her mind's eye outward.

"It's okay, Aunt Rachel. I've got you."

The vision grew stronger. Bodies formed in the mist, hazing her mind. She squeezed Josiah's hand. Holding her hand was something he'd done since the time he'd overheard her confessing to Sarah Anne that the visions scared her.

"What's going on?" Cur asked.

She shook her head. The words couldn't get past the power of the vision.

"She's having a vision."

"What the hell?"

A distant part of her mind recognized Cur's shock. Her world diminished until she was standing in a meadow looking through the transparent walls of a shack. Inside stood three men. Two she couldn't see; one she could. The one she could see was very scary. There was no doubt he was wolf. No doubt he was ancient. His face was horribly scarred. His eyes were cold and held the promise of death. She could sense he was facing enemies but he wasn't afraid. Resolute. He was resolute. He knew what he was doing. He knew it wasn't going to make anyone happy, but he was doing it anyway. The wall shimmered and solidified until she couldn't see any more inside the cabin. She heard a door open, the scuffle of feet. She heard Cur's snarl and then a cry of "traitor." The fog wavered. A gun cocked. She could feel the threat. Someone was going to die. She screamed, in her mind grabbing for the gun. Not Curran. Not her Curran.

"Goddammit, Rachel. Come out of it."

The mist wavered and dissipated. Rachel blinked. When she opened her eyes, all she could see was leaves backlit by sun with specks of blue sky in between.

The sun was blocked and then all she could see was Curran's face. A dream. It was just a dream. The scent of blood spiced the afternoon air. Beads of sweat dripped down her brow. The world shook again.

"Rachel, look at me."

The world wasn't shaking. Curran was shaking her. She moaned, remembering the gun blast.

Curran shook Rachel again. Her skin was pasty white. Her claws gouged his arms, but she was with him. And she wasn't screaming. He didn't think he'd ever get the sound of her scream out of his mind.

She was having a vision, Josiah had said. She was a witch. A witch in the eyes of all werewolves was evil. Fine. He looked into her face, her terrified gaze, and he didn't care. He pulled her into his embrace, holding her face into the curve of his throat, rocking her. "It's all right, Rachel. It's all right."

"The traitor got you."

"What traitor?"

"The ancient with a scarred face. He betrayed you."

He knew only one werewolf that fit that description. Daire. The mercenary with no allegiance to anyone. One of Haven's Protectors.

Eleven

"You're sure she's talking about Daire?"

Cur glared at Donovan. "As sure as I am that I gave you that black eye."

Donovan bared his teeth. "One lucky shot does not a threat make."

"And suspicion doesn't make for conviction," Cur snapped back.

Kelon yanked Cur's handcuffed wrists up behind his back. If they had been regular human cuffs, he'd have broken them. "Until Wyatt gets back, it's what we've got."

Cur snarled. And jerked on his arms. The sons of bitches had taken Rachel from him the minute they'd arrived. He'd fought, but they'd had the advantage. He hadn't seen the assault coming. He was pack. Pack didn't turn on pack. Kelon just increased his grip.

"Settle down while we sort this out."

"There's nothing to be sorted. Rachel is my mate. She wears my mark. By pack law, you have no right to hold her."

"And in ordinary times, we'd concede that."

"But these aren't ordinary times."

Pain ground through his shoulder as Kelon wrenched his arm higher. He snarled at him over his shoulder. It'd taken both Donovan and Kelon to get the cuffs on him. He would kill them both when they took them off. "Fuck you both."

Donovan shook his head. "No, thanks. Now, focus."

He smiled coldly. He'd told Garrett it was a mistake to strive for more than they were. No pack would accept mixed-bloods. Here was the proof. "Uncuff me."

"Not until you get that temper under control."

"I'm in perfect control." For a man whose mate had been taken into custody. For a man whose mate believed he'd betrayed her. For a man who'd thought he could trust pack.

"Good. Then tell me what you know."

"Where's Garrett?"

"Busy."

Movement outside the window caught his eye. Garrett stood across the street, leaning against a post, a smile on his face. No one who saw that smile thought he was up to any good. Cur knew the instant Kelon saw what he did. The werewolf stiffened.

"Shit."

Donovan came over. "What?"

Kelon motioned to the window. "Looks like we have dissension in the troops."

Garrett touched his hand to his hat. As a gesture of respect it was lacking. A crook of his finger summoned someone over. Cur burst into laughter as Rachel came into view. Garrett had busted her out. Another crook of his finger and four more women joined Garrett.

"Hell, I'd say we've got a full-out rebellion."

Two of the women broke ranks. They had similar looks, similar builds and similar frowns. They headed for the front door.

"Your mates?" Cur asked, his anger at last having an outlet.

Kelon glared at him. "Yes. And if you've upset mine, I'll cut off your balls."

"I'm sure she's no more upset than mine."

Kelon frowned as the front door slammed.

"Kelon!"

"Donovan! What did you do to Rachel?"

"Shall I tell them?" Cur asked.

Kelon's hand slammed between his shoulder blades, knocking him forward. Donovan caught his arm and murmured, "Robin is pregnant."

Shit. Cur pulled himself up just as a small, plump woman burst into the room. "How could you, Kelon? We had a surprise party planned and now Josiah's crying, Rachel thinks we hate her and no doubt Curran wants your blood."

Yes, he did, but not right now. The rage he felt inside seemed out of place with a woman in the room, the words he wanted to say too crude. Hell. Cur wasn't even Robin's mate and the tears in her eyes made him feel as guilty as hell.

"Seelie, sometimes things aren't as clear as you'd like them to be."

Robin pushed against Kelon's chest. He didn't let her go. "And sometimes they're not as dark."

The other woman stood just inside the door, tapping her foot. "I want an explanation, Donovan."

"So do I, but Cur isn't cooperating."

"His name is Curran," Sarah Anne said, coming through the door. "Not Cur. Please use it."

Donovan cocked an eyebrow at him. "You want to be called Curran?"

"Yes, he does." Rachel pushed past Sarah Anne and came to his side. She made a soft sound in her throat when she found the handcuffs. "Take these off him."

Shit. He'd never thought there'd come the day when women would fight his battles for him.

"Ladies—"

Before Donovan could finish the sentence, Lisa had filched the keys from his belt and tossed them to Rachel. With a growl, Rachel unlocked the cuffs. As soon as his hands were free, Cur pushed Rachel behind him, backing up until she was trapped between the wall and his body. As if on cue, Donovan and Kelon yanked their mates behind, leaving the other brunette and Teri standing in the middle of the room, alone and unprotected.

"Guess that makes us chopped liver, Heather," Teri said.

The other woman was Heather Delaney, Wyatt Carmichael's mate.

"Well, shoot." Heather huffed, putting her hands on her hips. "I'm telling."

Twelve

"TELLING what?" Wyatt asked as he came into the room.

Heather crossed to his side before he got more than one step in. To stop him? "Your Protectors left Teri and me exposed to threat."

"The hell you say." Wyatt glanced around. "What threat?"

Heather pointed at Rachel. "Her."

Wyatt tucked Heather to his side and walked to his desk. She went willingly. Tradition said human mates were frail and fearful, but nothing during Cur's time at Haven had given him the impression the human mates of the leader and Protectors were any less than werewolf mates. Though they were a bit more outspoken. "I'm going to gather from the excitement that you're Rachel?"

Rachel tilted her chin up. "And I'm going to assume from the fact I was taken prisoner and my mate handcuffed that your word isn't worth crap."

"You would be assuming wrong. Now, stand down all of you. I've just spent all morning with Buddy 'negotiating' his departure, and I'm not in a good mood."

"You should have let Daire kill him," Donovan said.

Wyatt growled. "Just for that, Donovan, you can pick up the tab for his moving truck."

"Shit."

Wyatt looked around. "Anyone else want to stretch my sense of humor today?"

No one said a word. Cur could see why. There was no sign of the benevolent leader about Wyatt today. He was all sharp edges just waiting to cut.

"Good." Wyatt pulled out the leather chair from his desk and dropped into it. "I get enough drama from the Carmichaels. I sure as shit don't need it from my own pack."

Heather slipped in behind him and started massaging his temples. Wyatt laid his head back against her chest and sighed. "Thank you."

Cur couldn't ever remember a leader allowing his guard down to this extent.

Different, aren't they? Garrett asked.

Too different to trust, maybe, Cur shot back.

If that were the case, we'd be dead already.

That was the truth. Cur would be dead for defying the Alpha Protectors, Rachel for kidnapping Josiah, and Garrett for freeing Rachel.

"If you two are done chatting among yourselves?" Donovan asked.

Cur smiled. So the Protector could sense energy. "For the moment."

"I'd like to ask some questions," Wyatt cut in.

"Fire away."

Wyatt sat up, catching Heather's hand in his for a kiss before moving her aside. "Of Rachel."

Cur felt Rachel stiffen. "What if I don't want to give them?"

The response was immediate. "You're welcome to leave."

Sarah Anne gasped. Josiah growled. Megan wailed, "Auntie R!"

Wyatt winced and glanced at Garrett's small family. "We would all appreciate it, however, if you chose not to leave."

"What kind of answers do you want?"

"Honest ones."

Rachel stilled. Cur could imagine what was going through her mind. The fears eating at her decision. Should she tell the truth and be ostracized? Should she stay quiet and be banished? He squeezed her waist.

Can we trust him with the truth about her powers? he asked Garrett.

She has powers?

Yes.

I trusted him with mine.

Cur bent down and whispered in her ear, "It's your choice. Whatever you decide. You're not alone."

––––––––

SHE wasn't alone. Rachel absorbed that truth, holding it to her. She had a mate. Whatever she decided affected him, too. She looked around the small group, feeling the honed focus of the men, the sympathy of the women. When her gaze met Sarah Anne's the other woman smiled. When she met Teri's, the other woman took a step forward.

"Since I'm the only one here without a mate to keep me in check, I guess it's my job to moderate this discussion."

"I wasn't aware I asked for a moderator," Wyatt countered.

She tucked her short hair behind her ear. "It's your lucky day. I'm working for free. Which is a good thing, because after buying off Buddy, you probably couldn't afford my rates."

The joke got a weak round of chuckles.

"I'm not up on all my werewolf prejudice and superstitions, but I'm gathering any sort or ESP is met with suspicion, even in ancients."

"With good reason, when you consider traditional pack hierarchy," Kelon interjected.

"Well, I think it's a lot of bull when you consider the evidence."

"What evidence?"

"The interbreeding of species seems, through anecdotal evidence at least, to produce more often than not a stronger breed with unique skills."

"I'm not strong," Sarah Anne interrupted.

Teri sighed. "I did qualify with a 'more often than not.'"

"She did, seelie."

Sarah Anne cuffed Garrett, who simply chuckled.

"You do, however, throw children that are superior," Teri said.

"Good grief, now she has me sounding like a dog in a breeding program."

Teri continued. "In my other life, I was a doctor. My specialty was genetics. In a way, werewolves are conducting a selective breeding program, but they're focused on old traits, ignoring nature's efforts to evolve."

"I knew you were a throwback," Lisa told Donovan.

"Tell me that tonight in bed."

"Shut up," Wyatt cut in, sitting forward in his seat.

Teri dipped her head. "Thank you."

"The only pack that's accepted the packless lost is Haven." Teri waved her hand, "By the way, I hate that description."

"It's no one's favorite," Garrett said.

"I'm just not sure you all understand what you've got."

Wyatt stilled, his tension spreading to the others in the room. "Tell me."

"By taking in the lost, by not discriminating against those with psychic abilities, you've got an edge no one else has."

"I don't understand."

"You all revere and fear the ancients for their skills, some of which are psychic. Historically, the reason these skills exist is because the ancients have an incredible amount of time to develop them. But by dropping prejudice and starting over, you all have the potential to define yourselves in a way other packs can't."

"She's right," Daire said, walking into the room.

Rachel stiffened. Any doubts Cur had that Daire was the person in the dream died.

"Garrett and Cur, here, are master telepaths." Daire explained, "Each strong in his own right. With the proper training, I'm pretty sure they could take out ten Protectors at a shot."

Rachel didn't take her eyes from Daire. Her fear tainted the air. She backed into Cur. He put her behind him, meeting the raise of Daire's brow with a lift of his lip.

Wyatt exchanged a glance with Kelon and Donovan. "Master telepaths?"

Kelon swore. Donovan clenched his fist. "There isn't exactly a way to measure these things."

"Actually, there is," Daire countered.

Wyatt waved his hand to Rachel. "Then what is she?"

Daire took a step forward and held out his hand. "May I?"

Rachel shook her head.

Cur linked with Garrett. *Monitor?*

There was a second's wait and then Garrett came back, *Done.*

Pulling Rachel into his side, Curran bent down and whispered, "Let him."

Her brown eyes met his. The fear within tore at his conscience. "Trust me."

After a few seconds, she nodded and held out her hand. Daire took it. No one seemed to breath as Daire measured Rachel's worth.

Daire released her hand. She slumped against Cur, her heart thundering against her ribs, her breath coming in short gasps. Daire grabbed a chair and slid it over. "Sit down."

It was an order. Rachel obeyed, clinging to Cur's hand all the way.

Cur exchanged a glance with Garrett. Garrett shook his head.

"What is she?" Wyatt asked.

"A low-level seer whose skills are developing randomly."

"What does she see that she fears?"

"Me betraying Haven."

Thirteen

"No way!"

Teri's denial broke the silence. Chairs creaked and floorboards groaned as everyone reeled in shock.

Rachel felt Teri's glare like a blow. "How could you?"

She tried to push out of the chair, but Daire was before her and Curran beside her. Unless she wanted to crawl through the wall, she was trapped.

"I didn't do anything."

"You couldn't see Daire betraying anyone. It's not in him."

Rachel didn't know what to say. "Daire saw what I saw."

"And what was that?" Wyatt asked.

"A moment, a fragment in time."

"But not the whole picture?"

She shook her head. "No. I never see the whole picture."

Daire caught her eye. As much as she wanted to look away, she couldn't.

"If you were trained, you might."

She didn't know if she wanted to be trained, to see the future in its entirety. "I'll think about it."

"I'd think it beats the half-ass messages you get now," Cur said.

She spun on Cur. "I said I'd think about it!"

Holding up his hands, he backed off. "Fair enough."

"Tell me, Rachel, do you think Daire will betray Haven?"

She didn't know how to answer. She just shrugged.

Garrett was the one who answered for her. "She doesn't know. She's literally at the mercy of these visions. It's why she ran with Josiah. The dreams, in her interpretation, told her to."

He made her sound like a pathetic idiot.

"How would you know?" she snarled, her claws extending.

"Cur gave me permission to enter your mind."

"What?"

Curran's hand on her shoulder kept her in her seat. "For protection, in case Daire really is a traitor."

Was she supposed to be grateful? Shrugging off Curran's grip, she jumped to her feet, not caring that she stepped on Daire's toes. Not caring that she was making a spectacle. She was fed up and she wasn't taking this anymore.

Daire stepped back. Rachel moved into the center of the room. The door was only eight feet away. Between her and it were Sarah Anne and Teri. Her friends. "All right. I have prophetic dreams. I can't control them, and lately I can't trust them, but that doesn't make me a mental petrie dish in which you all get to indulge your need to experiment."

Garrett stepped in her path. Slamming her hands into his chest, she had the satisfaction of hearing him grunt, but he didn't budge. Behind her there was a growl. Curran playing knight in shining armor. Well, it was too late. He'd betrayed her more than Wyatt.

Garrett inclined his head. "I'm sorry."

"I don't accept your apology."

Garrett looked over her shoulder at Cur. Rachel warned, "Don't look to him for help. I don't accept his, either."

She stormed out of the building, slamming the front door in Curran's face.

How could he betray her like that?

Fourteen

SHE got as far as the middle of the drive when she realized she had nowhere to go. She'd just stormed out of the room containing all the family she'd ever had since her parents died.

"Damn. Damn! Damn!"

"I'd throw in another one if I were you."

She turned. Heather was behind her. "Yell if you want, but don't hit me. Wyatt would have a problem with that."

Rachel pushed her hair off her face. "I don't want to hit you." From what she'd learned from Sarah Anne, Heather had been good to her and Teri, giving Teri everything she needed to recover from her injuries and loss. Jesus! She couldn't believe all Teri had been through. "You've been good to my friends."

"Believe it or not, it's our intention to be good to you, too."

"Really."

Heather grimaced. "The boys can be a bit overzealous."

"Boys?"

Heather smiled. "I say that to get their goat. Especially when they're being particularly autocratic."

"They were certainly that today."

Heather motioned to a rock. "Mind if I sit?"

"Not at all."

Heather pulled off her boots. "These are killing me."

"Why wear them, then?"

"You mean despite the fact that they look great and make my legs look longer?"

"Yes."

"Wyatt told me when I bought them they were too small, and I don't think he needs to know he's right."

"He'll be able to scent your distress."

Heather smiled. "Not if I'm careful and not right away. I like the man to have to wait a bit before he gets to say 'I told you so.'"

Rachel felt silly standing while Heather sat. She took a seat on an adjacent rock. "What did you want to say?"

Heather rubbed her foot. "You're werewolf, so you probably understand a lot better than I do how deeply tradition is embedded in your culture. What Wyatt's trying to do here is good, but it flies in the face of how all of you were raised, so occasionally, he or one of the other Alphas screws up. It doesn't mean their intentions aren't good, or they truly don't want to integrate all of the pack. It just means, they're . . ." She shrugged.

"Human?" Rachel inserted.

Heather grinned. "Exactly."

"Does Wyatt really intend to welcome all of the lost that want to join, regardless of their differences?"

"He truly does."

"That's going to be a mess."

"At first, absolutely." Heather spread her hands, indicating Rachel's position. "Consider yourself Exhibit A."

"Touché."

"Thank you. The situation is further complicated by the fact the Carmichaels have declared a blood feud against Haven and we just discovered an unknown wolf has infiltrated the human gang in town and was spying."

"For what?"

"We don't know. He got away, but you can see how your arrival and your dream caused a bit of an uproar."

Yes, she could. "Maybe I should take that training."

Heather nodded and fished in her pocket. "Maybe you should but in the meantime, take these."

The keys jangled as Heather passed them over.

"What do they go to?"

"The guesthouse behind the main house. It has a big soaker tub, which Sarah Anne is filling up right now. You're welcome to stay there as long as you want."

Rachel closed her fingers around the keys. She guessed she had a place to go after all.

Fifteen

THE house was empty when she got there. The tub was full and big enough for two sporting an infinity edge that let her slide all the way down in the water right up to her chin. She closed her eyes, breathing the rosemary scent of the bath salts Sarah Anne had put in. Listening to the fire crackle in the small wood stove, letting the moment of peace flow over her. For the first time in weeks, she could relax.

"If I climb in there with you, are you going to drown me?"

Curran. She sighed as her mark warmed that first tiny bit. "I haven't decided."

"Open your eyes and tell me that."

The minute she opened them she knew it was a mistake. Curran stood beside the tub, hands on hips, legs slightly apart, naked and aroused. Above the sharp jut of his cock she could see the laddered layers of muscle over his abdomen. Above that there was the clear delineation of his pecs. Her pussy clenched. And above that, her heart twisted. The apology she hadn't accepted was in his eyes.

"You don't play fair."

He shrugged. "Did you really expect me to?"

Had she? She tilted her head to the side, studying him, studying herself. Whereas she'd grown up loved, she knew from Sarah Anne that Cur hadn't. He and Garrett had had to fight for everything they had. And once they'd obtained it, they'd had to fight again to hold on to it. Cur had grown up packless, truly one of the lost. But he was still a good man. Misguided sometimes, but still good. "No."

She moved to the side. "And if you come in, I won't drown you."

He didn't move.

"I thought you wanted to come in."

"I do."

"Well, it won't happen if you don't take that first step."

"If I come in, I'll make love to you."

"I understand."

"I need to know something first."

"No, I'm not a virgin."

Living among humans, she'd tried to adapt their ways. After a couple of brief, unsatisfying affairs, she'd decided some things weren't for her. Curran waved her statement aside without a smile or a growl. "Neither am I."

She blinked. Whatever was on his mind was serious. "What is it?"

"Are you going to leave me?"

The question lodged between them, brutal in its honesty, stark in what it represented. Curran's pain.

She slid forward in the tub and wrapped her hands around his ankle. His expression was shuttered. His posture braced. Did he really think so little of her that he thought she'd leave him over what happened in the main house?

The answer when it came was humbling. He didn't think so little of her. It was himself he didn't see as a prize. And now that she had a flimsy excuse, he expected her to take it and bolt for greener pastures. She shook her head.

"We're mated, Curran. There's no do-overs."

"I don't want you just because I put a mark on you."

"Then you should have thought about that before you marked me."

"I wasn't thinking of anything then."

She tugged on his ankle. He teetered, but quickly regained his balance. "I think you were thinking a heck of a lot more then than you are now."

"What do you mean?"

"Then, you thought I was a person you could admire. That you wanted. Now you think I'm some petty individual incapable of making a commitment."

He slid down into the pool, his gaze guarded as it met hers. "You didn't mark me."

She rolled her eyes. "Is that what's bothering you?"

"Yes."

"Do you remember at all the time you marked me?"

His lips took on a sensual fullness and red tinged his gaze. "Yes."

She closed the distance between them, sliding her bare thighs over his, shivering as the hairs on his thighs tickled hers. "Then you'll remember you had me a bit distracted."

One of his hands cupped her hip. The other cupped her skull, tilting her head the way he liked. "I did, but that doesn't answer my question."

She couldn't remember what the question was, with his cock snuggled against her pussy and his mouth a hairbreadth from hers.

Looping her arms around his neck, she brought his mouth to hers. "Ask me again."

"Are you going to leave me?"

"No." She had questions of her own. "Are you going to give someone permission to play in my mind again?"

"Never."

"Good."

His cock caught under the hood of her clit, stretching the delicate flesh exquisitely. She shuddered and moaned. He bucked and groaned. His mouth bit at hers in hard, demanding kisses as he rocked her on his cock.

"I want you, seelie."

"Yes." She wanted him, too. His tongue slid into her mouth, gliding against hers, coaxing forward the response that was only his. He kissed her until she was breathless, until she was so hot, she was rocking on his cock like a wild thing. Wanting him in her, wanting him.

Water sloshed as he turned her around. "Brace your hands on the side."

A shudder took her from head to toe. He was going to take her the traditional way, the position symbolic of her submission, his dominance. Her womb clenched.

His chuckle vibrated against her spine as he kissed his way up to her nape. "I'm glad you approve."

There was the hot, moist touch of his tongue and then the graze of his teeth. Her pussy burned. Her mark burned. Her heart yearned.

"Curran."

"Yes, seelie."

His cock settled between her legs, centering on her pussy before pushing in—a slow, steady possession that left her gasping in shock, pleasure.

"I love you!"

His hips bucked against her, driving him deeper, faster. His fingers found her clit, rubbing gently before pinching lightly in rhythm with the pulse of his hips.

"I love you, too."

She took him to the hilt. Her claws scraped against the pool's edge. Her clit pulsed and ached. Her pussy rippled and begged. He pulled out, leaving her empty, wanting, needing.

Never. The thought whispered into her mind. *I'll always be here for you.*

And he was. In her mind, in her body. Filling both beyond capacity, giving her what she wanted. Need spiraled high, tighter. She could feel his pleasure echoing hers. His fingers left her clit. Something warm drizzled between her buttocks. His fingers found her anus. Pressed.

Tradition.

Her muscles parted. Pleasure, dark, forbidden but oh, so glorious, rippled over her skin.

His free hand slapped her ass. Ripples of delight spread deep. "Push back."

The guttural order just fueled the fire within. She was close, so close. His fingers worked in and out, stretching her, preparing her while she pressed back and squirmed, needing just that little bit more to come.

"Curran!"

"What?"

"I need to come."

His fingers left her ass, only to return to her clit. This time as if sensing her need, they weren't so gentle, pinching and tugging in time with the violence of her desire. His cock pressed against her anus as he gave one last slow twist to her clit. Her world shattered. His cock eased in, parting her for another, darker invasion. She bucked away from his fingers, driving back on his cock. The pleasure and pain blended with her orgasm, driving it higher, driving her mindless. She needed more. He gave it to her in steady thrusts until she had him all. He parted her buttocks, grinding in that last inch, imprisoning her hips between the edge of the tub and his cock.

"Again." He muttered in her ear. She shook her head. Though her clit throbbed and begged, her ass burned and pleaded, her womb wept and cajoled, she shook her head. It was too much. Holding her hips, he drew her away from the edge. His feet spread her legs. His hand left her hip.

"Yes."

The first slap on her clit was a tease. The next a command. The third an order that ripped her orgasm from her. Screaming his name, she came, bucking on his hand, riding his cock as he shouted his own release, sobbing as the hot jets of his seed coated her passage. She collapsed against the side of the tub, her muscles Jell-O. His still-hard cock slipped from her ass, leaving her hungry.

He turned her over and sat on the tub. She straddled his lap. Holding his gaze, she aligned his cock back with her ass and slowly lowered herself. It burned. She didn't care. Fires leapt in his eyes. When she had him as deep as she could take him, she moved the hair away from his shoulder. Leaning in, watching him watch her, she whispered, "Mine."

He howled as he took her mark. Made love to her as she licked it and when the storm passed, he was still there, holding her close, soothing her body with his hands and her thoughts with his mind.

"I love you." She breathed the words against his skin, feeling his hands tighten on her back.

"I love you, too."

There was a sadness in the declaration that she didn't like. "What's wrong?"

His right hand cupped her cheek. "I wanted to offer you a future, but I don't know what tomorrow will hold. Haven's future is uncertain."

She cupped her hand over his, pressing his fingers to her. "But we're not."

"No. "

"I bet you've made more with less." Throwing one of his favorite phrases back at him, she smiled into his eyes.

Curran smiled back in that way that tugged her heartstrings. Half grin, half endearment. "You'd win that bet." His expression sobered. "You're all I need, Rachel. If you want to leave, we will."

She turned her head and kissed his palm. "Thank you, but it's not necessary."

"I mean it."

She had no doubt he did. It would kill him, but he would do it. For her. There was no greater proof he could have given her of his love.

"This is our home, Curran. It's worth fighting for."

His smile grew at the word "home." Against her stomach his cock hardened, but what she couldn't look away from was the love in his eyes. Pure, unconditional love. For her. Forever. No matter what.

He held up his palm. There was the slightest hesitation, before he drew his claw across it. "Then we'd better make it official."

How could he doubt she would want this? He was hers. She was his. No matter what happened at Haven in the future, this was as it should be. She ran her nail across her palm, slicing it open, placing it over his mark. He did the same to hers. He leaned in. She stretched up. Their lips met. Parted. She took his breath as hers as their hearts blended in a whispered promise that would last forever.

"My soul to yours. In this life and the next, we are bound."